PROWLER BALL

A YANKEE STATION SEA STORY

JOHN M. BUSHBY

"Obviously I was challenged by becoming a Naval Aviator by landing aboard aircraft carriers and so on."
Alan B. Shepard

"My soul is in the sky"
William Shakespeare, A Midsummer Night's Dream

"Up there the world is divided into bastards and suckers.
Make your choice."
Derek Robinson

"Fight to fly, fly to fight, fight to win."
U.S. Navy Fighter Weapons School, TOPGUN.

"We train young men to drop fire on people. But their commanders won't allow them to write fuck *on their airplanes because? It's obscene!"*
Colonel Walter E. Kurtz, in Apocalypse Now, *1979.*

For

Rebecca, Heather, Geoffrey, Alexandra, and Walter

Contents

The Blue Box 1

Alameda—12 September 1972 6

Pacific Blue—12 to 26 September 37

Subic Bay 70

Welcome to Yankee Station 81

Home Front 94

Trick or Treat 101

The Da Nang Gang 123

Back on the Line 150

Steel Balls 178

Hong Kong Phooey 187

Thousand Plane Raid 199

Losses 210

Prowler Ball 222

Carrying the Melon 230

A Peace of What? 237

Coming Home to a Foreign Country 244

Death and Remembrance 248

Epilogue — Ho Chi Minh City 1994 252

Author's Note 258

A Short Glossary of Naval Terms 261

THE BLUE BOX

Call me Pierre. Some years ago—forty-one precisely—having completed my advanced flight training and having been assigned to a U.S. Navy electronic warfare attack squadron, I deployed aboard *USS Enterprise* for the air war in Vietnam. At that time, I thought that I would chronicle my experiences and feelings and then come back from combat and write the great American war novel. That was not to be. The war itself seemed to sap my resolve to write. I filled notebooks with scribbling, but nothing congealed that made sense. My mind was fogged by the experience and for long years thereafter I was plagued by a kind of remorseless fatigue when I thought about telling the story that kept me from making any sense of what happened and most importantly, why?

My real name is Walter Geoffreys. Pierre was the squadron nickname, bestowed on me by my friends and lived up to after a night of debauchery in Hong Kong. I was born in 1948, a native of New Jersey, and a true baby boomer. After, my tour in Vietnam I returned to the states I listened to some bad advice which led me to resign my naval commission, something I still regret. And yet, though I may have left the service decades ago that brief and chaotic year in Southeast Asia has never left me. My experience in Vietnam and the surreal aftermath in which I found myself left me in limbo. I have been caught between pride and confusion, honor and duty that have shaped my personality. My confusion and ambivalence that can be best attested to by the series of catastrophes that have resulted in my many failed personal relationships. I returned "home", but once back, I never knew what home really was or where I fit in.

By the time we sailed from San Francisco, the war in Vietnam had become nightly fodder on the news channels and the ensuing battles in the streets of America between the anti-war protestors and the "silent majority" were as intense as jungle firefights. But like Ishmael, I wanted to go to sea, to fly combat aircraft and observe at least some of the "watery part of the world'. Moreover, my ambition since boyhood was to fly and most particularly fly from an aircraft carrier going in harm's way.

Now, all that physically remains of that time are inside a large metal box. The box has traveled with me through the years, through all the relocations and all the marriages. It went in and out of moving vans and storage sheds where it remained, often ignored but not forgotten. The squadron riggers had spray painted the exterior royal blue. Now it is scuffed, its paint peeling. Like a treasure from the Valley of the Kings, it is a sarcophagus, inside a trove of artifacts, letters and photographs.

The exterior of the box is stenciled on the lid and sides with my name, LTJG Walter Geoffreys in large white letters along with "VAQ-131", my squadron's designation. In the center of the box is a decal bearing a Trojan Helmet with a lighting bolt, the squadron insignia. Strangely, this one part of the box appears almost new. The design was devised by one of our squadron's talented parachute riggers. He had conceived it from the cover of a pack of Trojan condoms. Retraced and colored in, added a red lightning bolt and it became the symbol of the VAQ-131 "Lancers". Our radio call sign was "Skybolt" and we thought that we were the hottest bunch of *shit-hot nasal radiators* that ever came into the fleet.

The contents of the box are slowly deteriorating with age. When I lift the lid of the box I am confronted with things that once seemed so important, but now seem irrelevant. There are letters, postcards, and clippings along with a flying helmet and oxygen mask, my parachute harness and an old pair of nomex gloves that are folded and stacked inside. Several notebooks, their pages filled with my scribbling wait for my editing. Long ago, I extracted my old flying boots, which were probably the most comfortable shoes I have or ever will have owned. Over the years the stitching had dissolved from exposure to JP-5 jet fuel. When I took them out to wear for a hike in the San Diego foothills they disintegrated off my feet as soon as I took a step. There are bits of uniform, although where my blues, whites and khakis might now be is a mystery. There is a plastic box filled with rank insignia, some medals, NFO wings, and a gold chinstrap for my bridge cover. Dress gray and white gloves, several piss-cutters, belts, buckles, and assorted other uniform items are also there.

These items maintain a silent testament, but the memories, the truths of the times that these things represent, are fresh and alive. Some are as indelible as the image of seeing a wingman's plane explode and burn in mid-air.

After four decades, the mention of Vietnam hardly produces a raised eyebrow, unless you are of a certain age. The vehement reaction to the war that back in the 1960s incited thousands of young people to mob the streets of American cities appears only in old footage shown on History Channel specials. I read a headline for an ad in the New York Times recently, where Alex Trebek, the host of *Jeopardy* was touting contestants to "Win a trip to exotic Vietnam and Cambodia". I thought, gee, I had already won two. The current generation can be forgiven its short-term memory; it is focused on other wars. It grew up on 9/11, the Iraq invasion and the tribulations of war in Afghanistan. But for some, having been sent to Vietnam and having fought in that place, their memories linger like they were yesterday. They all left the place with battle scars—some visible to all, but most of them are still burdened with indelible traces of war that, forty years later, provoke extreme emotions of pride and regret.

Perhaps, had I not served, I would have grown to be less judgmental, perhaps more forgiving and certainly more easy-going. Perhaps I would not have become the person who constantly looks for the "divert fields" in every situation, the person who does not press home until he knows that all the options have been weighed and considered. The process of becoming a Naval Flight Officer molded me in certain ways, and like metal rods bent to fit a specific function, I have remained fixed and cannot easily realigned.

I learned a lot at sea. It was a graduate level course in applied realities—places, people, and things. It was there that he learned that the four-letter word fuck was one of the most universal of all words in the English language—for in its various forms it can be a noun, a verb, an adjective, and in some cases, it simply it expresses all that could be said to describe a lousy situation. It is true. You can use fuck to describe sex or say it loud when you bang your thumb with a hammer. There is fuck it, when you are frustrated, and fuck you when you are angry. Then of course, there is fuck me when you screw up or are depressed. The action word, fucking is both a sex act and also a descriptor of magnitude, like, that fucking asshole, where the size of the problem is what you want to convey. After a couple of weeks at sea no conversation could be completed without at least a dozen or so fucks thrown in for good measure.

Then there was the booze. At sea, we regularly drank ourselves into oblivion, and yet for the most part, we remained functional. By law US Navy, ships are dry—well, supposedly. Even so, there are enough ships damaged in collisions and other errors of seamanship, that are committed by totally sober officers to make one wonder if a few drinks might have not serve to lessen the anal-retentive tensions of some of those skippers. But in Vietnam we drank non-stop, even before flights; some of us had to have a shot— or two in order to make the climb up to the flight deck. Booze came aboard the ship at every port of call. Hidden contraband, it was stuffed into duffels and shopping bags so as to elude the eyes of the Officer of the Deck. Once aboard, hiding it became a cat and mouse game to evade the patrols of Master at Arms. In our quarters, the J.O. bunkroom, we filled our safes with booze bottles and left our side arms and secret material out on the desks. Some days, aircrews manning up for flights had the shakes from hangovers so badly that they couldn't strap themselves in to their ejection seats without extra assistance from the line crew. They would sit in the cockpit, inert and with sweat streaming from their pores as the enlisted men helped with the straps and buckles.

There are more stories in this battered box than can ever, or should be told. On long nights the ghosts of the past rise from the box and come to visit me. So here is my story of my time at war Once upon a time, we were young men and sailed west with the setting sun, as far as it would go. We were proud. We carried our flag and they hoped that courage would not fail us.

ALAMEDA—12 SEPTEMBER 1972

The room was hot, airless, and rife with the smell of sex—hot sex, urgent sex; sweat sticking to our bodies' sex. It had been explosive sex, quickly begun, quickly done, and then quickly resumed. It was not sex from need or from love, but it was sex because sex was easier for both of us than talking. The bedside clock read three-fifteen when, spent and vaguely anxious I woke. I lay there for several minutes and watched her sleep. She was breathing softly her tousled blonde hair splayed over the damp sheets. As I thought about getting up and leaving I realized what a sonofabitch that I had become, and how I had done so in record time. What the hell was I doing with this woman? Groping in the dark and trying not to wake her, I found my clothes, dressed, and slipped from her bedroom.

I would have liked to say that the evening had begun innocently enough, but that would simply be another lie to pile upon the small mountain range of lies that I seemed to be building during the weeks leading up to the Westpac deployment. Two of us had crossed the bay from Alameda and wandered into the Iron Horse in Maiden Lane, off Union Square that afternoon, bent on some kind of "last night in port" adventure. My friend, Al "Red" LeBaron had led the way. Years before, he had been stationed at Treasure Island and he knew San Francisco better than anyone in the squadron. Since I had joined VAQ-131, LeBaron had become a mentor to me. He liked an audience and I was a rapt one for him. As a lowly Lieutenant (junior grade), I was sorely in need of an education in the realities of life and he was there to teach me.

There had not been much of a plan for the evening. We were due to sail the next morning. Given that, the skipper had declared that the official workday for the squadron should end at noon. The idea of drinking away the afternoon and getting a decent dinner before reporting back to the ship seemed in order. Perhaps I thought, we might drift over to that English Pub on Geary Street and see if those two Mexican girls were there.

The last time that we were in port, during the long weeks of pre-deployment work ups, we had a good time with the pair. They did not seem to care that we navy men were Anglos. They found us amusing, I suppose. They had even taken us to a sketchy bar in the southern part of the city where our white Anglo skin stood out. In the smoke filled bar and sensing resentment in the crowd of macho Chicano drinkers, we bought a round for the place and then the crowd left us alone. It was our money and our willingness to part with it, that seemed to enhance our personalities—an important fact of life that I was to take with me to the Philippines.

Al was a good ten years older than I. A lieutenant commander with two tours in F-4s, he stood nearly six foot six, and with his shock of orange hair, he had quickly become known around the squadron as the *Red Baroon*. The red came partly as a commentary on his hair and mostly because the only winter flight suit in the rigger's inventory that would fit his frame was bright orange. Wearing it made him look like a pumpkin. Al never just talked to people, he orated. He often spoke in stentorious tones offering comments as if they were imperial dictates, so the sobriquet baroon was derived from this buffoonish and imperious character and the orange flight suit. Like everyone else, he had to have a nickname and LeBaron just became baroon. Who knew who came up with it, but it stuck. What made it all the funnier was Al's expressed desire to always go first cabin, as befitted someone with such regal presence. First class on everything was his motto. That being the case, we decided to begin the afternoon in one of the trendier watering holes in town.

We ordered a round and had barely started drinking, a vodka martini for the Baroon and some decent single malt for me, when two very lovely ladies approached our table and asked if they could join us. At first glance, they looked like sisters, or perhaps even a mother and daughter act. Either way, they were stunning, and getting pleasantly blitzed so we felt that we had hit the jackpot.

"Hi, my name is Basia. That's Polish for Barbara." She was tall and thin with long blonde hair down her back to her waist. Her smile was ten yards wide, and she made me feel like I was the most important man in the room. At the time, I was married with a one year old, but my wife was back in Whidbey Island, though she was an attractive woman, never in her life could she have looked like this one who was now stroking my hair.

"Please, please sit down," I heard myself say.

"Thanks, this is my friend, Laura," she said, reaching out an arm to indicate a slightly older, brunette version of herself. Laura smiled at both of us and then sat next to Al, in the process of which her short skirt slid up to reveal a pair of very tan legs.

They seemed honestly happy to be with us, and, if their smiles and laughter were any indication, we were in for a very pleasant afternoon, and if luck held, a long evening too. It only dawned on us later, when a matter of money arose, that we were just two marks who had "navy" stamped all over us.

More drinks came and they were followed by hors d'ouevres and then more drinks. By the time that the sun had set, we were well lubricated with alcohol, and we found ourselves jammed into a cab on our way to Fisherman's Wharf. In the back seat, perfume filled our nostrils and naked female legs surrounded us. There never were two sailors who were ever more willing to be seduced than we were. Irish coffees at the Buena Vista followed a lavish dinner at Alioto's. When the pair asked us back to their apartment for a nightcap, we were more than willing.

"You boys are a lot of fun. I hope you don't mind, but our place is kind of small, and the rent here in San Fran is just a killer." It was Laura who left the rest of the question unsaid, but the two of us were more than happy to contribute to the pair's well-being and, after squeezing five twenties into each girl's hand we were on our way to paradise.

It was a walk-up apartment just off Van Ness. The girls shared a two bedroom flat that was decorated like a bad trip and festooned with the psychedelic paraphernalia that abounded in the Haight. Once inside, they both wanted to get high and offered us a bong, but neither Al nor I wanted to risk it. "I'll stick with booze," I said. Basia shrugged and went to the kitchen to retrieve a jug bottle of Mateus from a tiny refrigerator and poured each of us a glass. Soon the grappling began, and Basia led me to her tiny bedroom. It was cluttered with all the makeup junk of a single woman and lit dimly lit by a rose-colored floor lamp. These were the days long before AIDS, so sex was simpler and not as structured. "If it moves, fondle it", was a phrase of the time. As Basia closed the door, I looked back to see Laura with her face in Al's lap.

I crept about the cluttered space hoping that I would not knock something over and cause an alarm. Al must have left the apartment sometime before, because there was no sign of him anywhere inside. Him vanishing like that without a word was annoying and I was a little miffed that he had not tried to wake me and take me along back to the ship, but then I thought that perhaps he was embarrassed by the events of the evening. LeBaron had let his guard down, in front of a junior officer, and a friend.

I found my way out of the apartment and down the stairs to the street and stepping into a warm September night, I started walking. I had a mental picture of the city's street layout, and I walked down the side street toward Van Ness. Around three a.m., near the Hamburger Hamlet, I found a lone cab cruising. "Alameda Air Station," I said. The words came out from crusty lips. I still had the taste of Basia on my breath and my throat was raspy from the booze. As the cab toured through the quiet streets, I kept trying to remember her face. It was already becoming a blur as I thought of her, as for her name—Basia? Well, maybe it was for tonight, who knew what she might call herself tomorrow?

I felt lousy and my heart was heavy. Was I a heel, a sonofabitch for cheating—well maybe I was. But right then I felt no remorse at this breach of my marriage vows, it was nothing. What had happened was an interlude; something elemental that was of no consequence to my marriage or my wife back in Whidbey. The girl meant nothing to me, no more than the pictures of the naked women in the pages of *Playboy*. There would be time enough for remorse if I made it back from Vietnam.

Tonight, on this last night, I felt free of any conventions, free to act on a moment's notice, with no regrets. It was as if I had been told that I only had a short time to live—and maybe, indeed that was the case. Meeting and bedding the girl was as easy as ordering another beer. Tomorrow, well, it was today now, I would be at sea and before nightfall hundreds of miles from home, somewhere out on the North Pacific, headed to—well, who knew what?

In truth, I sorely missed my wife and I desperately wished that she had flown down with the other officers' wives to see me off. Then perhaps she could have shared and understood something about the adventure upon which I was embarking. Going to war was not a selfish choice; it was my profession, and something she well knew. But, she had chosen to stay at home. She and our child were back in the in the navy housing at Ault Field, Oak Harbor Washington. Our duplex was on Glacier Court, one of dozens in a development built on Whidbey's old seaplane base. As important as it seemed to be with my wife one last time, I had also wanted to see my daughter, now just a year old.

Leaving home had been too hectic, filled with too much of the bravado that the military poured on to deployments. The band-playing and flag-waving was necessary so that the men would get on the plane that took them from home and not break down emotionally. I suppose that all armies and navies have performed that way down through the ages, otherwise most of soldiers and sailors would get cold feet and simply and perhaps wisely, refuse to go. So, at the last moment there had been no room for emotion, aside from the traditional "Anchors Aweigh" and a few hasty kisses and hugs. The navy had arranged things that way, just like in a movie script. Still, she was back there in Oak Harbor, not here at the pier for me.

That morning, I had ducked out from work and called her from one of the phones that lined the pier. I knew that there would be no time the next day to speak to her. The ship due to depart at 0900. We spoke for the last time, until well, who knew, perhaps never again. It had been soft talk, husband-and-wife talk, no controversies, and no recriminations. Up to that moment, we had thought that as a couple we had all the time in the world, but it seemed that we only had the time the long distance operator would permit us. And yet, I knew, or at least I felt, that there was an even chance I might not return. It was not as if I was headed off for a business meeting in Cleveland; combat aviation was an unforgiving profession, and anything could happen.

It was a long drive from the Hamburger Hamlet across the bay and to the Alameda gate. By the time the cab dropped me at the carrier pier I was feeling ambivalent about everything. The release that the sex had provided was fleeting, gone now and replaced by a growing sense of unease. Ahead of me were months at sea, months in which I might find success or failure in a world in which failure was not an option. Would I measure up? Would I do my job and do it well? Could I live up to the uniform that I wore? For two years, since arriving in Pensacola right out of college, I had been trained and honed for this moment. Like so many who went before me, I had willingly joined these Spartans, a society apart from the civilian world with strict rules and mores and a special sense of honor.

———

An angry red sun rose over the Gulf of Mexico. Already the damp heat of the night was being scorched away by another summer sunrise in Pensacola. There were three of us sharing a tawdry room in the San Carlos Hotel. I wondered how many aviation cadets had, like us sweated through a sleepless night in this room? The walls looked as if it they had not had a fresh coat of paint since before Pearl Harbor. Tobacco stained, yellow plaster walls, dark mahogany furniture, and an aging ceiling fan, with one rasping blade, served as décor. Plaster was peeling from the ceiling in the shadowy corners. Air conditioning was something rumored for the future, so ventilation came through the large screened windows that were wide open to permit a gasp of tropical air. It was our last night of freedom, and none of us had slept very well, despite the vast quantity of beer that we drank while cruising the bars the night before.

I could not sleep so I sat up watching the night pass. From the easy chair near the window, I looked out as dim shapes on the street below took on definition as the light increased. My roommates, fellow officer candidates, lay sprawled across the beds, oblivious to the new day. I could not even remember their names. We had arrived together, strangers embarked on identical journeys. We met on the plane from Atlanta. Needing a place to stay until it was time to report to Naval Air Training Command the next day, a helpful cabbie had steered us to the San Carlos. It should have been obvious to us that he was getting a kickback for each young victim his delivered to the place, but we were just naive.

The hotel lobby reminded me of the set for *To Have and Have Not*, complete with the battered tables and slowly turning ceiling fans with bamboo blades. The hotel was used to arrivals like us. The place had been putting up would-be aviators for decades, and so the dour desk clerk sold us a suite for the night at twenty-five bucks apiece. We did not care, and, after tossing our bags into the room, we headed out to the street looking for the nearest bar.

The next morning found our trio hung over and wobbly as we ventured outside the hotel into the rising heat. None of us could face breakfast. I had been able to bolt down some rancid-tasting coffee from an ancient urn in the hotel lobby without heaving it up. Our orders said to report to the Naval Air Training Command by noon on 30 June 1970. Pensive, and not knowing what else to do until that time, we flagged a cab and piled in for the ride to the main base. The cabbie was a scruffy young man who had the feral look of an emaciated Lee Harvey Oswald. He turned to the three of us and asked, "Are you sure you want to go there? There's still time to go home, maybe even make it to Canada."

This seemed like crazy talk to us, had we not come to this sweatbox to become Naval Aviators? Nervously, we laughed his question off. Twenty minutes later the cabby was gone and we were standing in front of a rambling brick building with colonnaded galleries on either side of a white portico. All the buildings here looked identical, as if this were some kind of college campus plunked down along the Gulf of Mexico. Above the building's double doors hung the insignia of the Naval Air Training Command, below that was a sign welcoming all to the Indoctrination Battalion.

Everything had the feel of arriving at small town college on a sleepy summer's day. Across an expanse of green grass, I spotted people lounging at a swimming pool. Around me several of the other candidates were hefting suitcases, some had even brought golf clubs, and one fellow had scuba gear in a large duffel bag—this was the Florida Gulf Coast, after all. I felt a little left out, since all I had was a small gym bag containing a change of underwear and a Dopp kit. Something had warned me to travel light. As I approached the entrance to the battalion, a senior officer candidate met me. He was wearing pressed khakis and like a tour director stood there before the door and ushered we new arrivals into the building. He looked very officious and he was carrying a clipboard with a list of the names of the expected members of the new class. I stepped up to him along and gave my name.

"Oh, yes. Here you are," he said, as he checked me off. There were over a hundred names on the long list the candidate officer held. Then, using his pencil, he pointed over his shoulder at the door and said, "Just go inside and introduce yourself, one of the instructors will help you and show you where to settle in." Then he gave a wry smile and went on to the next man. Funny, at the time I thought, he didn't look like a sadist.

Gamely, I walked up to the door and looked to my right. There, beyond another row of neat brick buildings, was a stretch of azure blue, Pensacola Bay. Maybe, my naive civilian brain thought, maybe this weekend I would be able to go out there to the beach. This was, after all, an officer-training program, not Parris Island. Without another thought, I reached out and opened the door. I remain uncertain as to what hit me next, the wall of noise or the sinewy forearm of a Marine drill instructor. Perhaps it was both. One moment I had been smiling at the beauty of Gulf of Mexico and the next I was staring helplessly into a pair of reflective sunglasses that resided under the razor-edged brim of a Marine campaign hat.

"Get out of my way you horrible fucking beast!" The voice came from a slit just under the sunglasses. This aperture bore some resemblance to a mouth, and, since the sunglasses were directed at me, I was certain he must be the aforementioned beast. Instinctively, I glanced down and there observed the polished black shillelagh tucked under the man's arm, I was certain that there was a grenade attached to its thick end.

"Are you eyeballing me, maggot?" The slit moved again.

"No, sir!" I managed to squeak out. Although this was my first face-to-face experience with a Marine, I had read enough to know that, in my position in the US military at that moment, anything in uniform ranked above me and thus deserved a "sir" when speaking to it. Apparently not too many of my fellow arrivals had put the word sir in their replies, and this somehow made me stand out a little—not always a good thing in such circumstances.

"What is your service number, shit for brains?" The slit had opened and spoke. In it, I saw a row of teeth. If they had been filed sharply like a cannibal's, I would not have been surprised. This question baffled me at first, as shit for brains was not what my family had usually called me during my twenty-two years on the planet. Though I did know a lot of numbers, phone numbers, addresses, historical dates, but this number, which appeared on a corner of my orders, was not one for which I had any recollection. Well, the man was impatient, he was a master gunnery sergeant, after all, and as for me, well it seemed that I was obviously a shit for brains maggot. He grabbed the orders from the death grip in which my fingers held them and looked at them. Then he produced a red, permanent, felt tip marker and stenciled the number from the page across my forehead.

"Now, maggot, maybe *you will* fucking remember it!" Then someone else grabbed my arm and shoved me into a room. Four bunks lined the walls and three other similarly stunned maggots stood at attention while one of the other Marine gods yelled at them. Like the song said, "I wanted wings."

We were one hundred and ten young men that checked in to the Indoctrination Battalion that morning. Athletes and engineers, recent college graduates and a few enlisted men hoping to become officers, all of us were hopeful and we all wanted to earn those vaunted wings of gold. We were designated class 27-70, just another in a long line of volunteers for the naval air service. Almost immediately, some of the group had regrets. Within a few days, the winnowing began to show. More and more people decided that the world they had entered was not for them and DOR'ed, dropped on request. They were not all weaklings; several were noted college football players, used to the celebrity they had previously enjoyed that the Marine drill instructors ignored. A small number simply did not have the anthropomorphic characteristics required of a military aviator, and some were just scared shitless. During the next ninety days of training the class was whittled down so that on October 23, 1970 we were thirty officer candidates who stood on the parade deck and received our commissions as ensigns. Of these, less than half of that number actually won our coveted wings.

———

Back on the east side of the bay I got out of the taxi, paid off the driver, and walked to the double chain link fence that separated Naval Air Station Alameda from the rest of the world. Despite the hour, there were a number of people in the area. Some were loved ones, seeing off their departing sailor and some were just gawkers, come to see a ship go off to war. But there was another group, a crowd of scruffy people, hippies mostly, with posters and signs. Their signs read "SOS—Stop Our Ship" and other injunctions against the ten-year-old war in Vietnam. The civilian gate guard eyed them dubiously and checked my ID then waived me aboard the station.

Floodlights covered the pier, throwing shadows between the long, low buildings on the shoreward side. This was the same stretch of concrete and macadam from which in 1942 sixteen Army B-25s had been hoisted aboard another carrier, the *USS Hornet*, that Jimmy Doolittle then led on to raid Tokyo. For aviators this was hallowed ground, for who knew how many other men last touched American soil here before going off to die in some far away jungle or ocean. It wasn't hard to find my destination, the hulking grey shape of the *Enterprise*, with the huge illuminated "65" on the side of the carrier's island, stretched to the end of the pier. The officers' brow was located just forward of the island and towered up four stories to the quarterdeck. It took all the energy I could muster to climb those four flights.

I croaked out "Lieutenant junior grade Geoffreys" with, "Reporting aboard, sir," tagged on as I threw a salute to the fantail and stepped aboard. The OD nodded disparagingly at me, another late reveler returning. He showed me a weak smile as I stumbled off across the jammed hangar deck and found my way up the ladderway toward the junior officers' bunkroom and into bed.

Warships are not quiet places, something is always happening and sleep comes only to those who, in the space of a few instants, can drown out the constant banging of metal on metal or the heavy vibrations of engines and propeller shafts. The sounds of the ship preparing to put to sea woke me, and by 0630, I was dressed in a working uniform of wash khakis and on my way to the dirty shirt wardroom for breakfast. As I sat and ate several other officers drifted in to through the chow line, responding to the stewards' repeated chorus of "eggs to order, sir!" Fried eggs, scrambled eggs, eggs with peppers and onions, hard-boiled eggs—the place was cholesterol heaven.

Sitting there downing eggs and coffee, tucked just under the forward catapults, the spirits of the men were high; there was an eager anticipation of leaving port. The dirty shirt wardroom was the best place on the ship for fliers to eat. It was so named because officers who were in working uniform or flight suits could eat without the prissy formality of the main wardroom. Besides, it was always open. In the main wardroom, the meals were scheduled and white-jacketed stewards served the officers "Russian style" from silver salvers; up in the dirty shirt it was simply cafeteria style. Around me my fellow breakfasters scarfed down their food, navy fashion—we ate just as fast as one could, in case flight quarters was called and then one wouldn't get to eat again for hours. This was not a restaurant where one could linger over coffee; it was functioning and pulsating part of the ship's internal systems, designed to quickly process food into its sailors. As soon as I was done, I ducked out of the forward hatch and climbed into the portside catwalk to steal a quick walk on the flight deck. From the eastern sky beams of sunlight shot overhead and struck the windows of buildings in San Francisco, across the bay. They gleamed brightly; each pane of glass reflecting golden sunlight against a backdrop of clear blue California sky. Weather-wise, it was going to be a perfect day in the Bay Area.

Movement across the water caught my eye, and I watched the sleek gray shape of the *USS Bainbridge* as it slid out from the piers at Hunter's Point. She was headed for the Golden Gate and open sea. Once clear of the bay, she would loiter off the Gate until the *Enterprise* came out, and together they would head for the far side of the Pacific. The *Bainbridge* and the cruiser *Long Beach* were, like the *Enterprise*, nuclear-powered. None of the ship's needed to be refueled and in theory we could stay at sea for years running on our uranium cores. The navy often liked to demonstrate our combined power by photographing the three ships steaming together. There was one famous shot of the three ships steaming together. In the photo *Enterprise* with the equation $E=MC^2$ spelled out by groupings of white-uniformed officers on the flight deck and the two other warships on either side that made it to the front pages of several newspapers.

On deck, the air was sharp, clean, autumnal air. I drank it in. I wanted to remember it all, to etch my brain with the clarity of that scene. Along the seaward side of the *Enterprise* a line of Coast Guard crash boats had taken up position to prevent any vessel from getting too close to us. Beyond them bobbed a small flotilla of canoes and rowboats filled with wildly attired protesters shouting, "Stop this Ship". Under any condition, San Francisco Bay is not a tranquil stretch of water and they were soon tossing precariously in the choppy water of the bay. With the breeze rising, the seaworthiness of their overloaded craft would soon be in doubt.

Apparently, the objective of this tiny fleet was to somehow impede the progress of a seventy thousand ton warship using several twelve-foot aluminum canoes. I stopped to wonder if any of these foolhardy mariners had been among those people I had seen in the early morning near the main gate. Still, it was a sight to behold, and I watched with amusement as the coast guard began to clear the way for our ship to commence movement. Without warning, the coast guard crews throttled up and began to circle around the clusters of canoes: at first exhorting them over their loudhailers to exit the area, but when that failed, speeding around the tiny boats and swamping them. Then they went about plucking the dunked protesters from the cold bay while crewmen from another coast guard boat retrieved the empty canoes and stacked them on its afterdeck.

The morning began in dramatic fashion and much more was in store. Down on the carrier pier another scene was playing out. Orders were called out over the ship's intercom to prepare for sea. The civilian dock crew began to move the shore side gangways clear. As the final warning was sounded for all crew to return aboard or miss the ship's movement, feverish last minute hugs and kisses were exchanged between departing sailors and their wives or sweethearts. From behind the crowd of well-wishers there came a sudden rush of young women who surged toward the after brow. In a few seconds, several of these women had chained themselves to the brow railing. They were waving signs and wailing about the immorality of the war in Vietnam.

At the far end of the pier a local TV news crew, on hand to film the sendoff for the evening news, was attempting to find a location from where they could film the canoeists in the water. Some of the Stop Our Ship protesters ran up to the TV crew and alerted them to the commotion further back on the pier. But before they could react and reposition their cameras, the Alameda Air Station's Master at Arms van appeared. Its doors were flung open and a shore patrol unit sprang out and surrounded the women to the brow. Before the women knew what was happening, the Shore Patrol team had clipped the chains with bolt cutters and tossed the women into the back of the van. An instant later the van, its tires smoking and screeching, disappeared through the crowd toward the main gate, as the news crew dashed up to the now empty brow. It was all neatly done and there was nothing to film for the news except the tearful families on the pier, sobbing and waving goodbye to their sailors.

At last the order came down from the bridge to single up all lines and with tugs in place on either side of the ship's bow, one pulling and one pushing, the carrier began to move into the stream. Through the steel under his feet, I could feel the vibrations of the propeller shafts increase, and at dead slow the carrier inched forward. Aboard the *Enterprise* there was little ceremony at the departure, and, except for the Alameda Air Station band playing "Anchors Aweigh" on the pier, there were no other farewells. The captain had not issued any orders for the officers and crew to form lines of white uniforms, a maneuver known as manning the sides, for leaving port. It wasn't as if we were actually stealing away, but the war's unpopularity at home, especially in the ultra-liberal San

Francisco Bay Area, forced the navy to downplay our departure. The Vietnam War was now in its tenth year, and the civilian population was not about to cheer any more of the nation's warriors as they were going off to the other side of the world. This was a far cry from the rapturous ceremonies for deploying troops and sailors following 9/11, but that was far in the future. In 1972, if you were in the military, much of the public seemed to blame you for the evils of the unpopular war. To avoid controversy, even the *Enterprise*'s departure had been set for mid-morning. The navy sought this time so as to avoid any rush-hour traffic jams on the city's majestic bridges as much as to allow for low tide to let us slip beneath the spans without incident.

As embarked squadron officers on a carrier, there was not much for us to do during the port exiting maneuvers. Our jobs only got serious once we began flying, for the rest of the time we were merely passengers on a boat ride. Like vacationers departing for a tropical cruise, several of us made our way up to the open areas on the island known as Vultures Roost from where we could watch the scene in the bay unfold. Soon the catwalks and weather deck areas on the island were lined three deep with khaki-clad officers. It all seemed to be going by too fast. First, the ship eased under the Bay Bridge, and then Alcatraz, its walls streaked with seagull droppings, passed astern. With the city on the port side, only the arch of the Golden Gate and the open sea were before us. There is a sense of infinity as you look out under the span of the Golden Gate at the open sea. It is as if you are about to step off into another universe, and for a second I shared those feelings of uncertainty that I suppose the early explorers felt as they sailed out into the ocean and beyond the familiar fringes of coastline. The escorting tugs soon dropped astern, giving us a short salute on their horns. Then the ship picked up speed as the ocean rollers began to buffet the hull. The soft shore breeze fell away and was soon replaced by a stronger and saltier ocean wind as the flight deck went under the orange span. From above, several well-wishers on the Gate's walkway waived down at us, while a solitary protester made her contribution by dumping her week's garbage from the bridge. The brisk wind took most of it off toward the Marin shore, with just a few soup cans managing to clang off the flight deck. It came to me, just then, that this was real. That this event, me going off to fly in combat, was almost foretold— beginning with a birthday wish just eight years before.

————

In the summer of 1964, I turned 16—old enough to obtain a student pilot's license, but not in New Jersey to drive a car. For most of the last months of that school year, I had been teaching myself the principles of aircraft navigation. Since the beginning of high school, I had become a voracious reader and I would routinely stop in the Towne Book Store to find something new to read. In those days, the store was on the west side of Broad Street in Westfield and had a rear entrance through which I would pass on my way home from school. I read everything that smacked of adventure or swashbuckling, but mostly I read about aviation and aviators. One afternoon I found a small book tucked into one of the shelves on the topic aerial navigation. It described using vectors and wind vectors and how they affected the way an airplane behaved as it flew and tracked over the ground. I bought it. For the next few weeks, I spent my leisure hours reading about and learning to draw wind vector diagrams on notebook paper using a ruler. Since I had grown up around boats, the concepts of wind and drift were not new to me, and I had a good idea as to what happened to an airplane as it sailed through the ocean of air over the earth. At the same time, I also learned that real pilots had other tools to help them with this, and he was eager to learn what they were.

Prowler Ball

Ever since I could remember, I had absorbed everything that I could about aviation. That my father had flown in the Second World War fueled part of this interest, but as I was growing up in the fifties, the stories of Scott Crossfield and all the other American test pilots out at Edwards Air Force Base were front-page news. I devoured their stories, and my tiny room at the back of the two-family house, which we shared with my grandparents and aunt, was filled with airplane models. Hanging from my ceiling was an air armada of combat planes from every era. I patrolled the periodical racks of Meisel's newspaper store each Sunday morning, when I was sent to buy the stack of newspapers that our household consumed. The *Herald Tribune*, the *Sun*, the *Newark Daily News*, and the *New York Mirror*—the entire stack of newsprint filled my arms or my bike's basket. Stacked in along with them, and the fresh coffee cakes from the Robert Treat Delicatessen, were copies of *Air Progress*, *Sport Planes*, and *Flying*. Each issue of *Flying Magazine* had ads for the line of Jeppesen flight computers and other tools of the trade. I knew that if I was to be a real pilot, then I needed those. So, when my mother asked what I wanted for my birthday that summer, my choice was easy.

My earliest dreams had always been about flying. I yearned to soar high above the maple tree and lilac bush that fringed our small back yard. Back then they seemed enormous, guarding the night sky. Night after warm summer night, I would lay at the foot of my bed by the open window and watch the navigation lights of the DC-7s and Super-G Constellations as they sailed high above the tree branches and gained altitude. They were real airplanes, with real pilots flying from Newark Airport bound for exotic destinations, Denver, Albuquerque, or San Francisco, or maybe even further. On still nights, when the breeze came from the east, I could hear their engines rumble. A low rumble at first, barely audible, and then, as they powered up for takeoff, the roar would increase, and then there would be a few moments of silence until, appearing overhead, I could again hear their throaty drone and see the blue exhaust flames from their reciprocating engines. These were magic flying chariots heading off to far-flung places, places of romance and adventure—I wanted so much to be going with them. To this day, the word Albuquerque still conjures up memories of those nights at the window.

On The first of July 1964, my mother said she would take me to pick out a Jeppesen computer so I could have it for my birthday. The closest place I could think of to get one was Hadley Airport in South Plainfield. My father and I had often gone out there on weekends to watch planes take off and land, and I knew how to get there. In 1964, Hadley was truly out in the middle of nowhere, on the fringe of Piscataway, near abandoned Camp Kilmer. In her Olds, my mother drove us out early one July morning. Like most July days in New Jersey, it started off warm and slightly humid, with the inevitable prospect of a thundershower later in the day.

Though it had been in business since the twenties, Hadley had never been a prosperous business, just grass and gravel runways dominated by a large Mobil Oil sign and two old hangars. Skirting past a few planes parked near the gas pumps, we parked in the gravel lot. There was an iron pipe railing separating a concrete walk from the parking area upon which fliers and customers would sit and shoot the shit about planes and flying. But on this morning, the place looked deserted. Behind the railing was an old-fashioned nickel coke machine, the kind that had a top lid that you had to lift to get your coke bottle. They were suspended from an aluminum grid. Once you paid your money you had to snake the bottle through the maze until it finally popped out.

That morning I looked at the open expanse of grass where a few planes were tied down, waiting for their pilots to show up I was getting excited as we walked in the door marked office. Inside, what passed for the office was a two-tiered affair with the business side raised three feet from the entrance and a glass counter, housing flying paraphernalia of all sorts and separating the customer area from the staff. There was no sound in the place, just the aroma of stale coffee and cigarettes. Dust clung to most of the surfaces as if it had been applied with a spray gun. A steel trash can in one corner held what appeared to be a week's worth of used coffee-stained paper cups and sandwich wrappings. Somewhere above a horsefly orbiting the room droned. I paid it no attention, as there in the glass case was a Jeppesen Slide-Graphic computer. The price was $17.95, which was expensive enough in those days. I made a beeline to the counter and was excited when I saw it there. I began pointing to it, oblivious of the two men seated above me on the raised platform that defined the office. In an excited voice, I told my mother that this was what I so desperately wanted, along with a plotter and maybe a chart, so that I could practice navigation for real.

Like most mothers, mine often indulged me when she could and, smiling at my obvious joy at finding the thing I wanted, she spoke to the two men. Up to then I had ignored them in my rush to the counter. As my mother discussed the transaction with one of the men, the younger of the two spoke, "Want to go for a ride," he asked. His name, I learned was John Nemetz. He was a lank young man in his twenties and wore a fresh white t-shirt and khaki trousers with a full head of blonde hair that he kept pushing up from his face. He was the man who would become my primary flight instructor.

"A ride, in an airplane? How much would that cost?" my mother asked with just a touch of hesitation in her voice.

"It's thirteen dollars an hour, but we'll try a half hour and see how it goes," John replied.

I didn't have any money with me so I looked at my mother for an answer. Then she smiled, and with a nod from her, I followed John out through a door and into the hangar behind the office. Hadley airport remained a holdover from another era of flight. Most of the planes there were built in the late forties and early fifties. It could have been the area's major airfield, but Newark had eclipsed it decades before. Still, it had a long and colorful history and had once been a stop on the pre-war airmail routes. But now in the early-Vietnam era of aviation, business jets were being introduced and new executive airports were being built, and Hadley's short grass runways could not keep up with progress.

Stepping through that door into the hangar brought me into a soon to be lost world. There, I was in touch with the sweet perfume of oil and aviation fuel, leather and doped fabric—the stuff from which the heroes of my youthful mind had sprung. Even now, next to the scent of lilac, these toxic substances have remained my favorite aromas. As we went through the hangar, ducking under wings and around the propellers of a dozen parked planes, I was in awe. John led me to the two-story rolling doors on the far end of the space. Grabbing the handles, he pulled and pushed on the tall doors until they rolled back, allowing a flood of sunlight to splash into the gloom. And there by the door, painted the brightest canary yellow, was a Piper J-3 Cub, the most primary of trainers. The uninformed about aviation call any small airplane a Piper Cub, and most of the time; they are wrong, it is just like calling any big truck a Mack Truck. But this was the real deal, built by the Walter Piper Company in Lycoming, Pennsylvania.

John pointed at the wheels and had me pull out the wooden chocks, and then with one hand he lifted the tail and walked the light airplane onto the apron. "Know what this is?" he asked.

I thought he must be kidding, didn't everyone know what this was, I thought. "It's a J-3 Cub with a sixty-five horsepower Lycoming engine," I replied with confidence.

"Good, well then let me show you how to pre-flight it."

And he did, and so I learned about freeing control surfaces, draining the fuel sump, checking oil, gas, and looking for nicks in the brass-edged wooden propeller. At last, he said, "OK, you climb in the back seat. That's where you solo from, so you should start there." Solo, I thought to myself? Solo? When would that ever happen?

John then showed me how to work the simple magneto switch and the throttle. It was all ridiculously basic compared with an EA-6B Prowler, but it was real enough. With switches off, he pulled the prop through for a couple of revolutions. "See those little pedals just behind the rudder pedals? Those are the brakes. They aren't like brakes on a car, and we only use them sparingly, so you have to be careful with them. Now use your heels and stand on the brakes with all your weight, and put the magneto switch on 'both,'" he instructed.

Then he spoke those fateful words, "Switches on?" "Switches on," I replied, and, then pushing all of my one hundred twenty pounds of weight onto my heels to hold the brakes, I cracked the throttle a quarter inch.

With one hefty swing of the prop the engine caught. There was a small puff of oily smoke, the thin sheet metal engine cowling shuddered and rattled, and bits of gravel pinged along the underside of the fuselage from the prop wash. John ran around and was in the front seat in a flash. Then, turning to me, said that he could now release the brakes. I relaxed my legs and slid my toes up on to the rudder pedals. John adjusted the throttle, and we began to move. We taxied out past my mother, who now was watching dubiously, if not anxiously and perhaps doubting her wisdom in agreeing to this adventure. I waved bravely, and John advanced the throttle to take us out to the pasture by the north-south runway. A pair of goats chewed on the weeds in the field and looked on us as noisy interlopers. In the run-up area John showed me the procedure for checking the engine by running up the power to a thousand rpms and how to check the dual magneto gauge to see if there was a loss of power in one side or the other and to apply carburetor heat, and lastly to move the stick and rudder pedals to assure freedom of the controls.

There was no radio in this plane, and Hadley had no tower. It only sporadically monitored the standard Unicom frequency of 122.8 MHz to listen for approaching airplanes. There was no one to call for takeoff clearance. That being the case, there were none of the formalities of a controlled field, so take off clearance involved us making a series of S-turns on the ground, while looking toward the downwind leg of the approach to the runway. We looked and looked again, but there was nothing in the sky that morning. John then looked over his shoulder at me and took us to the end of the runway. We turned to a one hundred and twenty degree heading and John pointing the nose down the center of the cut grass pushed the throttle ahead. Instantly, the Cub's tail came off the ground. The stick stood straight up in my hand and cinders flew up and hit the underside of the plane like gunshots.

"Just put a little back pressure on the stick," John yelled over the roar.

I put a finger's worth of pressure on the stick, and we started to climb. John tapped the airspeed indicator on the panel in front of him and yelled again, "Climb and glide at sixty-five," then he said, "It's your airplane," and he let go of the controls. I was flying! The next thirty minutes passed in an instant. I held the stick in my right hand and gripped the knob on the top of the throttle with my left. At John's direction, we turned and circled, climbed and twisted through the air. I was beside myself with joy. Nothing was ever to be the same to me again, no woman would ever have an effect on me that could compare to what I felt that instant.

As the half hour ended, John coached me through the approach and landing, while at the same time teaching me how to side-slip: a very valuable technique for light, tail wheel airplanes and used to lose altitude smoothly in order to make a flared landing. The Cub was so light it wanted to stay in the air; it had to be brought to the ground. Touching the ground was both elation and let down. I had at last flown an airplane, but now that I was back on earth, I wanted to be back up there. Every moment being on the ground meant that I was missing something.

John didn't say anything to me as we taxied in and parked the airplane. He walked on ahead and into the office; while combing back his full head of lank blonde hair with his fingers. My mother was smiling, either from pride or a sense of relief that he had returned alive, asked me how it was. My face was alit and my grin almost slapstick. I was filled with joy and my face told her all that she needed to know—words would not come.

Back inside the office, they were toting up the bill. John had taken a black leather-covered book from a shelf and filled out the first page. "Hadley Field, 30 minutes, effects of controls," he wrote in a new pilot's log.

Handing it to me as he took the money from my mother's hand; "Coming back?" he asked.

"When can I?" I replied, and so the adventure began.

That July and most of August went by. I raided my savings account and the stash of change that I kept in my room for the $13 that they charged for each hour of dual instruction. On the days that I had a lesson, I would get up early, pack a couple of sandwiches in a bag, and take off on my bicycle for the airport. According to the FAA, I might have been old enough to fly a plane, but in New Jersey, I was a year too young to drive a car. I rode my old three speed "English" bike, that my grandfather had always called a wheel. And so on flying days I would pedal my butt the twelve miles out to the airport from the house. In those days, the roads cut through a still rural stretch of New Jersey countryside and traffic was sparse. I would speed along shady streets out Old Raritan Road and through the wilds of South Plainfield and in an hour or so arrive at the field. I soon became known as the kid among the other fliers and hangers on there—a sobriquet that was neither derogatory nor particularly gratifying.

The weeks went by as I learned to handle departure and arrival stalls, full stalls, sideslips and turns, glides and climbs, and then at last it came time for John Nemetz to let me solo. I worried that he might back off his promise to solo me before school resumed in September by saying that as a kid I needed more time. So it was with some misgivings that, on an August morning, I told my parents that I was going to solo and that they should come out to watch.

As usual with my achievements, the old man had not said much about the flying; he left all that fuss to my mother. Outwardly he seemed supportive, but since he never said much or gave me credit for doing a good job, it was hard to know if he was happy about the whole process. Still, he and my mother drove me out to the field, and I was happy to see that they brought along the family 8mm movie camera.

When we arrived my parents stayed outside near the car as I went into the office to check in with John.

"So what are we going to do today?" he asked me as he stepped up to the counter. I was crestfallen, could he have forgotten about my going solo, had he misgivings? I would be shattered if I had made the old man come out here and not solo.

"You said today was the day I would solo," I ventured.

"Hmm, we'll see" was his laconic reply.

John told me which of the several Cubs we were to use and sent me out to do the preflight and release it from the tie-downs. I could not even look at my parents as I passed by. They stayed near the blue Oldsmobile and did not even acknowledge that we were related.

The first fifteen minutes of the lesson went like all the others, smooth and easy. We took off, went around the pattern, and made a touch and go. Two more times we took the little Piper around the pattern with John saying little and sitting sideways in the front seat so that I would have a clear view ahead.

As we approached to land for the third time I flared the plane to just enough to let the wheels kiss the ground before applying power for another takeoff. John said, "Let's make this one a full stop."

Making a full stop only required that I close the throttle and pull the stick all the way back into my lap. We landed with a thump and rolled ahead for a few feet.

"Take me over to the tetrahedron," he instructed.

My heart and head were in a whirl—was this it? We taxied up to the yellow metal structure that sat at the crossing points of the two main runways. An ancient aviation device, it was designed to point to the direction of the prevailing wind to assist planes like the Cub, that wanted to land but were not equipped with radios, to identify the correct runway for landing. The yellow monster was fifteen feet long and could be seen easily from any point in the landing pattern.

As I stopped the Cub alongside the tetrahedron I was still not sure what John intended. Maybe he wanted to move the pointer, although there was not much breeze today and what wind there was seemed almost vague as to direction.

"Ok, drop me here, and take it around on your own. You know what to do. Make a full landing and then come back and pick me up. And remember, without me in the front seat the plane will be a lot lighter."

With that said he was out of the plane and stepping away under the wing. I grinned as wide as my mouth would allow and pushed the throttle gently ahead. In those days there was no real checklist prior to take off. Later on, as a military aviator, I would be bound with kneeboard-mounted checklists and would spend hours memorizing them, but on this balmy August day all I needed to remember was "climb and glide at 65."

I made sure that there were no other aircraft in the pattern and taxied to the takeoff position. Whether John had called my parents over or they knew enough to come out to the tetrahedron I never found out. As I raced forward down the runway, I caught sight of them standing with John at mid-field with the movie camera pointed at the Cub and me.

I sang and whooped all the way around the pattern. The J-3, without John's weight in the nose, climbed like a rocket, and I was at the pattern altitude of nine hundred feet by the time I reached the far end of the runway. I remembered to extend the length of the legs of the pattern so I would have time to make sure that I was ready for the landing. I wanted it to be perfect. Looking back now, I realize that never before or since was I as confident in my actions as I was on that day. I had drilled the process long enough, and I could feel the controls as an extension of me. I loved what I was doing and what it meant to be the only kid in my school that next year to have soloed an airplane.

With John out of the plane, the Cub floated and did not sink as fast when I pulled back the power. If I didn't correct the approach, I was going to land long. Without another thought I quickly reverted to a sideslip. I pushed right rudder and left stick. At one hundred feet I relaxed the controls, and the little craft swept low, and the wheels hissed as they met the patch of gravel in the touchdown zone.

John came over and spoke to me, saying that he thought I was just a little high on approach and then sent me off for two more circuits. I had finally made it. Each of the next two trips around the pattern was like the first, but better. I had officially joined the flying fraternity, and nothing could change that. However small and feeble my first efforts that day might be, they were the same as those of Lindbergh, Rickenbacker, Bader, and all the rest when they started out. They had their solo day, and, if I was to never have the breadth of their experiences, at least I knew what they knew on their first day in the air.

To celebrate that day, as a family we went out to eat. I do not remember where, though, maybe to the Lido Diner or to Swingle's

Diner, our family's two regular spots on Route 22. The movie my father made still exists along with a couple of snapshots of John and me standing next to the plane. More hours of flight training, ground school, and advanced training were in the future. John taught me a lot in those early days. Mostly, he helped me to see the world in a new way. He helped me into a world far beyond the confines of home and school, and a little of him is still with me.

About a year later, when I was finally taking my FAA written exam, I ran into John at the FAA office and testing facility at Newark Airport. The offices were housed in the original terminal building. It was an Art-Deco masterpiece topped by a forties-vintage control tower. The tower was not in use any longer, having been replaced by a new structure able to handle the increasing number of jets at the airport, but inside the building it was still 1940. Art Deco murals and bas-relief sculptures brought back the days when an airline trip was still an adventure, and something for which you wore your best suit or dress—far from the bus-station atmosphere at airports today. As I was getting set to take my exam, I saw John in the hallway. He was there to take his instrument written exam. He then told me that he had gotten a job as a ferry pilot taking planes from the Piper factories to locations around the US and overseas and needed his instrument rating. He then beamed his toothy smile and wished me luck. Later that year I learned that John had disappeared over Greenland ferrying a new Piper to Europe. He was the first of many friends that I was to make and to lose during my aviation career.

———

Hours passed, and it was time for lunch, I was feeling famished, something about being underway at last. The crowd of men had thinned as the coastline receded, and I took a last long look toward the north. The long arm of Point Reyes was faint in the sea mist. A thousand miles beyond that were my wife and daughter, and now I was off to war. At that moment, I felt very sad and wondered for the first time if I had made the right choice in joining the navy, or was I just being selfish in pursuing what I wanted.

"You look worried, so what are you thinking?" The question came from a voice to my left, and it startled me back into the moment. I turned. Al LeBaron stood there appraising me.

"You look wrapped in thought. Worried?" he asked.

"A little, I was just thinking about my family back in Whidbey. You know. I was wondering if I would ever see them again."

"Let me give you a piece of advice. It might sound a little harsh, but there are going to be a lot of things that will happen from here on out. Some good, some bad, some simply inexplicable, and some of them can kill you. Who knows what we will run into, it is different every time. But there is one thing that will really drag you down and make the things we have to do even harder. That is worrying about home. Just don't. The best advice I ever got back in '66 when I made my first deployment was to consider myself already dead. Stop worrying about if you are going to come home. That is out of your control. Just go with what happens. Anyway, there is a lot of fun to be had in Westpac, despite the war." LeBaron smiled, "You look hungry—let's get some lunch."

No mention was ever made of the events of the previous night, perhaps that was best. I took one last look northward and followed my friend down the ladder and off to the wardroom.

PACIFIC BLUE—12 TO 26 SEPTEMBER

Now that we were underway, our air group had ten days to fine tune ourselves as a cohesive fighting unit. For the last nine months, officers had been transferred into the squadron from the replacement air group and as a squadron; we began to work together as crews. A few of found ourselves shuffled into new crews but at this point everyone was eager and if there were some rough edges between us, they were quickly smoothed over. Prior to our deployment, there had been two work ups at sea off the California coast. These were short periods, mini-cruises in fact, where we flew from the ship, became used to shipboard routines, and learned about our sister squadrons, who they were and how they and their airplanes operated. During this time at sea all of us became carrier-qualified for launching and recovery from and to the ship. It was an intense time of air ops, catapulting from the ship, learning the appropriate patterns for landing and generally getting used to operating at sea. We then went ashore and spent another two weeks at Fallon, Nevada, again at an operational pace, flying day and night and working out other operational kinks.

Fallon had been an education on many levels, a grad school course in air combat. It was the longest time that as a squadron we had been away from Whidbey, and we were meeting our future shipmates, so it was also a time for sizing each other up. More than that, we had to learn to trust the other men in the other units, trust that they knew their jobs. Out there in the high desert we conducted round-the-clock operations, simulated alpha strikes with all the air wing's planes launched to bomb isolated Nevada mountaintops, night formation flights to ensure that we could stay together when the weather was foul and the chips were down. We still had time to play though, and that was part of the learning process as well.

Fallon was blessed with two casinos; one was a glitzy if rural version of the large gambling halls in Reno, the other a ramshackle roadhouse on the outskirts of town. In those days, the base was much smaller than it is now, and people didn't view the town as a particularly attractive duty station. It was dry and dusty and there appeared to be a high level of cancers among its residents. The navy was constantly rotating people in and out of the base for training as the war went through its oscillating cycles of intensity. Tradition had it that if you were a navy flier and you wanted to go out to gamble and have some drinks, and still keep most of your bankroll, you went to Mom's Roadside Inn. This was the dive outside of town. Mom's had been a hangout for countless numbers of naval aviators.

The walls of the place were covered with framed photos of Mom, a septuagenarian crone, seated in the cockpit of A-6s and Phantoms and wearing a flight helmet. The large domes of the helmets dwarfed her narrow wrinkled face to the point of absurdity. Every unit that had passed through Fallon had a plaque with its squadron insignia hanging on the walls. Actually, since prostitution was legal in many Nevada counties, the place began as a cathouse, and Mom had been the madam. But time passed, and she and the girls got older, and in order to keep the money coming in, she turned the place into a bar and casino. Some of the girls remained, in their forties now, still attractive and flirty, and served as croupiers and ran the games. You could get a steak for five bucks, gamble all night at the dime crap table and the quarter roulette wheel, and never lose more than ten dollars. It was great for us, since most of our money was sent home to our wives and families. As we played, Mom would come around; walking slowly with the aid her cane, carrying stacks of drink tokens and pressed them into our hands. It was safe place to drink and gamble and very tame, and we all got home without losing our shirts.

Our squadron was designated as Tactical Electronic Warfare Attack Squadron 131, or, in navy jargon, VAQ-131. The V indicated that we flew fixed wing aircraft, the A, indicated that our role was attack (as opposed to fighter or early warning), and the Q meant that we dealt in electronic warfare, but to our fellow aviators it all just meant *queer*. And queer we were. As such, we were viewed as the new Buck Rogers types of the fleet. The airplane we flew, the EA-6B Prowler was something brand new, an outgrowth of the tried and true A6 Intruder. The plane was created as an attack plane that instead of unleashing bombs, was designed to emit streams of electromagnetic radiation to suppress enemy radar-guided weapons. Some people thought we carried an arsenal of ray guns in the long pods that hung below our wings with which we would melt or sterilize enemy forces. Some thought we had a new kind of laser weapon right out of Star Trek, but in truth the system was much more prosaic. What made it all new however was that we were carrying the war—*the electronic war*—directly into battle.

What we did was called ECM or electronic countermeasures, and its practice had been around since the Second World War. Back then; bombers flying into Hitler's Germany would dump tons of shredded aluminum foil into the air. This chaff, or, as the British called it, window, fluttered about in the bomber's slipstreams and, because it was nearly weightless, remained aloft for long periods of time—long enough for enemy radar to identify the fluttering stuff as actual bombers and render anti-aircraft weapons useless. For what this chaff did was to reflect the beams of the ground-based radar stations thus blanking out whole sections of their search areas. Of course, they knew the bombers were in the air, but not precisely, where they could be found. That meant that in a Germany, with ever decreasing supplies of fuel, fighters, and pilots, that they could not defend the targets the bombers were after.

In 1972, VAQ-131 was only the second fleet squadron to be equipped with the new EA-6B. Outwardly, the plane just looked like an elongated version of the battle-proven A6 Intruder, one of the most successful all-weather carrier-based attack aircraft ever built. The EA-6B however, had been designed from the airframe out to be something much different. For one thing, the plane was designed, not for a defensive role, but as an offensive part of the navy's attacking air force. The Prowler was built to accompany bombers to and from hostile targets, and carried aboard it *active* electronic jamming equipment to do that job. Before the Prowler, heavy bombers like the A3 Skywarrior were required to carry bulky and low powered jammers into combat, and their success was indifferent. But the Prowler incorporated the latest advances in its electronic weaponry—the ALQ 99 system that controlled externally mounted high power jamming pods with steerable antennae. Now we could fly with the bomber force and knock out the effectiveness of enemy radar as we penetrated an enemy country from the sea.

Before the Prowler, radar jamming had been simply a matter of brute force. To win the battle of the electrons you had to overpower the enemy, megawatt for megawatt. For any radar to be effective, it must send out a signal, have that signal hit its target, and then return to the originating site. It is like hitting a tennis ball against a wall; the distance it has had to travel weakens the return bounce. It is simple physics, really, but where it gets lethal is that by matching the radar's frequency and what is known as pulse repetition frequency (PRF), the game enters a whole new realm. Now, the jamming plane can effectively take over an enemy's radar and deny them the ability to control their missiles, guns, or fighters for the few precious seconds that it takes to acquire and shoot down the incoming force. Once the defensive array of weapons is penetrated, the target is wide open for destruction. For the Prowler, in terms of the Soviet-built arsenal it did not matter if the radar was land, sea, or air-based—we could defeat them all. But what we did best was to battle the Soviet-built weapon that had become the scourge of the air war in Vietnam—the surface to air missile known as the SA-2 Goa and the Fansong B radar that was used to acquire American targets. The SA-2, a telephone-pole-length weapon was hitting far too many American planes, and so the Prowler's weapon system had been designed to defeat the Fansong B radar that directed the missiles.

For the rest of Carrier Air Wing 14, as our air group was designated, the fact that we could identify and then effectively jam the enemy missiles was viewed as a welcome relief, spiced with some doubt. A lot of the "retreads" in the wing, those who had made one or two prior deployments, were skeptical of what we could do, even though we had demonstrated our abilities on the test ranges in Nevada. They had first-hand experience of radar guided guns and missiles over North Vietnam and though they hoped we knew what the hell we were doing. They required proof before they would trust us. The proof we would provide in a few weeks, when we entered the South China Sea and took up our war position on Yankee Station, north of the seventeenth parallel. As it would turn out, during the entire deployment, none of our air wing's squadrons lost a plane to enemy ground fire when we were aloft and jamming for them.

And now I was on my way to war in a world of khaki and blue. I think that I was born to wear khaki. As a kid, my mother bought me "chinos", as the washable khaki slacks were then called. My father forbade blue jeans for me, especially once I became a teenager and the distance between us grew further and further. As a naval officer, I enjoyed wearing the service dress khaki uniform we aviators wore most of the time. I still think it was the best looking suit of clothes I ever owned. Khaki blouse, shirt, trousers, socks set off with a black necktie, and for us, brown shoes. Aviators or Airedales were called the "brown shoe" navy by the rest of the fleet. We set ourselves apart, eschewing the blue dress uniform, and in winter weather wearing the oh-so-comfortable aviation green uniform that dated back to the thirties. The navy's color choices simply met my sartorial preferences much to the annoyance of my series of wives and girlfriends. Now I had to prove myself worthy of the uniform I had come to love.

———

They had been there in the lobby of the cafeteria all morning. I had seen them when I walked by for breakfast, but I was in a hurry to get to class and soon forgot about them. But then, as I returned to the building at lunch, their display caught my eye. Blue and gold on the brochure that had an illustration on its cover of a pair of sleek F-111s overhead a carrier drew me over to the table. A moment later a young lieutenant, wearing shiny new aviator's wings, was talking to me. Was I interested in naval aviation? Had I thought about entering their AVROC program, which would allow me to graduate from college with a commission and orders to flight training, if I would agree to spend my summers in Pensacola learning the ropes.

I told them I was a licensed pilot and had been flying since I was sixteen. That statement brought over another officer, this time a lieutenant commander who, in avuncular style, asked if I'd like to take a short exam to see if I could qualify for their flight-training program. They were going to be on campus for the next two days giving the tests to young men interested in a naval career. As I stood talking to them, several other students passed by glared at me and made soft mocking sounds about the military. This was 1966, and the war in Vietnam was not yet the divisive topic that it would soon become, but its unpopularity on college campuses was growing. Besides, Rider College, tucked away in the shadow of its more prestigious neighbor up the road in Princeton, was no hotbed of dissent. Most Rider students, like me, were there to get the necessary credentials to get a job in business, not light up the world with protests. For the most part we were the sons and daughters of blue-collar parents, the so-called silent majority and the first in our families to attend college so rancorous polemics were not in our makeup.

I went to take the test at the school's job placement office where the navy was given space to conduct the exam. Spatial relationships: identify the position of an aircraft relative to the ground; reading of instruments; and some simple math comprised the timed tests. A senior chief petty officer led me into a tiny room with a table and chair normally used for on-campus job interviews. He placed the test booklets on the table and told me he would come in at the end of each timed period to collect the exams and grade them, while I worked on the next section. Then he left, and I started on the first section. It was all incredibly easy and my answers came without much thinking. When I had finished all the sections, he asked me to remain in the room for a few moments while he finished the grading. I sat there for about ten minutes and then there was a knock on the door, and he asked me to come out. The small reception area outside the interview room was now lined wall-to-wall naval personnel as I emerged. They were all smiles and the senior officer, that same friendly lieutenant commander, stepped forward to shake my hand.

"So you aced the test," he gushed. Immediately they all wanted to know when I could sign up. Since I was a freshman and had been on campus little more than a month, this all seemed a little sudden, I had no experience with being the "belle of the ball" and I told him I needed to talk to my parents. They were understanding and loaded me down with reading material, brochures and application forms. I went home the next weekend to proudly present the opportunity to my parents. My mother didn't say too much, but my father, in his inimitable burst-my-balloon style grunted, "Well, who is going to pay for your uniforms and stuff, and how are you going to earn money over the summer for college?" Clearly, he was not enthusiastic about me becoming a naval officer, but then, at this point in our filial relationship, he never expressed enthusiasm about anything I was doing or might plan to do.

Three years passed, and I forgot about the navy and gave little thought to the war. I was dating my future wife and making dean's list grades. I had a regular part-time job making oil burner nozzles at a factory run by a few ex-Nazis. My plans were simple, I thought I would graduate near the top of my class, get a great job, and get married. There was only one tiny flaw in the plan. Though I could not imagine that the Vietnam War could go on so long—but it did.

In my senior year, just before Thanksgiving, the navy was back on campus. This time there was a new set of recruiters, ones who did not rise to the bait of the jeers from the mostly anti-war students as they passed the tables with the brochures about naval aviation. But my head was still full of dreams of flying, and when I stopped at their table to talk to them, they were pleasantly surprised. I expect they found college campuses less than hospitable. In due course, they looked up my test records and invited me to come down to Lakehurst and visit with them. In truth, despite my high grades and the slew of companies coming to campus to recruit, I knew that if I did not sign up to fly, I would soon find myself up to my ass in some rice paddy. In any event, how much longer could the war go on? After all, flight training would take two years. Well, I signed up, swore to uphold and defend the constitution, and when I graduated I had orders to report to Pensacola by 30 June. It was a good thing that I had volunteered, for only two weeks later; they had the first draft lottery since the Second World War. The drawings were by birthday and mine, July 7 was a winning number—fifty. For me there was no doubt about being drafted, and if I hadn't signed up with the navy before the lottery, with such a low number the navy would not have accepted me for the program. I had dodged a bullet, of sorts, there would be others waiting. Still I had won a lottery of sorts—they kept the war open just for me—anchors aweigh!

———

Apparently, ours was not going to be any record-setting crossing of the Pacific. Ten to twelve days sailing from San Francisco to Subic Bay, the ship's captain had announced on the evening of our first day at sea. By then we were out on the broad North Pacific—deep, very blue water chilled by the arctic that swept down from the northern horizon. Soon though, we would alter course to move further southwest into the warm seas of the South Pacific, and then to war. For the ship's company, those sailors and officers assigned to the ship and not to a squadron, normal at-sea routines set the pattern of these days. For as many days as we were at sea, theirs was a kind of routine job, albeit seven days a week and twenty-four hours a day. For the embarked squadron personnel however, the two weeks of crossing the ocean meant there was no flying, and so any semblance of the normality of daily flight operations was suspended. Still, the job of maintaining aircraft readiness was paramount. Who knew what emergency might require the launch of aircraft to defend the ship? The Russians liked to fly their giant turbo-prop Bear bombers out from their bases in Siberia and attempt to intercept American carriers headed to the war zone. It was a decades old game, and for that there were two F-4 Phantoms kept in readiness on the flight deck. In any event, planes that don't fly seem to develop problems, hydraulic lines leak, pressurized gasses seem to evaporate and metal rusts, so maintenance had to be at top level, because once we reached Subic Bay all aircraft had to be up to full combat operations.

In the navy all aviation officers have two jobs, in the squadron you are a division officer first, and an aviator second. That doesn't mean you can slack off as a flier in favor of your work, it just meant that you are on duty around the clock, day in and day out. When we left San Francisco, I had just been reassigned from the stultifyingly tedious duty as the squadron communications officer, to a job in the maintenance department. The communications officer job is a thankless one in which I had been responsible for all the secret material and daily message traffic that flowed in and out of the squadron. It was a job in which a young officer can manage to sink his career by losing or mislaying some piece of classified material, and there were reams of papers stamped, Confidential, Secret, Top Secret floating around. After moving to the maintenance department, I was named the aircraft and power plants division officer, a much less ethereal kind of job. There were thirty mechanics who maintained the planes for which I was now responsible. These men kept us flying. This was not a trivial assignment, inasmuch as I was not only responsible for the work they performed on the planes, but for their well-being and behavior as well.

The assignment brought with it its own small chain of command. I now had two grizzled chief petty officers—old men it seemed, in their mid-thirties, to supervise. In truth, as in all services, it would be these experienced non-coms who kept me in line—*up to a point*. In any unit it is the chiefs and senior petty officers who are charged by the system with coaching young ensigns and lieutenants (junior grade) as to what should and should not be done, and how best to manage the men. I suppose that's been the way since Agrippa and his fleet defeated Marc Antony at Actium. Still, I was the one who would be held accountable if hydraulic systems leaked or engines were not up to performance. After all, we were here to fight a war.

The ship had been cruising at a fast pace, cutting through a half dozen time zones as we headed southwest. One of the *Enterprise*'s propeller shafts had been slightly damaged months before, bent slightly off of true, and though the ship should have been sent into dry dock for repair, the exigencies of war kept her at sea. When the ship made full speed, the vibrations from the turning shaft could be felt everywhere. I had grown up on boats in the waters around New York Harbor, Raritan Bay and Sandy Hook and had seen the ocean in various light conditions, but the North Pacific had the bluest water I had ever seen. The air, scrubbed my miles of open sea had no scent to it. We were in an indigo world, slashed with whitecaps and crowned by deep azure skies streaked by high wisps of cirrus. Piles of cumulus clouds filled the horizon, and the wind coming down from the Bering Straits sliced through the cotton of my summer uniform. Being out on the flight deck or simply standing by one of the open hangar deck doors was chilling because of both the drop in temperature and speed of our passage.

An aircraft carrier going to war embarks nearly five thousand men all jammed into a very small space. We were crammed into a length of eleven hundred feet of steel, and yet finding a quiet spot to think or write, was easy enough. Among the stacks of gear stowed next to the starboard-side hangar doors or along the bulkheads of the sponsons, there were many places where one could find some solitude. Several times I stopped in a special spot that I had found near the number three elevator to get my head straight. From there, when the hangar doors were open, I could watch the sea and sky, alone, unobserved, and uninterrupted. Men were working all around me, and I just appeared to be another clueless JG staring off to the horizon. I was of scant interest to them.

My home and office at sea was the junior officer bunkroom on the O3 level, just below the waist catapults on the port side of the ship. It was a six-man room, just forward of the air operations plot room and across from the sanctum of Admiral's Country, sometimes called boy's town. The interior was metal and linoleum decorated in the attractive gray and institutional green so beloved by naval designers. In a strange way, our little haven was very neatly isolated from the normal hubbub of the ship. No one with any sense hung about or ventured into Admiral's Country—those rarified spaces reserved for the commander of Task Force Seventy-Seven, when he was embarked. Most fore and aft foot traffic took the starboard passageway on the far side of the ship. We found our little haven ignored for the most part, especially by those snoops employed by the XO sniffing for contraband booze. The space we shared had six bunks stacked in twos, two sinks, six desks, six large wardrobes, and a couple of air ducts through which fetid air was recirculated from space to space throughout the ship. My bunk was one of the few had come with its own special décor, installed by me predecessor. It was an intricately designed montage of photographs that would have been appropriate to a cathouse in Pompeii. He had installed posters boards all around the bed, full of photos—all of naked women. The other denizens of the junior officer bunkroom had not seen the wall covering when we selected our bunks, nor had I, at first, but now, far at sea I counted my blessings and took full advantage of the scenery.

There were six of us living in a space that might, just might fit a pair of Volkswagen Beetles. The navy calls beds "racks" and for a very good reason. Each pair of bunk beds has a thin mattress supported by a steel slab. They were built into the bulkheads and were immovable. Heavy blackout curtains were hung that surrounded the bunks, like Pullman berths. This afforded some privacy, but they were there mostly so we could sleep when others were up. The best part of this arrangement was that I could read in bed without waking the others and lose myself in the text. Each of us had a desk which came with a safe, some shelves, and drawers, along with a tall wardrobe for hanging our uniforms. The bunks were set in each of three corners of the space with the forth set aside for the pair of sinks. The middle of the space was filled the block of six wardrobes. Once we emptied our blue metal cruise boxes and filled our lockers, the room looked like your average college dorm of the era—if you ignored the side arms and flight suits.

An officer's rack was his only truly private space on the ship, and mine was a bottom bunk under Bill Woods. Across from me, on the lower tier, was Dan Miller and above him the brand new squadron air intelligence officer, or AI, an ensign named Rick Adamson, but everyone in the squadron called him Clete.

Clete had joined us just before we deployed and reminded everyone of Ichabod Crane. And Ichabod would have indeed been his nickname, if we all had not seen the movie *The Hospital* in the ready room one evening during workups. In the movie, a character that looked even more like our hapless AI kept ranting that he was the "Paraclete of Kaborka." Given the creative powers of the assembled aviators, we dubbed Adamson The Clete, which quickly became just Clete. Clete's main problem was that he was a Mormon and in truth, not a very good one. Rumor had it that he had failed on his required mission to convert his quota of gentiles to the magic underwear squad. There seemed to be a surprisingly large contingent of LDS types aboard *Enterprise*. And an elect cadre of the ship's over-eager population of the Angel Moroni's followers relentlessly hounded poor Clete. He was ordered by them to perform some act of atonement to make up for his failings of faith, but the kid was more afraid of them than of the wrath of Moroni. Perhaps they wanted him to find a couple of extra wives when we got to the PI. It's not that I had anything against the Mormon's who sailed with us. Before I met Clete, I had not given that religion much thought at all. I had taken time in college to read the *Book of Mormon* and it made about as much sense to me as did *Mein Kampf,* and where as the one has the ranting's of one of the most evil men ever born, the other basis its tenets on a guy named Smith who looks to an angel named Moroni to show him where some gold tablets are buried in rural New York State. The whole time I read I just couldn't get the refrain from Shirley Ellis' *The Name Game* out of my head.

In the other corner of the bunkroom, Phil Celsius had occupied the lower rack and Tom Evers the one above him. Phil was the most patrician of the six of us. He had elegant manners and his uniforms had been specially tailored. A fastidious and well-groomed man, he seemed old before his time although he was only twenty-five at the time. He was a graduate-level brown-noser of the first water, who routinely curried favor with any senior officer, commander and above, through whom he could better advance his career. Phil was married to a stunning red head, an ex model from I Magnin in San Francisco. She is tall, with very long legs and green eyes, like emeralds. Phil, as rumor has it, had lent her out to some of those same senior officers in the hope that his wife would pillow talk his way up the chain of command.

Heading out to war, the J.O. bunkroom was a Spartan place. Entertainment, such as it was, relied on a couple of cassette tape recorders that offered occasional background music. There was no place to get new music until we hit the Philippines, so if your roommates loved The King and you didn't, well it sucked to be you. Most of us brought piles of books with us and these did circulate among the squadron's officers. As time went on, those titles that implied the most pornographic content attracted the largest followings. The worst of the situation was the fact was that there was barely enough whiskey hidden in the safes to make the ten-day passage. We had to ration our supply to make the journey.

There were two major defects of the J.O. bunkroom. The first involved our proximity to the communal head and the showers that serviced this section of the ship. These were located down the main passageway and one knee-knocker forward. For anyone to successfully negotiate the dozens of knee-knockers, essentially oval-shaped steel openings in the bulkheads to which emergency hatches could be secured, one had to walk like a hurdler, rhythmically thrusting one leg out over the steel rim and moving into the next section of passageway. It's done easily enough, and with practice I never had to think about my steps, even when I was drunk. The only drawback was that there is no chance to set your pace, and stumbling sleepily and banging your shin was often the fate of the uninitiated. The second drawback, one that was far more serious, was the fact that the J.O. bunkroom sat directly beneath the flight deck. Admittedly, there was sixteen inches of armor plate in the overhead above where we sleep, but then just above that steel plate were the tracks for the number three and four catapults.

During carrier qualifications, we J.O.s had learned to sleep through the bangs and roars of multiple launches and recoveries. It was either that or go crazy. Then again, some of us had already begun to demonstrate odd behaviors since going to sea. There was one not-so-obvious benefit of our location. As I mentioned earlier, we were adjacent to the combat operations center and across from the admiral's spaces. Being so close to Flag Country kept the master's at arms and the ship's X.O.'s coterie of spies from prowling around looking for booze and the location of our weekly smoker. None of these creatures of the night wanted to "discover" anything illicit that might impinge on the character of the occupants of the Flag Quarters so they stayed away.

One of the realities of shipboard living, something that I had discovered while we were on our first at-sea period back in June, was that if one is survive, an officer needs to develop a few trusted accomplices among the petty officers. The phrase "I'll scratch your back if you scratch mine" includes extra liberty chits and excused duty to those enterprising petty officers who just happen to have access to such things as a film projector and the appropriate smut movies to go with it.

Since my original assignment had been as the classified materials officer, it fell to me to find the X-rated movies. One might think that an impossible task on a warship far at sea, it wasn't. Had I any real scruples, I might have demurred; many other officers, straight-laced and prudish or religious, did refuse. Ironically, many of them managed to drop in when we were showing a film. It did not take long to find the appropriate scrounger among our senior enlisted men or, as the navy dubbed such individuals, a cumshaw artist. I found my main cumshaw contact in a garrulous and totally corruptible first-class petty officer named Denver.

Denver could locate anything, for a price. We quickly came to an understanding. I was clearly going to be his meal ticket for favors and liberty and in return, he would to his best to make sure that this JG's shipboard life was made easier, and we each made out by the deal. For him to operate he had to have friends all over the ship. It was Denver who first introduced me to the Filipino mess stewards. Each embarked squadron had to provide at least one steward from its own company to serve in the mess. Aquino was our squadron's sole donation and he worked in the dirty shirt wardroom. Aquino's reputation was enhanced amongst his peers since, through Denver he had made solid connections to the officers they all served. Through him, they could ask for and receive favors. Life aboard ship is like a small and genteelly corrupt town; you go along to get along. From the first day at sea, I never had to worry about my laundry going missing, my bedding not being changed, or not getting an extra slice of cake and ice cream at dinner.

But not all my fellow officers saw it that way. In the wardroom, I often grimaced as I watched as some of the other officers acted pompously toward the stewards, who as junior enlisted men often had to put up with a tremendous amount of bullshit. These officers barked at the stewards and generally treated them like personal servants. They acted as if they were British officers serving in India under the Raj. Perhaps in another age that might have worked, when flogging was part of life at sea, but these men were not servants, they were shipmates, embarked on the same warship and assigned to a support role so we could fly. Some of these officers remained ignorant of and oblivious to these young men, and they never took the time to find out that indeed many of the Filipinos had graduated from medical school or law school, and were only in the navy in order to get their US citizenship. Once they had that status, they could go back to the Philippines and demand premium salaries as Americans. The navy, in a vestige of the time when the only job on ships for blacks was in the galley, had kept the Filipino steward process going. But I took the time to remember their names, ask about their families, and, so, over time I reaped my rewards by treating them like people.

During the long crossing much of the day revolved around meals. Food and eating becomes a fixation of sorts. The dirty shirt wardroom was just down the passage on the port side from the bunkroom. Three meals a day plus nightly movies kept the place busy. Just forward of the wardroom was another space filled with lounge chairs. It was a nice place to spend some time in the evenings. If you closed your eyes you might think you were home in your own living room. That is, until some announcement came blaring over the 1-MC from the bridge.

Every other week I had the squadron duty, a task that falls to lieutenant commanders and below. Without any flight operations, that meant sitting for twenty-four hours in the ready room and manning the telephone. Since the phone seldom rang the most vital task of the duty officer is the selection of the night's movie. No other function seemed to be more critical to your standing in the unit. One's career might hang in the balance, especially if you gained the reputation for making poor cinematic choices. The movies, some almost ancient, and some from which the more prurient scenes had been snipped and the remainder respliced, circulated from ready room to ready room. If the duty officer picked a dud, he would not easily live it down. Artistic value was not appreciated, large amounts of exposed female skin, however was. Since departing from Alameda there were precious few decent movies aboard—and the admiral's staff always got first pick of the best.

"What's the movie tonight? Mr. Duty Officer!" Tommy DeAngelis, our squadron's X.O. snapped as he stepped into the ready room.

"*Two Lane Blacktop*, sir." I replied.

"Any sex in it?

"Some girls with bodacious boobs riding in cars with two bigger boobs from what I could tell, sir."

"You know, they've added a section to the fitness reports regarding movie selection at sea. It's right up there with airmanship, so you are betting the ranch on your choice tonight." The X.O. smiled when he said that, plopped into his chair, and pulled up the large red clipboard to read the day's message traffic.

All day long officers flowed in and out of the ready room. This was our home, our living room, and our rec room aboard ship. Like all the other ready rooms on the ship two massive coffee pots had been lashed to the bulkhead, and it was my job as the duty officer to keep them fresh and hot. Truthfully, what that meant involved sending the poor seaman assigned as my runner to refill the massive urns from the fresh water taps in the galley and shovel the ground coffee into the drip pans, while carefully avoiding adding too many of the ship's complement of roaches to the mix.

As the duty officer, one can either direct the center of squadron activity or end up becoming be set up to be the butt. Today, it seemed, I was to be the butt. Around 0830 another runner brought the daily stack of messages and memos from the CAG, the Air Group Commander. For the most part these were routine and directed the embarked squadrons to perform and report on certain areas of combat readiness. Nothing in the navy gets done without some sheet of paper being completed. Since we were not flying at this part of the transit, there were no orders involving flight, but it seemed everything else was fair game. There was one directive that was buried in the papers that morning. It advised each squadron to select a group of junior officers to report to the bridge for a rotation to stand watches to sight the mail buoy.

As the directive indicated, the mail buoy is a device to be air dropped ahead of the ship's course by a C-130, inside the buoy was the latest mail from the States. The job was to spot the floating buoy and then launch a ship's boat to recover it. The absurdity of the notion was clouded in very technical naval terms designed to sway the gullible into showing up in front of the ship's captain, binoculars in hand, and make himself a fool. This kind of gentle harassment was commonplace at sea. Young sailors on their first cruise are often sent off by their senior petty officers and chiefs to scour the ship in search of cans of magnetic flux, or lengths of waterline, or the ever-popular source of the cooling water for the hand rails. Of course, none of the senior officers in the squadron acknowledged the absurdity of the order. Instead they just smirked and buried their noses in messages or other busy work, all of which made it clear to me that this was just the trap that it seemed to be. I simply ignored the directive and, when one of the other J.O.s made a comment about it, I took him aside and "waved him off."

Later in the day the news circulated that CAG's own junior operations officer, an ensign with less sense than a doorknob, had indeed appeared on the bridge, binoculared and ready to stand the mail-buoy watch. CAG was chided all that day by the other senior officers on the ship about this I was not sure if we would see the young ensign in public for several weeks.

As the transpac continued various department heads from the squadron scheduled training that involved elements of the squadron, air wing, or the ship. There were also lengthy and humorless briefings from the embarked Grumman Aircraft reps, builders of the EA-6B Prowlers. Whether these Grumman guys were being punished by their employer by being sent to sea or were seeking a time off from their families was never clear. Each of them complained about their quarters, the food and the lack of recreational facilities on the carrier. Eventually the "Grummies" became mascots of sorts and occasionally whipping boys when the airplane failed to perform as expected. Each day at sea also brought another series of lectures as the ship moved five hundred sea miles closer to the combat zone. It was a surreal time drifting through a space between peace and war.

As we approached the combat zone, the meaning of time began to change. Hours ran together and the days of the week lost any relevance for us. An aircraft carrier never sleeps; there are people at work constantly, day and night. While underway, the *Enterprise* ran on three, eight-hour watches rotated through each day. This schedule changed to two shifts when we began combat operations then life continued on port and starboard twelve-hour watches. But such arrangements would always be irrelevant to me— aviators must fly whenever called upon, and it was rumored that *Enterprise* would be assigned to fly the midnight to noon cycle of combat operations. For those of us with divisional responsibilities, we simply had to handle them when we were not flying. Even meal times followed only a loose routine. The dirty shirt wardroom was open all day for officers in need of something to eat, and there was a standing order for "eggs to order." It turned out that I was eating several breakfasts each day.

When nightfall comes at sea, it descends as total darkness. I have never seen anything as black as the sky in mid-ocean. There was no light pollution in mid ocean and above deck lighting was limited to some red spotlights covering the landing area on the angled deck. The big "65" on the island, illuminated so brilliantly in port, remained dark at sea. And as we passed just north of Hawaii, heading ever south, the air began to lose its bite.

Many of the crew who were off-duty sought solace on the flight deck at night. It was the only place one could walk in the open, despite the jam of airplanes chained to the deck. On a transpac, the carrier serves double duty, acting as a freighter hauling cargo for forward bases. In our case, we carried a host of extra aircraft from the Alameda rework facility to be offloaded at Cubi Point in the Philippines. Each of these planes was wrapped in a bubble of white plastic sheathing and they sat like giant larvae along the flight deck edge waiting to hatch. At night I roamed the deck and leaned out to see the long phosphorescent wake streaming behind us. There were others out there, more souls lost in their thoughts and wandering from bow to stern and back again, adroitly stepping around the tie down chains.

There was a quiet anticipation in the air, especially among we nuggets. We had been trained and honed, but not yet tested. That made the cover of night the perfect time for reflection and philosophy. Several of us had found a favorite spot on the port side catwalk, just forward of our bunk room. The spot was a little difficult to reach from inside the ship. To find it one walked down to the head, past it through a half-high hatch, and then on to the open mesh steel catwalk—eighty feet below the sea was surging past the ship and creating a soothing background of swooshing water. In the darkness, the railing disappeared, and there seemed to be nothing but blackness between where I stood and the sea. From there, I could look southward and see the southern constellations as they began to rise above the horizon. Each night they stood a little higher, while to the north Polaris dipped lower and lower—we were nearing our destination.

For a few nights Paul Hazlet joined me in this quiet roost. We had taken to stopping out here after evening chow. Paul and I had arrived in Whidbey at about the same time and had just started to get to know each other. We both had children, each about a year old, and we had gone through the Replacement Air Group, VAQ-129, at about the same time. Paul was a Colorado boy, solid muscle and a broad chest, built like a bull—which seemed appropriate, because he had done some collegiate rodeo bull riding. It was from him that I earned the nickname Pierre.

It seemed we both went to college for business degrees and as it happened, our first conversations revolved around business, the stock market and the like. Both of us talked and talked, explaining our choices in life and what we hoped for the future. Somewhere along the way he started calling me JP, as in JP Morgan, and one night in the Mexican Village Bar in Coronado, as I lamely tried to sing along with the woman playing at the piano bar, it just became Pierre. At sea, the riggers took blue reflective tape and created the word PIERRE on my helmet. When they showed me their handiwork, I thought, well that is *me* from now on. With the night so black, that it was hard to make out the face of the man next to you. So, without the distraction of facial expressions we talked about everything, trusting in this visual anonymity to protect our privacy. This mid-ocean confessional was a way to say what you were thinking and feeling without judgment or stigma. It was strange that it was Paul who broke the ice.

"How do you know you love your wife?" he asked one night. We had been standing along the portside rail next to an enormous reel that held a hundred feet of jet-fueling hose. I had wedged myself into a comfortable spot out of the path of any of the other night wanderers and from where I could watch the night. The sky did not disappoint. Its show went on as it did every night, offering a view of the southern heavens that was magnificent. The Milky Way lived up to its name becoming a spectacular ribbon of white above our heads. I think I was beginning to grasp the concept of infinity, for nothing could be more immense, nor make me feel so small. Perhaps this was the best setting for truth telling.

"I don't know. I suppose it is just the feeling I have when I am with her and how bad it feels when we are apart. But if you are asking me what love means, then I have no answer." I had groped for this answer because the question seemed so close to the nub of my feelings right then. I was heading off to a place that the one human being with whom I had shared the most in my short life could neither know nor share. I had already stepped outside the bounds of the marriage with the girl in San Fran. Now, I asked myself, what did I feel for my wife?

"I don't think we have been married long enough to really know." Paul plunged on without acknowledging what I had said. "Betty and I are close, we have sex, but are we in love? Is that what love is? I don't know. We will be able to send mail when we get to Subic, and I have been struggling to write her each day while we are crossing this ocean. I find I don't have much to say. Oh, I miss her, but I keep asking myself if this is going to be a real marriage. How do the older guys do it?"

"Maybe you should ask one of them," I said. "That is, if they would or could tell you. I can't really see asking Ted or even the

Baroon. I think they would give you some offhand response and then give you a lot of shit about it later." We stayed there on that catwalk for a long time that night. Sometimes speaking, but mostly not, the endless sea absorbed our thoughts.

It wasn't all deep thinking as we crossed into warmer waters. Junior officers, especially those in the air wing, were supposed to learn something of normal shipboard life. Some bright light in the ship's exec's office thought of a good way to accomplish that and so a series of tasks were assigned to the squadrons, which meant that the work fell to the least senior of the officers who had not been at sea before. So, off we went. One of our tasks was to inspect various and sundry areas of the ship that were generally out of our normal routine circulation. In this way we might learn something of the way the ship functioned. I found myself assigned to such duty and, along with a herd of about thirty other JGs, set out with a clipboard and a ship's company petty officer to lead me on my way. It would be unfair to describe this exercise as a form of black shoe versus brown shoe harassment, but it came close. To the uninitiated, being a black shoe refers to the shipboard navy, whilst we aviators wore brown shoes, some of which were outlandish, including cowboy boots and jodhpurs. We were just barely within regulations. My job that day was to inspect three areas of the ship, and so off I went, down several decks to one of the crew quarters to check the communal head there.

The toilets in the heads aboard the *Enterprise* were not made of porcelain, but rather, they were made of brushed stainless steel, and the row of them I encountered upon entering the space gleamed like polished silver. As soon as I stepped over the threshold into the head, the swabbie third class in charge of the space called his crew of three seamen strikers to attention. The young men stood proudly by their charges, and I immediately thought of the scene in *No Time for Sergeants* in which Andy Griffith presents his toilets for inspection.

Well, a toilet is a toilet, except in the navy. My orders were explicit. I was to inspect the underside of the toilet rims for fungus and other mephitic growths. So, there I was, a lieutenant (junior grade) with my head half-sunk into the bowl, checking for slime. I had to hand it to the men though; there was nothing but gleaming steel to be seen. I took my head out of the bowl and congratulated them on a job well done, then, following my guide; I headed off to the next inspection.

One of the big movies that year was *The Poseidon Adventure*. It involved a fanciful account of an ocean liner capsizing and thus forcing the survivors to exit the ship by climbing into the bilges, normally the bowels of the ship, but in their case, the bilges were up, to escape the inverted hull. So into the *Enterprise's* bowels I went. My next inspection was a spot eight decks below the hangar deck, just above the line of the ship's keel. My guide, an older second-class petty officer with a grizzled moustache and an expanding stomach, led me forward and down a stack of ladders to the bow of the ship. I could feel the rush of water just beyond me on the steel hull. We were standing on a deck about ten feet below the waterline in a space that was lit by a single emergency lamp. The deck and bulkheads were painted a deep maroon, which, on a ship in which baby-shit green predominated, seemed totally out of place. In the center of the space was a circular hatch that had been pulled open; the hatch lid was laid back on the steel deck. The PO smiled and pointed at the hole. I smiled back, and then it hit me—I was supposed to climb into the hole. My stomach lurched. I did not like climbing down or up very much.

When I was a kid, maybe eight or nine years old, my father, ever the gentle and doting parent was doing some repairs on the roof of our three-story house. To teach me to not be afraid of heights, he forced me to stand on the edge of the slick slate roof and look down. I remember seeing the toes of my shoes and, about ten thousand feet below, our back yard. I wanted to puke then, and I wanted to puke now, as I looked into the hole and saw a vertical ladder descending into a murky space about ten miles down.

The navy required that I make this inspection, and so I stuck my clipboard in my belt at the back of my trousers, swung onto the ladder rungs, and began climbing down past four decks. At each deck level a mesh net was strung to catch anyone who might fall. I thought of any number of ways that I could fall, miss the nets, and find myself a permanent addition to the ship, my broken body too messy to identify. An eon passed while I descended. My trusty guide followed, only a few feet above me and, I hoped, climbing down slow enough to not step on my fingers. At last I touched down in a tiny space the size of a large outhouse. Instantly the seaman who had been waiting patiently for me sprang to attention and declared, "Aviation fuel pump number one, ready for inspection—Sir!" In that tiny space his voice rang off the bulkheads. This was the pump that pushed highly flammable aviation gas up to the flight deck for the few piston-powered planes that came aboard the ship. We were now nearly forty feet below the waterline encased in steel. I knew why the space was so small and isolated. In the event of a fire in the pump, the entire space could be sealed off and flooded to extinguish the flames. Much the same could happen if somehow the hull cracked or we hit something below the surface. It would only take a few seconds for seawater to fill this void as the hatches above were secured and the three of us became entombed in the ship. Hmmm, I thought, not something to ponder too much at the moment, just get the job done.

The space was painted the same deep maroon; and in one corner sat a gleaming brass pump. The deck had been swabbed and was clean enough to eat off. In that respect, it was cleaner than most kitchens I had ever been in. I looked at the sailor and said, "Stand at ease." Then I walked the entire distance of four feet to the pump and looked at it. I kept staring at it for what I hoped was the requisite amount of time that would validate my inspection. It shone from hours of polishing with Brasso. I turned and looked around the space. There was nothing else to see, or for me to do. I looked at the two men with me, told them to carry on, and started the long climb back up to the top of the ladder.

If I felt somewhat bemused by the inspection of the pump, my last stop was gave me more to think about. I was slated to inspect the huge walk-in meat freezers. Outside the ambient air temperature was nearing eighty degrees, so when I walked into these spaces my mustache froze and my once limp and now sweaty shirt became stiff on my back. There wasn't much to see, just rows of frozen food products, hanging sides of beef and such. It was not much to inspect, then I came to another door. "What's in there?" I asked.

"Well, sir," replied the petty officer in charge of the space who was leading me around, "That's where we keep any dead bodies until we can off-load them for shipment home."

I thought for a long moment and then, in my best parade ground voice, simply said, "Carry on," I hoped I would not end up by becoming an occupant of the space.

We had been steaming southwest for nearly a week when the sudden alert came. Somewhere over the arctic, a satellite had picked up the movement of a Russian Bear bomber heading out over the Sea of Okhotsk toward us. The ready alert aircraft, two F-4 Phantoms armed with AIM 9 Sidewinder missiles, were put on five-minute standby. Up in the CAG's office some bright light with no concept of electronic warfare suggested that perhaps the EA-6B could be launched to act as an early warning aircraft. In one sense, this was not a bad decision, but using our radar detection systems, as a warning alarm was not our mission. We carried nothing that would stop or hinder an airborne threat like the Bear. However, "saving" the ship from a mock Soviet attack would be a feather in our squadron's cap.

Because of flight deck loading, our aircraft had been kept below and we were forced to man up on the hangar deck. This was not that unusual, what with a flight deck overcrowded with shrink-wrapped planes as well as the entire air group, but starting engines on a deck edge elevator was something new. Like all supercarriers, the *Enterprise* had four deck edge elevators that were used to raise and lower airplanes from the hangar deck to the flight deck. Normally the aircraft are not manned when they are lifted up, but on this day, we were pushed out onto the elevator to start up.

A thirty-knot blast of air blew alongside the ship as *Enterprise* turned into the prevailing wind. Gazing down through the strips of steel that made up the elevator's surface, I saw the froth of the ship's wake surging below my feet. As the canopy closed I looked to my right and saw the ten-foot high arc of the bow wave. If we were swept off this perch there would be no way to survive, even if we tried a zero-zero ejection. The force of the water along the hull would slam us into the hull and sink us like a stone. The auxiliary engine starter, known as the huffer, kicked in, and Jake started the port engine. At the same instant the elevator kicked in, there was a lurch as the ship pitched and then we rose up to the flight deck. The queasy feeling passed and next few minutes were filled with getting ready for flight, going over checklists, and entering the present position of the ship into the onboard navigation computer.

By the time all that was done, there was a plane director standing in front of the Prowler, giving Jake Beltran signals to move us ahead. I sat next to him in the command seat and monitored my side of the plane, to prevent our hitting any of the other parked aircraft. Jake gave the engines more power, and we inched ahead, turning and moving slowly until we were lined up with the number four catapult. Given that we carried more fuel and could stay aloft longer, one of the gas-guzzling F-4s had been re-spotted to the other catapult until we were airborne.

As we inched forward on the cat track, the nose tow linkage was lowered, and the white metal holdback was inserted into the shuttle. The concept of launching a sixty thousand pound airplane from a standstill to one hundred and thirty knots in less than three hundred feet involved using a steam-powered catapult built into the carrier deck to hurl the plane aloft. At full power, a jet the size of ours would simply dribble off the flight deck and into the water without the assistance of the cat. During the Vietnam Era steam catapults were highly reliable, not like the old hydraulic cats of the forties and fifties. Back then it was not unusual to get a cold cat shot—one with no real power—and then find you and your airplane in the drink. The flight deck crewman with the take off weight tote board held it up for us to see. It read "63,000"—sixty-three thousand pounds, our maximum take-off weight. Jake gave him a thumbs-up and the tote board man showed it to the shooter in the port catwalk. It was the shooter's job to adjust the catapult for our weight and then shoot us airborne when the catapult officer touched the deck and pointed forward.

I looked to port and the shooter's hands were raised, as if someone had the drop on him in a western saloon. Jake saluted the catapult officer standing just to his left. The catapult officer, in his yellow sweatshirt and protective headgear, raised his hand and made a circular motion with his finger. Jake stood on the brake pedals and pushed the throttles ahead to one-hundred-and-two percent. The cat officer tilted his head, listening for any misses or deceleration in our two P408 turbojets. Satisfied with what he was hearing, the cat officer executed a graceful pirouette and swept down to touch the deck and point forward. That was the shooter's signal. Instantly, he dropped his hand and pushed the launch button. Jake released the brakes and we held on. A second later we were racing toward the edge of the angled deck.

The normal routine for a catapult launch is to hold on while the aircraft accelerates and then say to yourself, "one potato, two potato, thank you God, I've got it" and then proceed with a normal climb out. We were climbing and I called out the takeoff checklist, "gear up," then "flaps." Jake reached over and, while he maintained pressure on the stick for a smooth climb, down and raised the gear handle and then slid the flap lever forward. We could hear and feel the clunking of the landing gear being raised and the whine of the flaps sliding into the flight position. "Shit." Jake was not a man who cursed very often, so when he said this so soon after takeoff, there was immediate need for concern.

At this point the management philosophy of the former Secretary of Defense, Robert McNamara enters into my narrative. McNamara was one of the Pentagon's Second World War "Whizz Kids" and the former president of Ford Motor Company. One of his famous directives as Defense Secretary was that as many parts as possible in the vast military supply system should be interchangeable. He might have thought of himself as a latter day Eli Whitney, but he was mistaken. The military equipment world was far too specialized. As laudable as his concept sounded, there were very necessary and specific differences in some parts. Grumman Aviation, the maker of the A6 Intruder, EA6B Prowler, and E2C Hawkeye, equipped these airplanes with very similar wheel assemblies. Similar, but not identical—the reason had a lot to do with braking requirements. The point for us, as we were gaining altitude in a now crippled airplane, was that where we should have three up indications on the landing gear status indicator. At this point in our climb to altitude, there were only two up indicators and one striped or barber pole indication, meaning we had a hung landing gear. Later it was determined that a wheel from an E2C, which was just too big to fit into our wheel well, had been installed on our plane. However, flying thousands of miles from land over the middle of the ocean, the cause of our problem was not paramount in our minds—the ability to land safe and dry back on the ship was.

The exigencies of our mission were beginning to fade as we attempted to slow flight the airplane and try to lower the gear normally. Jake cycled the gear several times. Each time the nose and left main mount acted as they should, but the right main gear remained stuck in the wheel well. Below us on the flight deck, the F4s remained waiting for the oncoming Russians, who were apparently late for the rendezvous. For us though, the mission was effectively cancelled. We could not climb high enough, nor fly at normal speed with this gear problem for us to make any difference. If we had been in a real war, there would have been no question about us being sacrificed, but we knew the Bear, if it arrived at all, was nothing more than a Cold War provocation.

Since we were the only aircraft airborne, we had the entire ship's undivided attention. Jake flew us by the windows of PriFly, the ship's control tower, so that our maintenance and safety officers could look us over. They confirmed what we knew; the right wheel-well door was open and the tire jammed. Jake tried some violent maneuvers to try to shake the wheel lose, nothing. Then he tried porpoising, dropping and raising the nose violently—again no luck. Now, as time passed and fuel burned this situation was becoming what one might call a non-trivial problem. Those scenes from Hollywood movies of planes making wheels up landings don't tell the whole story. Planes often disintegrated or exploded when trying those stunts, it was not an option we favored. Even if we could do that, where would we do it—in the ocean? We were too far from any credible base that might recover us and besides; we were flying a brand-new $23 million dollar airplane. CAG did not want us to ditch, or eject over the sea. Then, of course there was always the barrier.

The barrier was a nylon web net that was strung across the flight deck and rigged to the arresting cables. A pilot was supposed to fly his damaged plane into the webbing and the arresting cables would bring it to a halt. It worked, most of the time. And time, along with fuel were things we were slowly running out of. Jake and I reviewed our options. The one thing we were holding off doing was to blow down the gear with bottled nitrogen. This was the last thing we could do to avoid some kind of crash landing. The problem was that blowing down the gear was a final, one-shot solution. Once the gear is blown, and the nitrogen discharged, if the gear does not come down it remains stuck there and there is no second chance. We had burned down about ten thousand pounds of gas and would need to make a decision soon.

In the end it is always the aircraft commander's choice. Jake slow flighted the airplane, and, with wings level, he turned the landing gear handle ninety degrees to the emergency position and pushed it down sharply. We heard the nitrogen discharge and then felt, the thunking of all three wheels coming down. I looked over and saw three beautiful green lights on the landing gear indicator. After that ordeal the landing was a piece of cake. We came aboard and parked the plane, leaving the flight deck crew to tow it to the elevator and strike it below to change the wheel. In the end we learned the Bear never came south, it turned around and went home to Russia, something about a malfunction aboard.

SUBIC BAY

If there ever was a tropical location that should have been developed as a resort location, it was Subic Bay. At first glance it is an idyllic spot. Even the Japanese, when they occupied the Philippines in 1942 tried to turn fortified Grande Island at the mouth of the bay a place for their troops to relax. Subic is a wide and deep-water port that, instead, had since the end of the Second World War become the nerve center for naval operations in the South China Sea. Where swank hotels should have lined the sand with tourists frolicking at the water's edge, rows of gray ships lay along the wharves and quaysides stacked with supplies and the implements of war. On one side of the bay, a huge airbase sat atop the flat expanse of Cubi Point. From jungled mountain slopes overlooking the runways rows of white, colonial-style buildings, peeked out from under waving palm fronds. This was the official establishment that held the fleet administration, housing, hospital, and the quite infamous Cubi Point O club.

I had never been in the tropics before, and, aside from my brief sojourns in semi tropical Florida and California, I had not experienced anything like the decadent lushness of the Philippines. Late into our last night at sea, as the *Enterprise* cruised down the west coast of Luzon, we began to smell the land. The lush, dank, and sweetly rotten smell of the jungle wafted out over the calm sea to us. We could feel the land out there, nearly invisible with only the occasional light from isolated fishing villages to define the shore. Only the stars in panoply of the southern constellations noted our movement ever southward.

At dawn, we stood off the mountainous and jungle-shrouded coast of the Bataan Peninsula awaiting the harbor pilot. Once he came aboard, he would guide us toward our mooring. Despite the size of the harbor, there was only one place for a ship the size of the *Enterprise* to dock and that was at the Cubi Point carrier pier. As soon as we were alongside the pier, our cargo of shrink-wrapped replacement aircraft could be hoisted ashore for reassembly by shore-based mechanics. While we waited off shore for the final run into the harbor, I wandered up to the familiar catwalks on the island above the bridge. There were a few other officers there.

The view from that height was stunning. Jungle covered mountains trailing wisps of white cloud streaming down their flanks, an azure sea rolling to soft breakers that swept on to long runs of sandy beaches, sea birds wheeling overhead and all the while the growing expectation of a new adventure before me. For many of the crew, officers and men, returning to the PI was as emotional as leaving San Francisco. Lots of the veteran sailors had essentially two families—their legal, stateside family and the woman and gaggle of children for whom they felt some responsibility living here. They embodied the old toast given by sailing men for ages "To our wives and sweethearts—may they never meet." The pilot took his time and arrived thirty minutes late, having been located and brought aboard by helicopter. Soon he was guiding us through the entrance to the bay and then the ship swung toward a line of the yellow and red yard tugs that were standing by to nose into the carrier's bow and push us toward the carrier pier.

By four in the afternoon I was ashore and perched on a barstool in the Subic Bay O club, working on my second Subic Special. Like most tropical drinks, the Subic Special was a lethally sweet concoction made primarily of rum and laced with sugary fruit juices. The drink went down easily, like soda pop, and the bartender, knowing that we had been at sea for a while, kept bringing us refills. Downing several of these in a short time could induce a certain degree of social ossification that might require hours to sleep off. As soon as we could leave the ship Al LeBaron had grabbed my arm and guided me over to the Subic side of the harbor. We had the tenuous idea that we would stroll into the quaint village of Olongapo after becoming appropriately lubricated. "No one should enter that quiet and lush village sober," he intoned. Later I would find out the truth behind that warning.

The place had a sordid reputation, that I knew long before we left Alameda. There was a song about Olongapo, sung to the tune of "Little Town of Bethlehem" that extolled the vices of the place. I had been to Tijuana, but nothing could have prepared me for what lay less than a mile from the comfortable stool upon which I rested my ass. Still, the view from where I sat wasn't all bad. One of the sidelights and potential benefits of a place like Subic was that there were a hefty number of American women on the base, so one need not sample the Filipina talent. Some of the American women living on base were nurses, some taught school or had administrative staff positions, and some were the wives who accompanied their husbands who were officers aboard ships operating from Subic.

PROWLER BALL

What I had noticed, almost immediately upon entering the bar at the Subic Club, was the number of attractive women who seemed to be entranced by the club's wall of slot machines. Al told me that the navy allowed the one-armed bandits in the clubs and took a cut from the profits. The women who were sliding silver dollars into the maws of the machines were, in his estimation, officers' wives. Many of these women, whose men had brought them to this isolated enclave halfway around the world from home, and then promptly left for sea seemed lonely, and, between booze and gambling, they managed to lose most of their monthly grocery money. Once they had lost the money that they brought into the club, these young and not so young lovelies would drift into the bar and look for some companionship and perhaps a shoulder to cry on. "Targets of opportunity, my boy, targets of opportunity," he murmured as he surveyed the curvy blonde who, at that moment, sashayed past us toward an empty barstool.

For any officer, dating the "Subic widows" was a risky enterprise and one that required skills of subterfuge that most of us simply had too little energy to employ. While it would be nice to have someone close at hand to bed down when one was in port, it was simple to find a whore in town—furthermore, whores did not have husbands who, when cuckolded, might go for their sidearm to settle the score, and there was no assurance that the "widows" didn't have a dose of the clap. You had to be careful where you put your pecker in this part of the world.

When we had enough booze and felt that we could still walk, we headed off to Olongapo City for a night on the town. Taxi was the only way to go and there was only one taxi company, Blaylock. Blaylock, a retired chief, owned the cab company on the base, and, for a buck a head, his cabs ran from ships to clubs to the main gate. In short order I found myself reasonably drunk, standing by the main gate, facing what struck me as a carnival in progress. It was not quite Bourbon Street and far from Rio's Carnival. If anything, the Olongapo scene was a carnival of sin. Neon lights splashed over crowds thronging in the street, bodies weaving to the cacophony of sounds that blared from dozens of nightclubs playing a concoction of every type of American music. All the while, the whores from the bars sashayed and vamped their sex for the eager sailors. To enter this sybaritic world, my first step was to cross the bridge over Shit River.

The body of water did have a real name, the Olongapo River, but that seemed all too exotic to describe this slow moving open sewer. The river was the physical barrier between the base and the mainland. The smell from the water reminded me of my father-in-law's cow barn in mid-winter but what caught my attention were the canoes lined up along the breadth of the stream. Standing in each dugout was a young girl, looking coyly virginal and dressed in white. Each girl wore a diaphanous blouse that left little to the imagination. Each held in her hands a coolie-hat and shouted for us to toss coins down to them. With deftness worthy of any major league outfielder, they moved the hats quickly to intercept the cascade of quarters and half-dollars that the Americans on the bridge tossed down to them. As I passed, I saw several coins splash the surface of the water amid the floating turds and garbage. It was then that I saw the real truth of the scene, for next to each canoe a tiny brown head bobbed. Each girl's boat was accompanied on either side by their younger brothers. The boys held on to the gunwales of the canoes until a coin, badly aimed missed the hats and splashed into the river. In an instant the boys dove to catch the coin before it sunk into the deeper murk. It must have taken a combination of sight and feel for them to succeed, as there was little light shining downward from the bridge. In the end, I don't think those boys and girls missed many of the coins the crowd of sailors so nonchalantly tossed to them.

Across the river, all was chaos. It was a world that thrived on the vicissitudes of the war. There were bars for every musical taste: from the more sedate, forties-style places such as the Sampaguita Club, where Roggie and the Philippine Symbols sang torch songs and standards; to the various "shit-kicking" bars in which twangy country western songs were belted out by tiny Filipinas wearing cowboy boots and sequined hats; to the infamous New Jolo Club with its three floors of ever-escalating sexual debauchery—Olongapo had something for everyone.

The Baroon's plan was to take me through town and point out the best and the worst it had to offer so that I could make up my own mind as to how far I might be willing to go on subsequent visits. Olongapo's city fathers, corrupt officials of the Marcos regime, were making various improvements to the town's infrastructure. Al was quick to point out the changes that had taken place since his last visit. One of these new improvements was the paving of the muddy tracks that had for years passed as streets. Everything from curb to curb was still just dirt, so the shuffling feet of hundreds of stumbling sailors created a minor dust storm about two feet off the ground. Incongruously on each street being readied for paving—something national government had long promised—the reconstructed street level was being raised and would end up about eighteen inches above the sidewalks and entrances to the bars. Coming out of some bars you had to boost yourself up to get to the street, no mean feat when you are plastered. One was constantly jumping up or hopping down to visit the places. I had to wonder what was going to happen when the rains came in earnest. Worse was in evidence, however. Along with this potential hazard, a very real one existed at every intersection. Streetlights and traffic signals were scarce, and it took some doing to avoid the open holes in the road, which gaped and revealed water flowing in the pipes below. Stepping into one of these gaping holes was a one-way trip to the big adios. Looking down into the wash of water, one saw bits of foliage along with the odd dead cat or chicken.

The air was filled with the smell of braziers smoking as their skewers of meat was slow-roasted. Squeaky voiced vendors stood by their fires and called out "barbeque, barbeque." For the uninitiated, this may have sounded like an attractive invitation for a snack, and for some sailors the smell of the meat, singed over the coals might have been mouthwatering. In fact, however, the barbeque had perhaps until late that afternoon been any stray cat or dog that had been caught, skinned, skewered, and now roasted. Of course, these delights ran a close second to the ritual of feeding of baby ducks to a languid alligator which lounged outside one of the bars.

For the youngest and most naive sailors, those whose life experiences were by definition, limited and had been taken under the wing of their senior petty officers, liberty in Olongapo provided several rites of passage. The legendary feeding of the alligator was one such. For these kids, it was also a challenge of sorts. The alligator must have been a half-century old and lay day in and day out in an open pit along the Magsaysay Street sidewalk. There, in a large puddle of muddy water littered with tiny white feathers it maintained a vigil of the passing crowds of rowdy sailors. In a bid to make the scene tropical, or at least exotic its owners had placed some rocks and a few desultory plants in the pool and surrounded it with a low fence. Next to the fence sat the duck vendor, a wizened old man of indeterminate age with weathered, leathery skin and a single tooth protruding at a thirty-degree angle from his tobacco stained upper gum. He wore a greasy baseball cap that might once have borne the insignia of the St. Louis Cardinals, but was too dirty to know for sure. The young sailors were brought into line by their older mentors and encouraged to step up and, for a quarter, buy a duck to sacrifice to the gator. Lest one think that all the sailor had to do was toss the tiny fowl to the giant predator, further contemplation is required. Completing the rite required that the young sailor to put the tiny duck's head in his mouth and bite down to sever the head and beak from the duck's body. Then, without throwing up, the sailor was meant to spit the head at the gator's mouth and toss the still-quivering duck body into the pit. On a busy night this might involve the consumption of a hundred or more tiny chicks. Oh, how travel does expand the mind.

Al led me to a club on Magsaysay Street that he had visited in the past. The thing was that the owners often changed the names of the places to reflect what carrier might be in port at the time, thus the Big E Club might become the Ranger Bar or the America, depending on which ship was in port and which bunch of sailors they were trying to attract. God help everyone if two ships were in at the same time. Upstairs we sat at a large round table. Several others showed up, including Bill Woods, Hazlet, and a guy we only knew as Willie the Dick from one of the fighter squadrons. Once we sat down everyone ordered a San Miguel Beer. A swarm of bar girls appeared with a tray of bottles and glasses. Al whispered in my ear, "Never take an open bottle, make sure you see them open it in front of you, not at the bar—*and for Christ's sake make sure you never take your hand off of it.*" It was good advice, for within moments we were surrounded by tiny women in skimpy bras and G-strings.

"You *Enterprise* sailorman?" they asked in giggling singsong voices as they found their way onto our laps. Soon their tiny fingers were massaging our crotches, as they tried to grasp our beer bottles, which we kept waiving away. The girl on my lap smelled of cheap perfume and sweat. She wasn't attractive, but in a feline sort of way she exuded her sexuality and her availability. No one kidded himself. There was no allure here, everything was purely business. If you wanted a girl, you saw the Mama-san, a dragon-like figure in a flowing silk dress seated in an alcove at the rear of the bar. Two ugly Filipino men sat near her, muscle available in the event that someone wanted to avoid the pay-before-you-play policy of the place. She would look you over and set a price, depending on the looks of the girl, but you couldn't leave with her before midnight, since all the girls were meant to sell as many bottles of beer as possible during their shifts.

Everyone at our table seemed to be having a grand time. We laughed, the girls giggled, and the beer kept coming. Douglas MacArthur's family still had a stake in the San Miguel Brewery, so, in a way, we were all helping to pay the general back for his war service. All at once one of the girls jumped on the table and grabbing the beer bottle out of Bill Wood's hand, pulled off her G-string, revealing a tiny shaved twat and squatted on the open neck of the bottle. She rose up a little and with practiced motions swung her hips and swirled the beer in the bottle. Then she pulled it out of herself and tried to put it to Bill's lips. He fended it off with a swift swing of his hand, and the bottle fell to the floor and rolled under the table.

I had drunk way too much and to take a leak before my pipes burst. Spotting the sign to the men's room at the back wall, I got up and began to navigate toward it. All of a sudden I found myself escorted by a pair of the girls, each one taking an arm. They giggled even more as I staggered toward the head. They pointed down a dirty corridor, there was no sign, but the smell of urine and vomit told me I was on the right course. The urinal was in reality just a long trough of galvanized metal next to an open, floor-to-ceiling window, overlooking the street. As I stood there unloading the beer and rum, the two girls walked in and stood on either side of me. "Me hold it," one of them insisted. I brushed her off, I might have been drunk, but I wasn't stupid. There was nothing remotely alluring about the prospect of one of these whores holding my dick.

Back on the ship I tossed in my bunk. It was all coming too fast, a downhill slide into a world of sleaze, random acts of wantonness and debauchery. Is this what going to war meant? I had yet to see a shot fired in anger and yet, the men I was with, the behavior of the men I looked up to, seemed to exhibit a license that had no limits. Ted Steele, our operations officer, had often chided me when we were back at Whidbey. He thought I was wrapped too tight, that I acted too seriously and studiously as I went about learning my trade as an aviator. "You need to loosen up. Nobody likes a prude. It's a mark of a real man that you are a boomer on the beach!" he had said.

Was that it—my aspiration as a naval officer? Was everything a joke, something that could be washed down with more San Miguel or a shot of Johnny Walker? I didn't know. I had done nothing wrong in Olongapo. Yes, there were naked girls dancing on the tables, but I didn't partake or even think about buying one from the bar for the night. I suppose I was numb from the experience. Neither prudery nor even guilt had entered into my thinking; I was just becoming a little bored by it all. There was nothing much to be gained by paying for one of these whores. Worse still, most of them probably had either a disease or some nasty body vermin. The gaiety at the bar only lasted as long as the San Miguel. Lying in bed, my stomach, sour from the beer that mixed with the Subic Specials from earlier in the day, made me feel like retching. There were to be months more like this it seemed—I had entered a strange world indeed. And as strange as it was in the Philippines, I just wanted to get on with what we had come all this way to do. Not to fight as much as to know if I had it in me to do the job for which I had trained, or was I simply a smart kid in a nice uniform?

Welcome to Yankee Station

Autumn skies over Southeast Asia, clear and blue all the way north into China. At thirty-three thousand feet I could see up into the hill country of the Golden Triangle and down toward the haze that hung over the Mekong Delta. That first image remains indelible in my mind; we might as well have been flying over California, as being in a war zone, everything up here was serene. That image was to change shortly.

The skipper had wanted to give each of us nuggets a taste of the war and of flight ops in combat. I'm not sure what he intended to do if we screwed up. Each of the JGs found himself assigned to his crew for a hop, and, since the scheduling was done in no particular order, I found myself assigned to a late afternoon hop. The skipper had made several flights that day and the one I had been scheduled for was his last, just a few hours before sunset. The *Enterprise* was just getting into its wartime routine so there were a lot of these warm-up, low intensity daylight hops being flown by all of the units. It would be another week before we would take up our inexorable midnight-to-noon flight schedule that would last for most of the cruise.

From altitude the landscape of the Vietnamese littoral appeared as a hodgepodge of jungle and rice paddies. Roads, if you could see them at all, seemed to be mere trails. As for towns, whatever below passed for settlements seemed to be no more than smudges on the landscape. Major roads, two-lane thorofares left over from the French occupation, were empty of traffic. The NVA had learned not to move anything in daylight. For a few moments it seemed we were flying over a pastoral sixteenth-century world. Then the first call of "SAM, SAM vicinity of Dong Hoi!" broke the spell. Two sections of VA-196's A-6s had been hitting targets close to the coast and had spotted missiles airborne. We had our jammers on, but no telltale Fansong radar signals had been detected, so we had no sites against which to direct the jamming.

The skipper, Cowboy Bill Brewster, was a former SPAD pilot, a rodeo rider, and an all-around candidate for the real-John-Wayne-in-uniform award. To him, the idea of standing off a target to jam radars fell into a queasy area of wimpiness in which he had never truly believed. He was a born and bred Iron Bomber for whom flak bursts drifting by the cockpit were like extra olives in his martini. The basis of success in our mission depended on understanding the pure physics of electronic warfare. This meant that in order to successfully protect one or more striking forces we had to operate and attack the enemy's radars from outside the range of the missile envelope. The other, perhaps more pressing, argument for remaining outside of the 'death zone' was that the United States had only eight deployable EA-6Bs in the fleet at that time, and losing one to outright hubris was not going to be well-received up the chain of command. In 1972 we were flying the most expensive combat aircraft in the US arsenal and losing one for whatever reason was going to cause uproar. In fact, Cowboy Bill had already lost one EA-6B on a training mission up in Canada and losing another one so soon would raise eyebrows if not generate a board of inquiry. The cause of that crash outside Edmonton, Alberta was a design flaw in the cross air bleed system and not attributable to pilot error. Grumman had to scramble for a fix since it was their design that caused the problem. In the end, their fix, like so many they came up with during the cruise, involved the crew disabling one of their systems by pulling the circuit breakers once the engines were started.

Flying our airplane like a quarter horse rounding up strays; the skipper understood that and kept us in a long racetrack pattern just off the coast, while we jammed the weapon systems that covered the target area. The SAM2 missile had a range of seventeen nautical miles. In order to comply with the orders we had been given by CAG, we should have maintained about twenty miles off the coast. We had to stay just out of detonation range, as we knew that one of the missile batteries was sited very close to the shore. When flying, the skipper was one of those men who looked at rules and directives more as advisements and nothing to get too hung up about. So, on each circuit we kept our northern track at twenty miles off shore, but as we turned south, he veered closer to the coast so that the track was at some points just six miles off shore. We could see the surf line along the beaches.

Well, that was when the next barrage of missiles went off. A classic ground to air engagement, from the Vietnamese point of view—fire one SAM high, and, when the enemy dives, hit them with another one from below. This time, they were aiming at us, and not the four A-6s that were pulling off the now smoking target. They had lost interest in static targets and were now looking for trucks along the back roads. Sure enough, up came one SAM from the site close to the coast. I can't erase the image in my mind of a long cylindrical shape, the size of a telephone pole with fire streaking from its tail and a long plume of smoke drifting back toward earth. The skipper, no stranger to such engagements, but normally flown in aircraft a little more nimble than ours, casually turned us toward the missile; as it passed high overhead before detonating. He knew, as we all did, that the second missile we had to worry about, the one with our names on it. It would come at us from below. Sure enough, there it was, coming up from the jungle, moving in on us. Cowboy Jim banked sharply and again turned toward the streaking weapon. Maybe this is what he wanted to accomplish by having us fly with him that day. The SAM, with its tiny control fins, could be defeated. Like the puny front legs of a T-Rex, the SAM's control fins could not make tight turns, and it flew on past us and crashed into the sea. With a sigh that indicated our fun for the day was done, the skipper intoned, "Time to go home." We had been officially baptized.

Yankee Station was one of two ephemeral locations in the South China Sea created by some planner in the Pentagon. The other was Dixie Station. Obviously, Yankee Station was the northern one and denoted a place somewhere in international waters between Hainan Island—Chinese territory and bristling with SAMs and MiGs—and the coast of North Vietnam. The supercarriers were all stationed here, and flight ops ran around the clock. Normally two carriers would remain on station, one taking the day ops and the other the night strikes, while a third would go back to Subic for a few days of relief. Because of the intensity of air operations against targets in North Vietnam, only the larger decks were assigned here. Dixie Station, off the bulging east coast of South Vietnam, was home to the smaller 27-C carriers, the improved Essex Class ships, survivors of WWII and Korea that had been refitted for the larger jets of the Vietnam War era. These ships generally operated only during daylight and supported the troops engaging enemy forces in the south, and not venturing north at all. At the same time, because they were more removed from a threat of being attacked by missile-laden Komar patrol boats, they got the lion's share of the USO entertainment. Aboard the Big E, so close to hostile countries we had to entertain ourselves.

The entertainments most in demand were pornographic movies. This was the age of the eight-millimeter porn movies made in Southern California garages, or in Holland and Germany. The quality was poor, the girls not too beautiful, and the soundtrack, if there was one snapped and popped like Rice Krispies in milk. Having had the job of communications officer, I had also been dubbed the official smut officer, responsible for obtaining the best quality films for viewing by a select audience. Despite my advancement to a maintenance division officer, my success in managing the smut business ensured that I would not be permitted to shirk this vital duty.

The logistics of the smut operation were, in some ways, daunting. Not only did I have to secure a constant supply of new smut movies, as the audience demanded fresh faces, well not necessarily faces as they were the focus of the films. In any event, I needed a projector, a screen, and a place to show the flicks. As with all illicit and semi-illicit activities aboard ship, I relied on a senior enlisted man's help. Officers were not supposed to know about such things, or so the official view of our duties went. And among enlisted men, it was the boatswain mates who knew where and how to acquire such things. It only remained for me to find the right person, and collect the items or favors that I had in trade to obtain the movies.

Finding the right man was no problem; Aviation Boatswain Mate First Class Dan Denver was the man. He had joined the squadron two months before deployment and was a newlywed, married to a cute Filipina who worked at the Navy Exchange in Whidbey. Still, he had been in the navy nearly twelve years, and he had connections throughout the ship. As a cumshaw expert there was none better. You only had to mention that you were thinking of acquiring something when, abracadabra, up it popped. He didn't want money in return, just favors. Perhaps he might have extra liberty or use of a squadron vehicle when we deployed somewhere far from home. And, if you were a smart junior officer, you saw to it that there was a little extra for him in each deal—a box of cigars, a bottle of scotch, whatever might leave a lasting impression and a feeling of goodwill.

Soon after getting underway, Denver had located an eight-millimeter projector and, through the enlisted underground, access to a never-ending stream of smut movies. For these I traded some extra liberty time and a bottle of Johnny Walker Black. The two things he could not deliver were a screen and a place to show the movies, but I thought I had these covered.

It was rapidly becoming apparent that the junior officer bunkroom was going to serve as the squadron's members-only cocktail lounge, as well as our home while at sea. Since we were located in a part of the ship that the masters at arms avoided on their periodic sweeps looking for booze, our space evolved into the smut theater. And because there were no sleeping quarters on either side of the space, the soundtrack of the short smut movies would not interfere with anyone's sleep, nor cause any inconvenient inquiries. As for a screen, well the blackout curtains, although gray, had a certain luminescence in their fabric, which though shadowy allowed the picture to be large enough for the viewing audience to catch all the cinematographic detail.

Attendance at the showings of these films was by personal invitation only, with the exception of the residents of the bunkroom. No one objected to the showings, as we had all abandoned our scruples long ago—that is with the exception of Clete. He couldn't be locked out of his own sleeping space, and, although he whined a bit about the pornography we were showing, he really had nowhere else to go. The film festivals were held about once a month and then only on evenings when we were certain that there were no demands for flights or training. Filipino cigars and various whiskies were in ample supply; we even kept the bar stocked with our guests' favorite bottles, Ten High Bourbon for Ted Steele. By the end of the several reels of film, the air was foggy with tobacco smoke, which, fortunately, overpowered the smell of booze.

Most of the films ran for ten minutes at most, these were not of the *Debbie Does Dallas* or *Deepthroat* quality, so the sessions did not last more than an hour or, at most, two. Clete certainly was not a smoker, and it was clear from his theatrical attempts at coughing and gagging that he did not appreciate the smell of the tobacco. Since we used his blackout curtain as the screen, he would shun us and climb up into his bunk, ignoring the guffaws and coarse comments from the small crowd of maybe ten guests. What we didn't know until much later was that the grainy image of the film came through to the backside of the blackout curtain in reverse. There, behind the barrier Clete was feigning sleep. With a little imagination, he could find himself added to the cinematic image portrayed inches from where he lay.

———

Days began to run together, and the routine of flight operations created a kind of comfort. Each day you knew what you had to do and when you had to do it. For aviators, that is doubly comforting in that we know when we are at risk and when we are not. When the enlisted men began to snivel about being away from home—it had just been a month—it was hard for me to find much sympathy for them. No one was hurling them off into the night sky or shooting at them with flaming missiles. True, life aboard a ship was not like living at the Ritz, but they had warm bunks and good food, and though the work was hard, no one was taking shots at them. Those of us who over heard them griping simply listened and told them to get on with their work.

We had been at sea just long enough for the venereal diseases carried by the girls in Subic to blossom forth. All the officers who so indulged seemed to have heeded the warnings of the flight surgeons and used condoms, but several of the enlisted men, some so young that this was their first time mixing booze and whores, began to complain of pain in their private areas. As their division officers, they had to come to us and we had to sign off on their sick bay chits, so we soon became aware of the offenders.

This meant that as part of our daily supervision duties, we had to go back over the rules of port liberty with the entire division before each return to port. Since we did not use precise medical terms, these sessions were coarse, bawdy, and for the most part embarrassing to the men whose groins burned with the fire of Eros. Still, the navy had a policy for this kind of offence. You could get the clap or NSU (non-specific urethritis) twice in your career and nothing would be said officially, but the third time, or if you had to be taken off duty status because of the infection's severity, there would be a write-up in your file. Repeat offenders could even find themselves court-martialed.

We had also been at sea long enough for the most naïve of the young sailors to have fallen in love and want to marry some girl they had met in a bar. Tow-headed young sailors, fresh from Bumfuck, Missouri or East Jesus, Tennessee, would line up, their hearts on fire to get a marriage chit signed. They had stars in their eyes because they had met some hooker who did them up one side and down the other and now they professed undying love for the girl. Our job was to steer them clear from making this horrific mistake. It was hard work to dissuade them, they were in love—or so they thought. Pointing out to the sailor that their ladylove was at this moment probably sucking the cock of some other in-port sailor from another ship never had much effect. Nor was pointing out that the girl probably only wanted to marry any American she could seduce so he could get her a US passport, and oh, by the way, she would need one for her mother, sisters, younger brother, and aunts. All of who would have to be supported on the poor sailor's meager pay and housed in some dump back at the base. But such is the power of testosterone—it fogs the brain of young men, older ones too. Our best tactic in these cases was to find ways to limit any liberty for the kids when we were in port. A cruel punishment, perhaps, but maybe we helped keep some kid from the worst mistake of his life.

While we plied the open seas off the coast of North Vietnam, we were not alone. True, we had a series of our small boys— destroyers assigned to us as escorts and which followed us as we moved about launching and recovering airplanes. These ships provided the carrier with defensive firepower and, if called upon served as plane guards during flight operations. There to rescue anyone who had to go into the water while launching or landing. Supposedly, there was an attack submarine around, but we never saw it—of course, that was the point of it being underwater.

Our next closest companions were a seemingly endless series of Soviet AGIs, intelligence-gathering ships, which followed us day in and day out. They were built to look like fishing trawlers except for the forest of antennae that grew from their decks and masts. They listened and watched and when we launched, they would note the number airplanes, the types, side numbers and insignia, the ordnance carried, and direction of flight—then they would radio the North Vietnamese to let them know what to expect.

About halfway through our first line period, the *Enterprise* scheduled a stand down day. In the times of sailing ships, this was generally done as a Sunday tradition. In the days of sail it had been a time when the iron men who sailed the wooden ships would be able to write letters or to mend their clothes or simply have an extra ration of rum and spin a few yarns. The modern navy didn't operate that way, but stand-downs were good for morale, so after the obligatory safety briefings and safe-driving movies—*who cared about driving out here?* We all went up to the flight deck for a barbeque in the humid sunshine of the South China Sea.

Fifty-five gallon drums had been cut in half lengthwise and turned into charcoal grills. Cooks tended them, sweating over mounds of steak, chicken, burgers, and hot dogs. Long tables were set up with all the regular accompaniments, ears of corn, potato salad, buns, and the like. In the middle of the landing area, between the number three and four wires, another long table had been set up; it held a huge cake in the shape of the *Enterprise*. It was nearly ten feet long and covered in gray icing to match the ship. Whatever they used to make gray icing and worse, the black that they put on the cake's flight deck, we chose to ignore. Two cooks stood to either side of the cake cutting pieces of catwalk and hull for those interested in desert. There was vanilla ice cream in huge tubs that was melting to slush in the rising heat, despite being set in even larger tubs of ice.

Looking aft I could see the AGI increasing her speed and nosing closer, almost cutting between our escort destroyer and our ship. The plumes of smoke from the grills must have looked to the Russian crew as if we were on fire; that and the mass of sailors walking up and down the flight deck must have raised many questions. What they thought was happening was anyone's guess. The AGI closed to within a few hundred yards. I suppose the captain or the political officer had a whiff of the barbequing meats and, knowing what swill they fed their crew, didn't want to risk a mutiny, so the AGI suddenly heeled over and sped off toward the eastern horizon. Most of the *Enterprise*'s crew ignored the AGI's maneuver and went on with Frisbee and volleyball games, while one of the A7 pilots rode his unicycle up and down the flight deck. Apparently too much merriment was not good for the morale of Soviet sailors.

―――――

The day finally arrived. Our air group's first alpha strike was a big deal by anyone's standards: seventy or more combat aircraft going against one target to unleash tons of ordnance in the early morning. It was a brilliant autumn morning at sea. On the flight deck all the combat aircraft the ship could arm were spotted and ready to launch. Tankers were to launch first in order to be able to top off the F-4s and the RA-5C as soon as they reached assembly altitude. One of the fighter squadrons was assigned to provide CAP, combat air patrol while the other, the Puking Dogs, was to carry out iron hand against any anti-aircraft fire we might take. The rest of the attack force, A-7s and A-6s, were loaded with every type of explosive ordnance from the ship's magazines, snake-eyes, MK-82s, missiles, cluster bombs—everything. The target this morning was the port city of Haiphong, the gateway harbor of North Vietnam. Our only instruction was to not hit any Soviet or Eastern Bloc ships; everything on land was fair game.

The sequence of launching from the catapults went flawlessly. When it was our turn, we banged off the ship and climbed out. Moments later we were part of a swirl of jet aircraft swarming overhead. Like a huge air show, the sky was filled with airplanes turning and joining up into formation. Once everyone had joined on their assigned wingmen, we formed a phalanx of planes and set off northward.

This strike was supposed to be a big surprise for the North Vietnamese, but the Soviet AGI observers had been working overtime to log the huge number of planes in the air and radioed ahead to let their allies know we were on our way. The AGI could tell them we were coming; it would be up to the North Vietnamese radar operators to figure out where. That was the Prowler's job, to deny them the ability to react to the attack. The mass of strike aircraft seemed to fill the sky. Descending to five thousand feet, each airplane took up its assigned position. F-4s were flying CAP high above and doing a Thatch Weave while the A-7s fanned out on each side with a wedge of A-6s in the center. We took up station astern, so we could cover the mass of airplanes with our jammers.

We streaked across the open water. At this low altitude we could see the individual sampans, their crews wearing coolie hats and rocking gently in the swells of the Gulf of Tonkin, as they dragged their nets through the sea. We were approaching the target through the archipelago known as the Grand Norways in Ha Long Bay, jungle-covered islets of limestone karst that rose from the placid sea. Ahead of us the islands sat like green pyramids atop an azure sea— truly postcard material. That is, until the top of one of the islands erupted with anti-aircraft fire. From the peak of the island, dead ahead, green palm fronds flew into the air as puffs of white smoke and red lines of tracers spewed toward us. Their mistake was that they had fired too soon.

Seconds later, a pair of F-4 iron handers rolled in on the island. I watched as the dark olive lozenges of a dozen, MK-82, five-hundred-pound bombs sailed down from the sky. Then, like a tropical volcano, the islet's peak erupted in flame and boiling black smoke. The alpha strike air armada just sailed by unscathed. In my rearview mirror I watched the secondary explosions of anti-aircraft ordnance as the flames rose higher.

We pressed on, and within a few more minutes the docks and petrol storage facilities of Haiphong were burning. No one was hit, no one was lost—pretty good work for the morning.

HOME FRONT

We had not been too long at sea when problems back home on Whidbey Island began to evolve with tragic consequences. In the nineteen seventies one of the challenges we faced with being at war and trying to keep up with what was happening at home involved establishing a time line and sequence of events. There was no email, video conferencing or even telephone service then from a warship at sea. This was still the era when a two-way wrist radio existed only in the Dick Tracy comics. Once at sea, we were cut off and ignorant of much of what was going on in the wider world, especially with our own families. The only "news" we saw came to us via *Stars and Stripes*, the military's highly filtered mouthpiece. To avoid confusion and to make sure we did not miss anything all of us sequentially numbered our letters going home, and, for the most part, the wives did the same with mail coming out to us. Still, there were times when we would get a letter out of sequence, and it might be weeks before the intervening letter or tape recording would arrive that would clear up the mysteries. Ted Steele's wife was trying to buy a house, while we were out at sea and the sheaves of paper that he had to sign and send back to her, despite having given her a power of attorney in his absence, drove him crazy. Too often, an important document simply vanished in the mail and the process had to resume from square one.

Mail was notoriously slow getting out to ships in the Gulf and only the Red Cross, seemingly one of the least charitable of the charities, especially with regard to its support of service men, had the power to quickly communicate with deployed troops in time of emergency. The first instance of trouble at home arose when one of the sailors in the electronics shop was alerted by the Red Cross of the death of his mother. Through a naval message to the chaplain's office aboard ship, the charity passed the word. No other stateside entity had the power to verify there had, in fact been a death. He was immediately granted compassionate leave to go home for the funeral. That was the easy part.

The more difficult part was getting him off the ship and on to a flight to the States. Fortunately for him, we were in port at Subic Bay when the notification arrived. Orders were cut, he packed his sea bag, and he was ready to go, but there was no military flight available to take him home. It was decided that the only way home meant that he would have to go commercial, an eight hundred dollar fare. The kid barely had a hundred dollars on him, even though he had just been paid. We arranged for him to get a month's advance pay, still he did not have the fare.

Like all of us, he had been taught that the Red Cross would be there to help him out. That was their mantra, wasn't it? Well, charity for the Red Cross meant only that they would *lend* him the money, if he would sign a promissory note and pay interest. The whole arrangement would have come to nearly twelve hundred dollars when he got done paying them back—*some charity*. I had long harbored misgivings about the charity. My father had told me that the Red Cross used to charge servicemen in Europe for the packs of cigarettes that American tobacco companies had donated at no cost to the war effort and that they even charged for donuts and coffee that the Salvation Army always gave away. Once the squadron officers got wind of what the kid was facing we got together and pooled our cash, raising about a thousand dollars for the kid and sent him off to Manila to catch a flight home.

A second event happened around the end of October. This one was tragically sad. Being at war, all of us thought that if death reached out its cold hand, it would be for one of us, not for our families back in the States. One night, after another raucous party at the Cubi club, several of us returned to the ready room to check back in, only to find the Catholic Chaplain, a full navy captain who actually outranked the ship's captain, waiting for us. There had been a fire in a house back on Whidbey Island. How it had started, no one knew, maybe embers from the fireplace? It had been a wild and windy night in Puget Sound, and that seemed a likely scenario. The house began to burn, the wind whipping up the flames into an inferno. It was George Conlin, our maintenance officer's house, and his wife tried frantically to get their three children out from the flames. Two made it, but she went back for the third, an autistic boy of five or six; they never made it out.

Now, in an instant, he was a widower with two traumatized children ten thousand miles away who desperately needed their father. Shockwaves hit all of us. The ship's XO, who was generally perceived as an enigmatic and taciturn man, arrived in the ready room and immediately arranged for George to fly out from the airbase at Clark, just north of us. The XO arranged for one of our helos to take George up there. In a matter of hours he was gone, and all of us withdrew to our own thoughts of life and what it meant. That night a lot of emotional letters home were written.

————

Most of us lived in married officer's housing at Whidbey. For those who had never visited the junior officer's housing area on a military base before, their first glimpse might come as a shock. There are generally hordes of young children and babies everywhere. In the seventies the visitor might also notice that at least half of the young wives living there were pregnant while the other half we pushing strollers with squalling rug rats. At a cost of twenty-five dollars per birth, having a child while on active duty in 1972 was the only bargain that young military parents would find when came to having a family.

On isolated Whidbey Island, there were few choices for entertainment for the wives we had left behind. The toils of child rearing and keeping up their spirits for months on end were difficult. Besides, the average age of most of these service brides was twenty-four or twenty-five. Now, they were stuck living in a sort of sorority environment far from home. As the weeks and months went by, the deployed husbands began to hear whispers about what was happening back home. The women were lonely; they were also young and, until the day their mates left for the South China Sea, sexually active. It was no wonder that some extracurricular activity took place.

They were known across the fleet as Westpac Widows, young, and some not so young, married women whose husbands were at sea, ten thousand miles away. Every base that sent squadrons west to war had their little groups of Westpac Widows. At the bases near large urban centers, it was perhaps not so noticeable, but on an island in the middle of Puget Sound, the situation became notorious.

Soon, as with their departed husbands, the natural urges began to surface, and one by one or in pairs some of the women began to frequent the bar at the O Club, especially on Friday nights. The routine was simple: find a sitter for the kids, shop for something to wear, then spend the afternoon primping to look one's best. As evening fell, with the kids fed and the sitter in charge for the evening, they would drive to the O Club.

The word about the widows was out around the fleet. Each Friday, aircrews on training flights from bases all around the country would arrive at the transient line and park their planes. By evening, the line looked like a valet parking lot for naval aircraft. They had ostensibly chosen Whidbey Island so that the crews, flight instructors and student aviators could book enough flight time to complete their monthly requirements and to do a little cross country navigation along the way. The timing of their arrival was impeccable. All these flights seemed to arrive between four and six in the afternoon so that the crews could get to the BOQ and clean up for the evening ahead.

The wives who could no longer abide their loneliness would show up at the bar, alone or in pairs, around seven. There was always some local of band playing, and it was a rule of the house for local couples in the place to not notice who was with whom on the dance floor as the night progressed. By ten, the requisite pairing was accomplished, and then it only came down to whether the additional late night activity would take place in the visiting flier's BOQ room or, if the women who had pawned off their kids for the night, in her own bed at home. The wives were not the only women at Whidbey who played this game. Several of the female officers assigned to the base, many who were permanent residents in the Q, would show up as well, competing for the available male flesh.

It had long been a rule in families where deployments were long for the husbands and wives not to ask too many questions of each other, and it was a religiously observed practice to ensure that no pesky STD or other infection might develop to bring the marriage down. In the fleet, married officers observed the PCOD, or pussy cut-off date, to ensure that no disease contracted while off the field of battle could develop. This date was regularly pronounced by the flight surgeons to ensure that only healthy officers returned home. There had been some rare cases in which the virulence of an STD outbreak had kept an officer hospitalized overseas. The families were given sparse information, but the timing of the ailment in proximity to a ship's return often told the tale.

Telling tales was also how the word about the Whidbey Westpac Widows made it out to the fleet. Some of the aviators who had bedded the wives of deployed officers arrived as replacements for embarked squadrons. Not all of these officers kept their mouths shut about their stateside antics. Soon their tales of the romantic liaisons at Whidbey and other bases and amplified by fairly accurate descriptions of the women involved began to circulate. Rumor had it that there had been a few altercations between the cuckolded spouses and the interlopers, resulting in some bruising to both combatants. What was said by an injured husband to his spouse about these affairs forever remained under wraps—*of course, these same husbands might well be the ones who were busy satisfying their own needs with the bar girls in Subic, so perhaps a certain equality was achieved.*

There was one incident, or, really, a series of them, that went unknown until long after the Whidbey squadrons' return. There were only two OB-GYNs available at the base hospital, and they were kept busy. At one time or another, they had seen every dependent woman there. As was usual in the seventies, there were no female navy OB-GYNs. One of these young male doctors, known as

Doctor Feelgood, realized that his tour at Whidbey had landed him in a candy land surrounded with an ample supply of nubile female flesh. Perhaps that was why he chose his medical specialty. At any rate, he took full advantage of the fact that these attractive women were regularly spreading their legs for him. Some of them knew exactly what he was doing, but most proclaimed innocence when the facts finally came out. In essence he began by photographing the half- naked women, at first surreptitiously, then by using narcotics to put them out and pose them. It was never clear when he crossed over to actually arranging the orgies, but soon several of the women were calling on the good doctor at home for drugs and sex.

Feelgood's home, like many on the island was secluded in the heavy fir forest. It was perfect for these clandestine liaisons. He had fitted out the place like a movie studio, where drunk, drugged, or sober, he filmed the women having sex with him and several other men as well as with each other. What he especially liked to film were the pregnant women. He took shots of them in all poses. He did not discriminate, white, black, Asian; it didn't matter to him. Some were group shots with him, and some were of the women with each other. He was very ecumenical. When the women, awaiting the imminent arrival of their returning spouses, tried to break it off, he threatened to show their husbands the photos.

Feelgood was an enterprising sort, and he soon tired of the restrictions of navy life. After putting in his required time, he resigned and took his practice down to Seattle. Two years later, his body, containing five bullet holes, was found in his lakefront home amid piles of photographs of naked women. The Seattle police destroyed the photos. The killer was never found. When it all came to light I wondered whether my wife had been one of the women involved. It did not pay to ask, and I never knew.

TRICK OR TREAT

Oct
ctober thirty-first, Halloween, and the heat was nauseating. It rose from the ground as the sun cooked this part of the planet. It was so hot that the sweat ran down my sides from my armpits and, soaking my undershorts, oozed down my legs to make puddles on the concrete. The booze from the previous night kept me woozy—or was it the oven we were living in? Slowly, the alcohol cooked away; at least I wasn't puking out my guts like the two guys sitting under the wing of the A-6 parked next to us. They were in really bad shape. It's a wonder that they had anything left inside them to lose, but puke just kept coming up. When the tepid breeze that stirred the humid vat of air moved toward me, the smell from their vomit was atrocious.

We have been out here for over an hour, sitting in the only shade available—under the wings of our planes. We were supposed to fly them out to the ship once *Enterprise* cleared Subic Bay and flight ops could commence, but that was hours away. Looking over at the carrier pier I could see the island with the ship's number "65" still tied up.

Under our Prowler there were four of us, all from different crews, each of us had staked out our own spot of shade. I had my place next to the port main mount, and my flight gear was stacked behind me like an easy chair to give me a chance to get some more sleep. The concrete under my butt was still cool and damp from the previous night's rain—it was the only relief from the heat available. It hasn't taken us long to adapt to the Filipino method of dealing with humidity and the scorching sun—move slowly and stay in the shade. From where I lay, I could watch the ship, but there was no sign of movement, so it still would be hours. As time went by, the shape of the shade under the plane changed as the sun moved west. I thought I would be good for another three hours or so, after that, there would be almost no place to go.

Across the breadth of searing white concrete was the line shack. It was air-conditioned, but there was only room for three men inside. It was not a ready room. The poor bastards who worked out here every day were entitled to some relief. There was a soda machine inside and a head, although the smell inside the tiny toilet area was foul from puke and piss. If one of us got up enough energy to stand, the rest called out their orders for soda and received the finger in response. Then the energetic one would stalk off to get his bit of relief, only to return empty handed—it made more sense to drink the soda in the relative coolness of the shack than to carry cans out here in this oven.

We were in the asshole of the world. In the Philippines the hills are covered with magnificent jungles that run down to a translucent blue sea rimmed with snow-white sandy beaches, yet the fetid feces of their inhabitants have corrupted these islands. The town of Olongapo, across the bay, wallowed in its own sewage, human and otherwise. The incongruities of this location were staggering. There was a natural beauty, which overwhelmed the senses, yet the places touched by man seem to numb the soul with their squalor, excess, and depravity alongside saintly aspirations. The breeze rising from shore carried the stench of the raw sewage from Shit River. The two months that I spent out there showed me only the seamiest side of humanity, both of the Filipinos and us, their American "guests." But then, I was in a seamy profession—high-speed delivery of explosive ordnance to the indigenous population of a certain Southeast Asian country with opposing political views. Our job was simple—we were there to save a nation and its people from itself, by bombing it into formless mud—we were very good at our job.

This was our third in-port visit to the PI since arriving in September. For the nuclear-powered the *Enterprise*, Subic Bay was one of the few welcoming ports in all of Southeast Asia. Most countries objected to our parking eight nuclear reactors in their harbors, no matter how much money American sailors spend once they were ashore. The respite from thirty days at sea and war had been welcome, but it gave no sense of relief. Too much drinking and too many late nights had taken a different toll than flying. The nights had become early mornings, wandering through the squalid back alleys where the prostitutes lived. We came back soaked with sweat, alcohol, and cheap perfume; exhausted and in many cases dead broke.

Sailors and aviators treat port calls with the same high-speed intensity that they apply to combat. We just replace one kind of tension with another. After a couple of days sucking down San Miguel beers and watching the girls at the New Jolo Club eat bananas with their pussies, the comparative quiet of an Alpha Strike on the Than Hoa bridge seemed tame. Most of us became filled with remorse as the in-port period extended. The feeling is made worse every time we saw a round-eyed woman on the base. Most of the

Wave officers and nurses were a bunch of cock-teasers who were looking for a good time and someone to spend money on them. They are just prostitutes with a different pricing plan. The worst come-ons were the wives of deployed Seventh Fleet Officers. You can't really blame them. They had relocated out here only to find themselves abandoned by their husbands who were off sailing the seas. The long periods during which their husbands were at sea were made more endurable by booze, gambling, and the occasional roll in the hay with a virile young aviator. So every afternoon these women arrived at the O Club and got themselves genteelly blitzed while scoping out the new meat from home.

The cause of my pain on this Halloween morning had begun early afternoon of the previous day. Several of us had arrived at the Cubi Officer's Club around two. While some of the wives sipped their martinis by the windows overlooking the bay, Bill Woods, Paul Hazlet, and I settled into a booth in the main bar. A Filipino waitress came by pushing frozen margaritas for ten cents each, so we bought her entire tray, at least a dozen, and then ordered three trays of lumpia, a tray apiece. We ate the stuff like potato chips. Lumpia, for the uninitiated, is a snack made with native seasonings and filled with American ground beef—a cross between a spring roll and a taco.

By sundown we had boozed enough and decided that dinner would be a good idea. Prawns, the size of lobsters, and steaks were to be had for a few bucks in the club's dining room, and we filled up. After that we each grabbed a beer from the bar and took the obligatory cab ride to the main gate. Trusty Blaylock Taxis hauled us there for a buck a head. This was a simple approach for drivers and for us—they didn't have to run a meter and drunken sailors didn't have to do any math.

The main gate on the Subic side of the base opened onto Magasaysay Street, one of Olongapo City's main thoroughfares. During the day it is a sleepy place, but at nightfall the carnival begins. We walked across the low arched bridge that spans the Olongapo River, which serves as the border between the base and the town. The river was rife with raw sewage the rankness of which rose and mingled with the smoke from the street vendor's braziers in the humid air. Crossing the bridge we plunged into the crowd of vendors, sailors, and hookers. Each of us was aware of the ship's scheduled early morning departure as well as the stricture of the Marcos regime's imposition of martial law and midnight curfew. It was a particular sport of the dictator's military police to hunt down stray servicemen caught out past the witching hour. If they caught an officer in one of their sweeps, they took particular pleasure in alerting the offender's commanding officer of the transgression. For officers serving aboard the *Enterprise*, this meant an invitation to perform an obligatory "carpet dance" before the ship's captain. Being in hack with him for this kind of nonsense was especially tough since the captain, a former aviator himself, assumed that we were entitled to raise hell ashore after a combat period, but that we should be adroit enough not to get caught.

As we cruised down the street several of our squadron mates came out of the saloons that lined the street. From there we barhopped until the Red Baroon suggested that we top off the evening with a visit to the East Inn Club. Sleaze oozed from the East Inn Club like oil dripping from a '53 Mercury. It was no better or worse than any of the other hooker bars that had been frequented over the years since the air war in Vietnam had begun.

The girls at the East Inn were passable enough—by PI standards. They came in all sizes and shapes, some were even cute. The best looking of them were the youngest—fifteen to eighteen years old and fresh from the farm. Once they got to be twenty, if they weren't careful, they began to show the wear and tear of the life they led, and then the bar owners would send them back to wherever they came from and recruit a new crop. The most sophisticated of all of the bar girls were, in fact teachers by day. These few sometimes found a husband from among the sailors. Of course the sailor wasn't just marrying the girl, he was joining with her entire family of mother, sisters, brothers, and aunts, all of whom would be lining up for visas right after the wedding ceremony.

The club was the usual Olongapo dump inside—battered round tables with rickety chairs, loud jukebox music, and a strong aroma of tobacco, beer, piss, and sweat. We called for beers all around. As was the custom in these sleaze pits, the bartender arrived with a tray of San Miguel bottles. The routine was that he would open the bottle in front of you. If they delivered an open bottle you sent it back, for there was no way to know what might be in an already opened bottle. Then, once you had yours, you kept a death grip on it lest one of the bar girls, who had now descended on us like flies on shit, would get hold of it.

There was now a crowd of girls swirling and squirming around our table. "You want girlfriend?" they all asked in that singsong oriental lilt that seemed as much of a stereotype of their trade. "You want sucky-fucky?" It went on and on. Then they got to business and, grabbing our crotches and squeezing, they hissed, "Buy me drink?" So we did. It seemed natural enough for us; we were wasting time and money in the place anyway. The war had already trick-fucked us, that was not hard to figure out, so why not get trick-fucked by these whores. The girls drank some concoction of coke and jungle juice, but like all clip joints, their drinks cost three times what our beers did. Al waived over the girls and shelled out a sheaf of pesos. Being the most senior among us with three tours out here, we looked to him for some degree of guidance when ashore. Armed with their drinks, the girls came back and found our laps and began the crotch squeezing again. It was not much of a come-on. Sexually, these girls were pretty inept and, for the most part, they covered their pungent body odors with gallons of sickly sweet perfume. They touched us and giggled and we talked among ourselves. What worked in these places was what we called "pesonality"—if you had the pesos, you could get the girl or girls. These girl-women were like lap dogs, once you paid for one, she would not leave you. They squatted in your lap and rubbed away. Their favorite trick was to follow you into the men's room and try to hold your penis while you took a leak. Frankly, that was something I could do for myself.

As I was coming back to the table, one of the girls got hold of Dave Allen's bottle of San Miguel and jumped up on to the table. Like most of her co-workers she hadn't bothered with underwear, so it was easy for her to hike up her skirt and squat on the top of the bottle. The rest of us watched with more than idle interest as she proceeded to use the neck of the bottle as a dildo. Then she whipped the bottle from her vagina and tried to get Dave to drink from it. He slapped it from her hand, and the bottle crashed on to the floor. For a second she looked offended, but then with a gleam in her eye, she reached out and whipped Al's glasses from his face and folding them repeated the process pushing the frames all the way into her several times. With a flourish she pulled the optics, dripping now with her body fluids, from her twat and tried to put them back on Al's face.

Al was ready for her and, using his handkerchief, gripped the gooey glasses, wrapped them with the handkerchief and stuffed them in a pocket out of sight. He told me later that back on the ship he had set them in a glass of vodka and left them there for a week to make sure that they were clean.

It was time for us to leave. We had never planned to stay, and as we had an hour left until curfew, it was time to disentangle ourselves from the place. Amid a cacophony of calls from the girls, offering themselves for "Twenty P. I love you all night" and "You butterfly," we exited and headed to the base, but not yet to our bunks. Out on the street the night air was dank with the stink of exhaust; sweat, rotting vegetation, and the perpetual reek of sewage. Wildly painted jeepneys raced down the street filled with raucous sailors shouting and singing. The corner vendors shouted out "barbeque" and hoped one of us would buy some of their grilled dog or cat meat. I honestly wished to be back at sea, but it was the collective wisdom of the group that we needed a nightcap. Just because there was a curfew in town did not mean the bar at the Cubi club would close. As it turned out, things were just hopping.

At the O Club things were booming. One of the A-7 jocks had built a pyramid of champagne glasses at the curved end of the bar. The structure was at least four feet high, and he was filling the entire assembly by pouring wine into the top glasses and letting the wine flow down until the bottom row was filled. Of course most of the wine was on the bar and forming a growing wet spot on the carpet. When he judged his work done, he tossed the empty champagne bottles carelessly over his shoulder where they crashed and broke on the wooden stairs leading down to the lower dining area. "Casey's the name, flying's the game. Have some champagne!" he shouted.

To a bunch of drunks that seemed to be the height of hilarity, and I suppose it was—until next morning's hangover kicked in. It took a few more rounds of drinks before the real insanity began. One of the A-6 pilots decided that the glistening stack of champagne glasses at the end of the bar would make a great substitute for the ship's arresting barrier. In dire emergencies, when a wounded airplane just had to be recovered on the deck of a carrier, a nylon mesh barrier was employed. Attached to the arresting wires, this nylon mesh was held up by two pylons that normally remained retracted into the flight deck. To use the barrier, the pilot of the disabled aircraft had to put aside all he had been taught to do as a flier and fly into the erect webbing. Each naval aircraft had small steel protrusions on its wings leading edges to catch the nylon webbing, and once caught; the arresting wires would bring the plane to a stop. As the merit of using the champagne glasses was being deliberated, an exceedingly inebriated BN from VA-196 stepped up to test the arresting characteristics of the champagne wall and hoisted himself onto the opposite end of the bar. Immediately, a pilot from his squadron pulled him off declaring that only a pilot could make such a landing.

Amid a chorus of cheers and cat calls, up he went and lay on his back on the bar, his feet pointing toward the glittering target. All the drinkers along the twenty foot length of the bar grabbed their drinks while a self-appointed launch crew wetted down the bar top. Of course, the universally accepted lubricant was beer, and so everyone with a bottle in his hand sloshed beer over the smooth wooden surface. The two Filipino bartenders looked on stoically as they stood back against the back row of bottles. They were wise enough to know when not to interfere. As the beer sloshed and spewed everywhere, one of the recce pilots, a guy about six-four and two hundred and ten pounds grabbed the A-6 pilot by the belt and collar and began to slide him back and forth on the slick bar top to gain momentum. Beer was sloshing everywhere while two quick thinkers grabbed one of the bar's couches and slid it around toward the end of the bar giving the intrepid pilot a relatively safe place to land. Someone elected himself to serve as catapult officer and began to give the run up signal with his right hand.

The recce pilot had the rhythm down now, and, to a chorus of "one, two, three!" the catapult officer dropped his hand and the recce pilot threw his man down the bar. There were more shouts from the crowd followed by shattering glass and a heavy *whump* as the flier went through the barrier, hit the couch and went over the top coming to rest on the floor beyond. The champagne glasses did not survive and now lay in glittering shards all over the room. Everyone in the bar roared with delight.

It seemed that nothing could top that for the evening's entertainment, and the bartenders wanted to close up before anything more could happen, so with "last call" we all began the trek back to the ship. Well, we had a month at sea ahead of us during which we could to sober up. I wasn't troubled by being so drunk, the ship's early movement from port didn't require my participation, and we would be at sea long before I woke up.

For the most part the black shoe officers of the surface navy, the ones who actually ran the ship, preferred that air wing officers stay out of their way when entering or leaving port. For us that meant some extra leeway in terms of sleep and relaxation. Our squadron had only one airplane ashore, it had flown in to Cubi several days before we had arrived, and the squadron's XO and his crew were assigned to go ashore and fly it out to the ship in company with several other planes from our sister squadrons in the wing. This was a normal routine when leaving Subic Bay. Once the shore bound planes were recovered aboard, then all of us would proceed to Yankee Station for another forty-five days at sea.

The phone call came at zero five hundred. Shrill and insistent, all of us tried to ignore the persistent ringing of the phone. It had been a rule in the junior officer bunkroom to avoid or ignore the telephone. It always brought bad news. None of the six of us wanted to answer it, and, after the antics of the previous night, only a few of us were capable of even speaking. The ringing finally stopped, but thirty seconds later, it started again and would not stop. After an eternity my eyes opened into slits and revealed the half-naked body of Bill Woods lying on the deck in a sea of vomit with his arms wrapped around one of the head cans. Behind him a hairy leg, presumably Phil's dangled from behind the bunk's blackout curtains. I conked out when someone answered the phone. The next thing I knew I was being shaken awake by the newest addition to our happy quarters, Clete the abstemious AI was shaking my shoulder.

"Hey, wake up. You're going flying," he said in that sanctimonious voice that he used when proselytizing the gentiles.

"Fuck you," I replied and rolled over.

"Hey, I'm not kidding, you have go."

"Go?" I mumbled, "Go where?"

"The XO's lead NFO is sick. So you're elected. They want to brief in ten minutes. You got to get to the ready room." Then he crawled back in his bunk and feigned sleep.

Sick? I was sick. What good was I going to do, I could barely see. Now I looked around the bunk room. The other four were either truly unconscious or doing a great job of faking it. There was no movement from any of them. Clete must have seen me move while I was asleep and, knowing him, the sniveling little shit that he was, no doubt volunteered me to the XO. I had no time to spare, so I stumbled out to the communal head and showered. It was quick and did little to clear the fog banks in my skull. I wasn't very quiet or respectful of my bunkmates rest when I got back to the room to dress. Bill had managed to drag himself back into his bunk leaving a crusty trail of prawn laden vomit behind him. I pulled underwear from the drawer, clean and scratchy and fresh from the ship's laundry. The one-piece green flight suit that I pulled from its hook and stepped into was losing its battle with rot in this humidity. It never got to dry properly and the stains from my perspiration were turning to mold. It just remained to pull on my flying boots, lace them up, and then slide into my shoulder holster.

I made it to the ready room in fifteen minutes. It was empty but for two other officers, both who were newcomers to the squadron. The pilot for this evolution was a mustang commander and soon to be our XO—that is, he would be, if he could ever qualify in the airplane. This man had instantly earned the nickname Walrus, partly from the short beard and moustache that he tried to stuff into his oxygen mask, but also from the Beatles' song "I Am the Walrus," and we often just referred to him as *goo-goo katchoo,* as we thought the refrain from the song went. He had arrived aboard the ship with a bad reputation preceding him, and each day he was with us, it got worse. He was a florid-faced man who demonstrated a pure disdain for junior officers and, as it turned out, for me in particular, and he went to great pains to display his feelings. We determined that this attitude stemmed from his insecurities and the obvious fact that nearly all of the officers with whom he had contact were smarter than he was. Mostly he hated officers with college degrees, since he never went beyond high school. The other fellow was a new JG who was eager to get flight time. This kid had just come out of the RAG at Whidbey and was eager to get into the war. He would ride in the back seat, and, since I was the senior electronics countermeasures officer, I would run the mission—such as it was. I got the feeling that the Walrus was counting on me to help him find the ship at sea and, once there, get him safely aboard. Why hadn't I feigned sleep too?

The Walrus began in a lugubrious fashion to give the most cursory of briefings. In essence we would go ashore with our flight gear and wait until the ship was twenty-five miles off shore, then we would fly out to it and land—big mission. It was an unspoken rule that no flying officer was required to fly with another whom they thought was unsafe or unqualified. Its also a rule that is seldom invoked as it can cut both ways when you are ratting out a senior officer for being a turd of a pilot. At that moment, I didn't think I had a choice in the matter. This aspect of aviation lore had caused great consternation in our squadron since our incoming XO had failed to complete his NATOPS (naval aviation tactical operations) qualification in the EA-6B. Worse still, he had never carrier qualified in the plane. Someone had pulled strings for him.

His mediocre flying skills were sorely tested during his generally inept and often-dangerous attempts to land back aboard the ship. It was bad enough that he had to rely completely on his crew to preflight and get the airplane ready to launch, but once aloft and with only one set of controls in the plane, he alone maneuver the Prowler to a safe landing. Time and again he missed the target wire on the deck, and the LSOs (landing signal officers) would just keep writing him up for his lousy approaches. At one point the XO, a full commander, pulled rank and bit back at one of the LSOs, who was a mere lieutenant, for his comments. Well, that was not at all kosher, for the LSO, like an NFL referee was the final arbiter of an aviator's skill in landing, and the lieutenant mentioned the XO's tirade to CAG. CAG was having none of it and summoned the XO to his quarters.

All of our squadron's junior officers, who had to endure the XO's regular verbal assaults, reveled when we heard that the XO had been given a severe and nearly career-ending dressing down by CAG. Details of the XOs "carpet dance" circulated rapidly and was no doubt greatly embroidered by the time they reached us, but we were greatly surprised that it had happened at all.

CAG reaming out of the XO did not help his crew very much, in quite it just made life harder for all of us. He had to go through a complete requalification in the airplane, which meant that they had to fly with him as he learned what he should have mastered back in the RAG at Whidbey. We pitied them as they made training flight after training flight around the ship, doing touch and goes with him until, somehow, he got a passing grade. At the same time our own LSO and the Safety Officer had to mentor him through the NATOPS exam, not an easy task for them as the XO was a Mustang. He came from a breed of fliers that got their wings during the Korean War, but had come into the navy with little formal education. His flying before joining our squadron had been done in a series of prop airplanes such that the transition to high performance jets was a shock.

Barely able to stand, I was now beginning to wonder what I had done to offend God to have earned this kind of a penance. My head and body ached as if someone had used a two by four on me for batting practice. Death, even at the hands of someone so hateful as the XO, seemed a pleasant alternative. I needed something in my stomach, so if I got the heaves, then something would come up. If eating a sponge to soak up the booze would work, I would have gladly done so. The main wardroom was open, and despite its prohibition on flight gear, it was too early for any of the black shoe snobs to complain. I ate and the food sopped up some of the extra booze still sloshing around in my stomach, and the multiple cups of coffee that I drank gave my body enough caffeine to keep me vertical. During Walrus's two minute soliloquy that passed for a briefing, he had mentioned that our wingman would be a KA-6D tanker. That plane was to be flown by the two A-6 guys who were puking up their guts—not an encouraging sign.

Nine a.m. and we have been out here in the Filipino sauté pan for nearly three hours. The sun cooked the air into a quivering broth as it slowly ate the shade away. I was ravenous despite my breakfast, worse my thirst could not be slaked. I lurched to my feet and made my way, swaying in the heat, to the line shack. Inside the men waiting to launch us were hunched over a game of acey-ducey and enjoyed the sixty-degree blast from the window air-conditioner. The cool air turned my damp flight suit into a slimy green shell. At the water cooler in the corner, I gulped down cup after cup of chilled water. I looked, in vain, for a candy machine, anything would have done. As if reading my mind, one of the crew handed me a tray of iced donuts; they were covered with orange or black symbols. Nothing about their design registered.

"Trick or Treat!" he said with a bright smile.

I looked at him with glazed over eyes as my hand, as if operated independently, reached for one of the fat pills.

"It's Halloween Sir—you know, trick or treat?"

"Oh. Oh yeah, sorry, but that heat out there is a bitch," I mumbled and bit into the donut. I dallied as long as I could in the shack, and they let me have another donut. But they had business with all the planes parked on the apron, men came and went as the workday progressed and I could see that I was just in the way. Besides, enlisted men don't feel very comfortable when an officer just hangs around. Outside again nothing had been done to cool off the sun, but there was good news in the distance. The *Enterprise* was now in mid-channel and steaming out past Grande Island. Halloween, huh?—well maybe Hollywood should give up on ghouls and monsters. If they could capture the filth and degradations of this place and combine it with the way I was feeling, they could make a movie that would scare anyone.

The KA-6 crew had the sullen look of the condemned. The pilot had been sick again and the BN was very groggy and kept humming some song that was vaguely recognizable. The pair had been with the bunch of us at the bar in the Cubi O Club the night before. I didn't really know them, but I could only assume that they had been roped into flying at the last minute as I had been. On my way back from the line shack I had bumped into a RIO from the puking dogs squadron and I mentioned the tanker crew. He thought that anyone that sick ought to just cancel out of the hop. I agreed, they could go later. We did not need a wingman. He said that he had talked to them earlier, but they said the ship was short of tankers, and they were going to fly out hung over or not.

The line shack finally alerted us that we were a go. Manning up seemed very hurried after the hours lolling around in the heat. Once the ship cleared the harbor and dropped the port pilot, it signaled that we would have a ready deck in thirty minutes. We all got together again and re-briefed. There were several sections of two planes each. The tanker and we would go last. There was a huddle with the KA-6 crew just far enough away from where they had been sick so that the smell just melded into the rest of the stench of the islands. We reviewed hand signals and radio frequencies. There was not too much to talk about. The XO was senior man, but he was not about to lead the flight, he didn't want to chance any screw up that could be blamed on him.

We agreed that the KA-6D was launching with empty drop tanks and so would climb faster and, thus, should take the lead for our section takeoff. As Walrus was saying this, he kept looking at me, as if to assure himself of the flight procedures. I was getting a sinking feeling. He had no clue about executing a section takeoff. With his ineptitude at flying the EA-6B, I knew that he would not be able to stay on the lighter plane's wing. He was probably already envisioning the raucous stories that would be generated by the wardroom crowds about how he was sloppy in the air and how he struggled to maintain section integrity.

Since the Phantoms carried less fuel than we did and burned it faster, they had to go first and would be recovered as soon as they were overhead the ship. We carried a huge load of fuel and would be heavier. Once we got out to the ship, we would need to dump several thousand pounds of it, so we would be at the right weight for the trap.

For me this was to be just another hop, just fly and get it over with. But once we've trapped aboard the carrier, I vowed that I'd make sure to never fly with the Walrus again. He was an angry and disagreeable man—Captain Queeg was more likeable than he. I was dog tired, and the Walrus was nervous—surely not a great combination to have sitting on top of twenty-four thousand pounds of thrust. We took the air start, and then throttled around the horn as the most pleasant sound in the cockpit filled my ears as the onboard air conditioning kicks in. I brought the control panel to life with the master "on" switch and began the takeoff checklist.

"Canopies" ... "closed and locked";

"Wings" ... "spread and locked."

I looked out to the right and left to make sure the little red locking flags were down into their locked positions in the wings.

"Flaps" ... "down"

"Stabilizer" ... "shifted"

"Fuel" ... "checked"

"Fuel transfer" ... "norm"

"Controls" ... "unrestricted"

The Walrus "cleaned" the cockpit with the stick and pressed the rudder pedals. I could see the control surfaces moving out on the wing and in the canopy bow mirrors. Maybe I was feeling just a little better—or maybe it is the pure oxygen I was breathing through my mask.

"Aux brakes" … "fifteen cycles"

"Flaperon pop-up" … "armed"

"Antiskid" … "on"

"Seats" … "armed"

With the ejection seat now armed, I could blow myself out of the beast at any time, if need be. According to the manual all that is needed is eighty knots of airspeed, and you can make a safe ejection. I looked over at the KA-6 and had to nudge the Walrus. They were giving us the hand signal to taxi. Jesus, what the fuck was he doing? You have to keep one eye on your wingman at all times. I guess for today that means my eye, because the Walrus was out of his depth in making a section takeoff. The tanker started to taxi and called the tower. I could hear them on the radio. As section leader that was his job, I just monitored the radios and set the navigation coordinates of the airfield in our computer.

Most airplanes, when moving on the ground appear ungainly and awkward. Deprived of speed and with added the encumbrances of landing gear and external stores, they seem to lumber along. Fighters aren't so bad; their sleekness of design gives them a look of speed even when stationary, but bombers, well they look big and clumsy on the ground, like the fat kids at a little league practice. The heat from the KA-6D's exhaust turned the air between us into a watery, wavering curtain. Its wings appeared as bulbous accordions, and their clean aerodynamic lines were lost in a jumble of grotesque overlapping shapes. The KA-6's BN signaled; it was time to switch to tower frequency.

"Climax four, position and hold."

Slowly, we followed the KA-6D onto the east runway, and to my surprise, the Walrus tucked us into the correct position just behind its right wing. With our nose in the proper position, we could look right up the sweep of his wing and into the cockpit. Everything was just as it was supposed to be. By now the air conditioner has finally cut through the accumulated heat in the cockpit, and the oxygen has stopped the alcohol from killing any more of my brain cells.

"Climax four cleared for takeoff. Winds zero eight five at five knots. Altimeter two niner-niner eight," came the voice from the tower.

"Roger, Climax four cleared for takeoff. Two niner-niner eight." I heard as our leader acknowledged the instructions. In their cockpit the BN spun his finger in the air to indicate engine run up.

"Engines" … "one hundred percent"

"EGT" … "safe"

"Fuel flow" … "okay"

"Oil, hydraulic pressures" … "okay"

The Walrus and I looked over to see the tanker's BN drop his hand, as they started to move. Walrus eased up on our brakes, and we too began to roll. The takeoff was slow, very slow; my VW went uphill faster than we were moving. The thrust of the jet engines were straining to move us through the thick sea of hot air atop the wings. Like a giant claw, the fingers of the humid tropics were hold us back, denying us the cleansing act of flight.

I was watching the runway markers showing how many feet of runway remain. I ticked off seven thousand feet of runway left, and I felt as if we were standing still. The airspeed indicator was pegged at zero. Six thousand went by, and then at five thousand feet remaining the KA-6 seemed to lurch ahead as it began to break the hot air's grasp—now we had eighty knots and four thousand feet remaining. A hundred knots, one ten, and the airspeed needle jumped to one hundred and thirty knots, and I felt the sensation of lift, we were free—airborne. The KA-6 dipped slightly, no longer were we on a steady climb with them. I looked at our angle of attack indicator; it was just where it was supposed to be. We were only at two hundred feet, but we were climbing, and then, just ahead and to the left of our nose, a huge pillar of water rose and in it a white and orange drop tank was shooting skyward.

Up! We had to go up. Altitude is what we needed, and the fingers of hot air suddenly released us. There was no time to look at the fountain of water and the descending debris off our port wing. We had to climb!

"Gear" ... "up"

We shot upward, airspeed increasing

Fifteen hundred feet

"Flaps" ... "up"

With our wings cleaned up, we could now maneuver. Walrus made a shallow left turn, and we looked to where the KA-6D should have been, but there was only smoke and debris on the surface of the harbor. I had to take over the radios, because in that instant of calamity we became a flight of one.

"Climax Four, Cubi tower."

"Climax four," I replied.

"Climax four, continue circling the field. Maintain five thousand feet."

"Roger, maintain five thousand. Did anyone get out?"

"Climax Four, negative chutes."

We circled the crash site for another ten minutes looking for a parachute or a life raft, a man, anything. All I could see were chunks of what had a few minutes before been a flying airplane. Helicopters and crash boats had been launched with rescue divers aboard. Soon the fire trucks reached the site; and there was nothing left for us to do but press on.

The tower finally turned us loose, and I gave the Walrus a heading and we swung west to find the ship. Our mother ship was now fifty miles ahead waiting for its errant sons—two of which would not return. We flew on in silence, each caught up in their private thoughts. Each of us in the Prowler wondered what could have happened, what did they do that killed them? It was to be an easy hop, why did anyone have to die? My mind marveled at the speed of it. They were flying, we were flying, then they turned into smoke and debris—how did that happen? I asked myself, "Where did they screw up?"

We were professional aviators, and as such, the death of other professionals while flying was something that bore examination, a clinical dissection, so we could understand and so avoid our own deaths in similar circumstances. Now we had questions, too many questions, but in the back of my mind I knew the real answer: they were tired, sick, drunk, and hung over; their real mistake was in not saying no.

"Climax, Skybolt six one two," I radioed the ship. As we were now alone in the air, I used our own squadron call sign.

"Skybolt six one two, ready deck," the ship replied.

There it was, dead ahead; a long grey shadow on a shimmering silver sea. The carrier's wake was streaming straight aft as it kept its bow pointed into the wind. That piece of steel was our safe haven. Friends were aboard, hot showers and food were there, and it was our home. Our approach to landing would be zip-lipped—no extra radio transmissions. This was called a case-one approach, and we descended to pattern height as we headed to come up along the starboard side of the ship. Hopefully, the Walrus could fly this simplest of approaches. He had not spoken a word since the crash, not a good sign. All he had to do was fly a normal pattern, up the starboard side and break left a mile ahead. Landing should be routine. I keyed the mike again.

"Climax, Skybolt six one two, we are a single flight, the KA-6 crashed on takeoff at Cubi."

It seemed at once gratuitous, but necessary to make this radio call, and I knew it, but I wanted to be sure someone aboard the ship knew and not wait for an airplane that would never arrive.

"Roger Skybolt six one two. We'll pass that on to the squadron."

We were five miles astern.

"Hook" ... "down."

I looked down at my kneeboard, focusing on it for the first time that day. There on the flight information card that they had given us that morning, which listed the day's frequencies and call signs, was printed a big black cat with the caption Trick or Treat under it.

Trick or treat.

THE DA NANG GANG

The right fire warning light beat out a steady pulse and filled the cockpit with an angry red glow. Against the pitch black of the night sky, the indication that our aircraft was on fire was doubly fearsome. Fire in flight has always been a flier's worst fear. That was a lesson I had learned at an early age upon hearing my old man tell of how he had nearly severed his own leg with an axe to extract himself from his airplane's wreckage rather than burn in a crash. With his leg pinned in the nose turret of a flak-riddled B-24 as it limped home to England from a raid over Germany—two engines out and forced to make a wheels-up landing—he held an axe over his leg ready to chop it off rather than burn if the plane caught fire. In high performance jet aircraft, you seldom had time to contemplate such an action. Sitting atop an array of fuel cells filled with JP5 jet fuel and engines pulsing at temperatures of eleven hundred degrees, a fire meant that in a second or so you could erupt into a ball of fire. It looked like we had rolled the dice in this game of war and had come up snake eyes.

A few moments before, the four of us in our Prowler had been chattering aimlessly about food and wondering if we might find some cheeseburgers in the dirty shirt wardroom after we trapped back aboard the *Enterprise*. We had just completed another in a second of two night hops that night, providing jamming cover for several of our air group's attacks up along the North Vietnamese coast. At dinner, hours before we launched, I had asked Aquino, our wardroom steward, to save us some burgers for a snack upon our return. He smiled broadly and agreed then offered that he would even make us some French fries to go with them. It would make a nice change from the eggs-to-order that seemed to be our usual post-flight meal. Now it looked like all we might get to eat would be a survival bar from our life vests as we floated around the darkened waters of the Gulf of Tonkin in our rafts.

As the warning light continued to flash, I began to immediately read off the emergency procedures from the EA-6B pocket checklist that was attached to my kneeboard. Now, rapidly but with precision, Ted and I were doing everything we could to keep the airplane in the sky and avoid becoming a million glowing sparks floating down through the night sky into the sea like the finale at a Fourth of July celebration.

"Right engine off! Gangbar off!" I shouted into my oxygen mask's microphone.

Ted had beaten me to it, his twenty years of flying experience, from flying blimps to attack aircraft, instantly kicked into high gear, he was already two steps ahead of me. Instinctively I looked up to scan the rear view mirrors along the canopy bow to see if we had flames coming from the rear or underside of the plane. Behind us there was nothing but black sky.

"Any secondaries?" this time speaking to Phil and Shit-finger in the back seats. Back there, they were helpless; they could do nothing about the flight situation but wait for Ted's instructions to eject or without warning to feel the preemptory jolt of an emergency command ejection. If they had felt any thumps or bumps under them, resulting from internal secondary explosions, they did not say. If we were about to explode, we had less than two seconds to eject and avoid becoming part of the massive fireball when the jet exhaust burned through to the ten thousand pounds of jet fuel we still had on board.

"Nothing," Phil replied.

Shit-finger was still trying to find his pocket checklist from amidst the debris of flight gear with which he habitually flew. As usual, he was next to useless in the air.

"Climax, Skybolt Three." Ted was on the radio to the ship. Even on the darkest of nights, and tonight with no moon was especially dark and layers of overcast. All combat flight operations were conducted with a minimum of radio contact so that when a call like ours was made, flight operations aboard the ship was put on heightened alert.

"Skybolt Three, Climax—go ahead."

"Skybolt Three's declaring an emergency, we have a right fire warning indicator. We have secured the engine, no sign of fire or secondary explosions. Request immediate bingo." Ted was very crisp and clear as he communicated our situation to the ship.

"Roger, Three, standby for bingo instructions."

Well goodbye cheeseburgers, our request for bingo instructions meant we were going to be rerouted to the beach—a land base, and in this part of the world that could only mean Da Nang.

As soon as we saw the fire warning light, we all knew that we were not going to be getting back aboard our ship very soon, if at all. But now we were operating with a single engine, and that meant no shipboard landings. With the underpowered engines that Grumman had rushed to install in the EA-6B, so that we could be sent off to war, we would have been dead meat if we attempted a shipboard landing on one engine. With only the one engine turning, our sink rate would have been too high for an approach to the ship. If we had to waive off, it would just mean that another four aviators would be swallowed up by the Gulf of Tonkin—four more casualties to add to the growing list of men lost after completing another of the thousands of meaningless missions of blowing holes in the jungles of North Vietnam.

It wasn't that we were bitter about being here—it was our job. As professional naval officers, we conducted our part of the war under a professional code. But as intelligent men, we knew that was not how the overall war strategy—if indeed there was such a thing— was being carried out. Making a stab for the deck of the *Enterprise* in a single-engined EA-6B was not professional, nor even wise, and we were not going to be the first to try it. There is an old saying among aviators, going back to the days of the First World War, when planes were held together with fabric and wire: There are old pilots and there are bold pilots, but there are no old, bold pilots. That was an excellent maxim to remember on nights like this.

It dawned on all of us that perhaps, once again, Shitfinger had put his whammy on us, and we would, of course, forever blame him. But blame would have to wait until we got the limping airplane back on the ground. Aviators are often a superstitious lot, or at least they, like their seafaring ancestors, do not like to tempt fate. Some do not even like to have their photos taken before a flight. That superstition goes back to Manfred von Richtofen, who had his photo snapped just before he took off on his last, and fatal, flight. So, it seemed that flying with Shit-finger at any time, but especially in combat, was the ultimate temptation of fate.

Minutes passed when last the ship called back, and, as expected, Da Nang was our bingo field. I dialed in the TACAN frequency and set the field's coordinates in the flight computer. Instantly, Ted saw the fly-to solution appear on the flight video indicator in front of him, and he turned us south.

After several minutes, our heart rates began to normalize.

"Skybolt Three, Climax. Confirm your bingo is Da Nang, two zero five at eight zero miles. We are passing your status on to them. Contact Da Nang approach on button ten," came over the radio.

I answered the ship. "Roger, Climax—switching to button ten." Ted was intent on watching the exhaust gas temperature gauge to make certain that there was indeed no fire under us. With everything on the gauges looking normal, I punched up button ten on the UHF and called Da Nang.

"Da Nang approach, Skybolt Three." It was close to two-thirty in the morning, and I was hoping that I would be speaking with a GI controller. The war at that time was halfway into the Vietnamization phase, and who could tell if we would be talking to some ARVN controller with minimal English who was new to the job. With the pressure of an emergency, we did not need the added confusion of garbled communications. But then a groggy, but decidedly American, voice responded.

"Skybolt Three, ident—state your intentions."

I punched the IFF switch to identify us on Da Nang's approach radar. Ted was busy maneuvering the aircraft and hoping that whatever damage the fire had caused had not compromised the combined hydraulic system—the lifeblood of the airplane's flight controls. If we lost that, we would be in the water or end up augering into the dirt before we could land.

"Roger. Skybolt Three's a declared emergency. Fire warning lights and single engine. Request immediate clearance to land," I replied.

"Skybolt Three, come left to one-eight-zero. Descend and maintain five thousand."

Ted nodded to me and eased back on the throttle of the port engine. With only one engine, the airplane was sluggish and flew like a turd. The normally nose-heavy airplane began to sink like a rock. He added some power and, extending the speed brakes slightly, kept our descent to just above the panic level.

I got back on the radio, "Skybolt Three's out of one-zero-thousand for five, coming left to one-eight-zero."

The airplane had steadied up and, although the thrust was severely reduced, there was no need yet to jettison the heavy jamming pods that hung below the wings and the centerline and created so much added drag. Costing over one million dollars each, jettisoning them was a last-ditch effort to keep flying. We did not relish having to explain their loss to the air wing commander unless we felt it was the only way to keep from losing the airplane. CAG had been pretty direct with our skipper. When we first deployed to the South China Sea, the commander of our air wing, known as CAG-14, or just CAG, had half-jokingly told him that since our airplane and the jamming pods were so expensive, he wanted to remove our ejection seats and bolt down our canopies, and make us fly like kamikazes. He just wanted to ensure that we would do our utmost to bring our planes safely back to the ship and not scatter them across the landscape.

Things quieted down in the cockpit. Each of us was checking and double-checking everything before we pushed over for the final descent. With only one engine turning once the landing gear, heavy and unaerodynamic, was extended, the plane would fly like a rock. In the dense, humid air of the Vietnamese night, the plane's response to an emergency application of full power would be slow and unpredictable. If, for some reason, we had to wave off the approach to Da Nang's single long runway, it was an even bet if the Prowler would climb at all. We each had the sinking feeling that followed a rush of adrenalin. Somber in our thoughts each of us were wondering what had jinxed us tonight and whether Shit-finger, because he was not one of our regular crew and added, as a fourth-seat rider at the last moment, was indeed a real Jonah.

The radar in front of the stick on Ted's side of the cockpit painted the coastline near Da Nang. Thirty miles to go—show time! Checklists were reviewed with the two guys in the back, Phil and Shit-finger, each following along on their PCLs to make sure Ted and I had not missed anything. Approach gave us a new heading, and we flew south so that we could turn one-hundred-and-eighty degrees and land to the north. Everything normal, everything looking good, but I wasn't thinking about what we would do once we were on the ground. We still had to get there.

As we descended to two thousand feet and turned toward final, the approach controller turned us over to Da Nang's final controller. As instructed, I switched frequencies and called for final.

"Ah Skybowl tree, Dah Nang apoach," came the singsong voice of a Vietnamese controller over the radio.

"Jesus fucking Christ! Get us a fucking GI controller. I'm not taking this big ugly fucker in while some fucking local slopehead tries to fuck us up!" Ted shouted over the intercom. Ted remained rock solid on the controls of the wallowing airplane, he usually could handle anything, especially when things were going to shit.

"Da Nang, Skybolt Three requests a GI controller." I felt sorry for the kid on the radio. It was not his fault; his life was going to be completely fucked anyway once the US finished pulling out of this sinkhole. But at that moment it was our asses in question, so any sympathy I had for him was dispersed by the thought of all of us being squashed like a bug in the jungle below.

A moment later a GI controller, probably the same guy who had guided us on approach came on the radio and had us switch frequencies again. We were now five miles out from the field. The very last thing we wanted to do was to lower the gear. Lowering the gear or going dirty, as it was called, would put the maximum strain on Ted's ability to keep us airborne. When the new final controller came on the air, I wished we had stayed with the Vietnamese kid. This new guy's voice bordered on the hysterical, he seemed to be in a state of high emotion, and his voice came across the air in a high-pitched squeal.

"Skybolt Three, this is your final controller! Can you land?"

Could we land? What the fuck did he think we were doing, towing banners at the beach?

Asking us this question was bad enough, but what followed scared us almost shitless. Since we had not blown up over the Gulf, we had almost forgotten what had happened to cause this emergency as we worked to put the plane into a stable, safe-flight attitude. We still had the confidence of all aviators: somehow, someway, we would come safely to land. But as he continued to speak on the radio, we could hear him talking to the emergency rescue vehicles at the field.

He was almost screaming now, "We have and aircraft on fire and attempting to land," he went on over the air.

Fire! We weren't on fire, were we? Did he see flames from the tower; we were almost on the ground? All of us scanned the rearviews—no flames.

"Da Nang, six-one-three is single engine, no fire. Repeat no fire!" I wanted to wring this guy's neck, but that would have to wait.

The controller did not acknowledge my call but went straight into his approach script and cleared us to land.

Now a wounded airplane, one with little ability to maneuver, creates a fat and tempting target for any enemy. We were big, slow, and wallowing through the night sky like a dying duck. Below and in front of us the terrain was dense foliage opening to marshy land at the approach end of the runway. Suddenly, out of the darkness, heavy shooting erupted. Tracers streaked through the elephant grass south of the field perimeter. For all we knew the VC were probably monitoring the base radio frequencies. If there was any doubt about that, it was cleared up in the next instant, for out of the darkness came the flare of a rocket as a RPG shot up toward us. Its launch flash and fiery trail were almost instantaneous. Instinctively Ted pushed the nose down. We needed airspeed, but at five hundred feet, we had no maneuvering room no matter what our airspeed.

"Fuck me! Fuck me! They're fucking shooting at us!" Ted was shouting.

"Da Nang, Skybolt Three's taking fire from the approach end!' I had no idea what good saying this would do. I just did not want to die mutely in this iron albatross as it augured into a swamp. Maybe there were still some GI's around to kill those sons of bitches down on the ground.

Below us, more flickers of tracers streaked across the blackness and up at us. We were now so low that anything that hit the plane would bring us down, and, if we ejected at this point, we would be floating down right on top of the people who seemed very intent on killing us. There was no place to go but forward. Another rocket flared but it seemed to explode on the ground before becoming airborne. From my side of the cockpit I could see more tracers, but these had to be ARVN or Marines, because they seemed to be pouring fire toward the area from which the first RPG had been launched. Then, just as suddenly as the firing had begun, it was over, and we made the runway.

As we pulled off the runway, a gray navy truck drove out to meet us, and we followed it toward a row of sandbagged protected aircraft revetments at the west side of the field. Our canopies were opened, and we drank in the sick, sweet and dank air that hung over the land. As we shut down on the apron, a grizzled chief got out of the truck. He looked at the side of the plane and, somewhat dubious about our arrival, unlatched the side ladder and climbed up to speak to Ted.

"Evening sir, welcome to Da Nang. I understand that you've had a bit of a problem."

Ted gave him the run down on the situation with the plane, and told him that we needed to speak with the ship. Now that we were on the ground, we needed to get some mechanics out from the *Enterprise* to look at the plane. Walking around the plane, we looked for signs of fire, but there were none to be seen. We still did not know if there had been an engine fire, but whatever the cause of the night's problems, it looked like we were going to be spending the next several days on the beach. There were no qualified mechanics in Da Nang who could work on the plane, and the only spare parts for it were on the ship or back in Bethpage. Without a mech's sign off, we could not move the plane.

"Sir," the chief began, "it would be prudent to get this airplane parked inside one of these revetments as soon as possible. The perimeter of the field is hotter than it has been in years, and we are expecting incoming in about another half hour. Charlie is pretty punctual, but as you may have noticed, your airplane is a lot taller than the other structures around here. In short, sir, you make a pretty good target."

We needed very little encouragement from that point on. Up in the cockpit I rode the brakes as an APU hitched on to the nose wheel and pushed the Prowler back into the U-shaped space made by twenty-foot tall piles of sand bags. Once parked, we unlatched the engine bay doors, but amongst the myriad complexity of wires and tubing, there was no evidence of fire. We looked at one another and shook our heads, as the night registered as just another bad dream.

"There's a BOQ next to our radio shack. Once you have sent a message to your ship, you can find a rack and turn in there," said the chief. He had taken on the air of a hospitable innkeeper, but clearly we were going to be a burden to him, until we could get airborne and away from his tiny fiefdom.

There is something that happens to me after flying. Call it post stress syndrome or simply a let down from the exhilaration of the flight experience, but I have it every time I come back to earth. It is as if life on the ground can never quite measure up to the sensations and command of life in the air. Add to that the adrenaline rush of being shot at, surviving, and negotiating one's way through a major emergency, well, normal, professionally trained people can end up doing some very strange things. It was under these conditions that the four of us found the door to Da Nang's Red Dog Saloon unlocked. Before us the bar beckoned.

The interior place looked like any suburban US rec room. Cheap wood paneling from which hung an assortment of beer signs gave the place a familiar feel. We might have been in Chicago or Des Moines from the feel of it. The assortment of liquor at the bar assured our conviviality. We just assumed it was free and available to unexpected guests. With the necessary messages to the ship sent and the temporarily immobile airplane safely parked, we were free to indulge. Ted's favorite bourbon, the one we kept in the J.O. bunkroom for him, Ten-High, seemed to be in ample supply. The fridge was stocked with cold cans of Coors, within a few moments, the booze was flowing in on our empty stomachs, and we were becoming uproariously drunk.

We felt thaw we had been hard at it for some time, downing shots and beers, but the hands of the clock had barely moved. Shit-finger stood up and began a lunge toward the door, then stopped and looked at the three of us. He was making a course toward the open-air latrines just beyond the building that housed the Red Dog and the BOQ.

"I've got to piss." Shit-finger had spoken his soliloquy, and now he prepared to exit the stage. He had remained silent for most of the flight, and we tried to forget that he was with us. He had been drinking steadily since we found the bar, and now a latent streak of wily belligerence in him had begun to emerge. "An' if there are any gooks out there, I'll shoot their asses off!" he declared. With that, he pulled out a 9 mm parabellum automatic from somewhere and waived it over his head. None of us had noticed his gun before this. The rest of us carried the navy-issued airweight Colt .38s in our shoulder holsters, but Shit-finger must have kept this cannon zipped up inside his survival vest.

Shit-finger stood in the center of the room pointing the gun and taking imaginary pot shots at VC hiding behind the beer signs. Shit-finger was tall and athletic. He played a mean game of tennis, it was said, and although not muscular, he was certainly not someone with whom any of us wanted to wrestle. But with eighteen high velocity rounds of ammunition at his disposal, unleashing him into the night did not seem to be a smart idea, even to our alcohol-shrouded brains. But it was Ted who took action; while Phil and I sat, slack jawed. Coming from an almost prone position on the couch, he rose. As Shit-finger spun past him on his swirling game of shooting gallery with the beer signs, Ted grabbed Shit-finger by the neck with one hand, while with the other he crushed his fingers into his gun hand and, with a twist, disarmed him. Shit-finger slumped halfway to the floor, "You don't need the gun now, Shit-finger." Ted spoke softly, like a father to an errant child. We all waited for Shit-finger to regain his composure. With a slight whimper, he stumbled toward the door and out into the night. Ted checked the safety on the weapon and then pocketed the gun.

"Give him a few moments and then go out and see if he is okay," Ted said to Phil and me. Then he turned back to his bourbon.

Shit-finger's trail was easy enough to follow. Outside of the Red Dog, he had knocked over a trashcan and scattered its contents over the floor. Further down the passageway that led to the latrine something dark was spilled out on the linoleum. Whatever it was lay just outside the door marked with the name of some ARVN colonel. The door was closed, and it seemed as if the colonel was not at home. We were about to knock and go in when we heard the sounds of heavy banging coming from outside the building. Phil and I walked to the door and cautiously pushed it open. "See anything," I asked.

Beyond where we stood watching was a short walkway that disappeared into a narrow maze of metal troughs, each stood about thirty inches high. This was the open-air pissoir of the latrine. The place was roofed with corrugated metal that rang with the impact of raindrops from the slow drizzle that enveloped the airfield. Standing in the middle of the maze was Shit-finger, taking a leak. He looked like one of those Italian renaissance fountains pouring water from his prick. But instead of the troughs, he was pissing into a large potted plant. As we approached, he zipped up and looking very impish, pointed at the potted plant from which a small placard bearing the name of the Vietnamese colonel dangled. "Found it in the hallway, belongs to some ARVN colonel. Well, fuck him!" he said quite pleased with himself.

All of us were now running on empty, and although the booze had been good at the time, we needed sleep. We crawled up the stairs to an empty room, and each of us found a bunk. Shit-finger had come along quietly and was soon asleep on a lower bunk. Sometime later, there were sirens and the heavy whump, whump of a few explosions. They seemed far away. I was just too sleepy to move.

Voices drifted up to the open window from the outside, and I was still coming out of a dream in which I was making love to my wife, when, below me, I saw the coolie hats worn by black pajamaed women. "Shit! Look at that, VC!" I grabbed for my .38 as I jumped down from my bunk. Ted, as groggy as I was, grabbed my arm.

Ted looked out the window and saw the women. "Calm down, they are just the cleaning ladies. They might be VC by night, but during the day they clean the BOQ and get their rice bowls filled by Uncle Sam," he said calmly.

I looked out again at the slender women who were filing through the gate and heading off to their workplaces. They were so exotic looking to me, much more so than the women in the PI. For several moments, I just stood and stared at them. We had "checked in" to the BOQ after we extracted Shit-finger from the latrine. Saying that we had checked truly overstated how we got to find our beds. The duty officer at the shore detachment simply told us to hunt around the building find a room with no one sleeping in it. We had found an empty four-bunk room on the second floor and took possession of it. In it were bunks with mattresses, but no sheets or blankets. In a locker we found four flak vests and four helmets, very reassuring. But I did not feel reassured, and, after a sweaty night on a mildewed mattress, it came to me that at last Vietnam was my new reality.

The BOQ had no air-conditioning, at least not in this part of the building, which appeared to be older, almost abandoned and left available for transients like us. My body felt sticky, smelly, and I needed a shower. With no changes of clothes available, it seemed that I would be spending several days in what I was now wearing, so a shower was a necessity. With Ted smiling bemusedly at my recent bout with the invasion of the VC, and the other two snoring loudly, I set off for the lower deck and the head.

During the day the staff of the place appeared and there was a steward on duty at the desk. He gave me a quizzical glance when I

explained that there were four of us upstairs. No one had told him
about us. Still, I coaxed him out of a skimpy and raspy towel and
hotel bar of Ivory soap. When I asked about the shower, he just
hooked his thumb toward the passageway behind his counter. That
is where I went. A few feet beyond the desk the passageway ended in
a large, tiled shower room. It was like all the showers in all the BOQs
around the globe, side open and with no door. Along the walls were
two rows of showerheads. I found a row of hooks for my clothes and
the towel. There was a metal soap dish for the Ivory. I cranked the
faucet handles until a spray emerged from the showerhead. The
water was tepid, the stream a bit limp, but it was refreshing
nonetheless. I was enjoying the wash when I first heard the noise
behind me. With the splashing of the water I almost missed it, but
there it was again, a kind of high-pitched whistling, no, giggling. I
turned and looked toward the open doorway and saw two women
standing there. From their identical black pajamas, I took them for
some of the "enemy" who I had seen from my window moments
before. But they were already at work, ironing and folding other
officer's laundry and watching my nakedness with some curiosity.
Under the circumstances, their giggling seemed both appropriate
and somewhat expected. This war oscillated between the tragic and
the hilarious.

War produces many emotions, but I could only laugh as I
stood, buck naked, in front of those women, who at any time during
the night would gladly have blown me to hell. Either one could have
been among those who, last night, had tried to shoot us out of the
sky. Now that I was aware of them, they both stopped what they
were doing and came forward. I was not sure if this was the normal
practice in the Q, or if this was to be construed as a one-off business
deal, but the pair began to strip and seemed to be ready to join me in
the shower. I smiled but waved them away. "No money, no Ps," I

shouted over the sound of the running water, not from any sense of propriety, but I knew that in this part of the world, sex with GIs was a business proposition, and, despite a desire to wrestle under the water with these two, I hadn't the means to do any financial wrangling.

The pair looked very forlorn. Another customer had gotten away. I smiled at them, dried off, dressed, and made it back to the room. Phil was awake when I got there. He looked at me with my still-wet hair. "Find the shower?" he asked.

"Yeah, just behind the desk downstairs."

"I think I'll go down," he said. I nodded and looked at my watch. Three minutes later, we heard his voice at a loud pitch, and a second after that he burst through the door, naked and soaking wet.

"There are women in the shower!" he shouted.

I looked at him and then at Ted, and we both howled with laughter. I had begun to wish I had taken the pair up on their offer.

———

It turned out that we were to spend four days in Da Nang. Neither the cuisine nor the accommodations recommended the place as an attractive liberty port. When we weren't trying to find new ways of making hot dogs and cheese sandwiches taste like something other than their principal ingredient: cardboard, we focused on repairing our airplane. There was little, that we as the flight crew could do to fix whatever was broken. All of us were great at writing up gripes on sick birds, and most of us could give a mech a fair idea as to where he might begin his hunt to find a problem, but actually fixing a broken airplane was clearly out of our province. Long ago aviators with stricken planes could reach behind the seats, find some tools, and, with a little luck, a hank of wire, and some electrical tape go about fixing their problem and get airborne. In a complex jet aircraft, we fliers needed some help.

Help came late the next day. Two of our power-plants mechanics were heloed out from the ship, and they soon found the problem. They found it too soon—at least for them. Any time off the ship was a luxury for the enlisted men, even a trip to Da Nang. Aboard the *Enterprise,* they lived in cramped quarters, sleeping three bunks high with absolutely no privacy. Ashore, even in a pit like the base at Da Nang, they could have some breathing space, and, better yet, get something a little stronger than soda pop to drink.

They found that the problem that had caused the fire warning was that the insulation on the fire-warning sensor had worn off. This had resulted in our getting a faulty signal. Repairing the sensors in truth only amounted to a couple of hours work for them. But as experienced enlisted men, they stretched the repairs to two days, and, as equally good officers, we saw to it that they were well supplied with beer to ease their job. Even if it was 3.2 beer, it was going to be a long time before they were back in the PI, drinking San Miguel with the hookers. We were not able to help them with the hookers in Da Nang; apparently, the enlisted quarters did not have willing shower mates.

No one thought to ask the ship to send out clean clothes for us. We were still living in the same sweaty rags and had not found a washing machine to clean them. This meant that although, we could wash in the head only if we were prepared to stand around naked for a couple of hours while they drip-dried. So it was a choice of bearing our own manly, tropically spiced scent for three more days, or sitting around naked, like delinquent mental patients as our clothes moldered. By this point in the war, Da Nang had little of the amenities that it had boasted during the intense build up of US forces. Phil and I appointed ourselves the re-supply team and set about looking for necessities like deodorant, toothpaste, and shaving stuff.

We had very little money between the four of us, although it turned out that Shit-finger carried a couple of hundred dollars with him at all times. Dollars were good, but scrip was better. Our host, the chief, gave us a wad of the play money and told us we could get the things we needed at the Air Force PX at Dodge City West. He pointed vaguely down the road, outside the main gate, toward a cluster of buildings about a half-mile away. We had no transport, so off we went, walking out in the bright Vietnamese morning. The road ran straight along the top of a narrow dike. On each side of the road were deep ditches; beyond which was a sea of elephant grass stretching out to a distant line of trees. The air was soft in the early morning, and it felt good to be able to be out in nature after so long at sea. If it was not for the war, this place did not seem like such a bad spot.

We covered the distance to the buildings at a leisurely pace trying not to build up too much of a sweat. Once Phil and I approached the small cluster of structures, we saw that what had once been a barracks had been turned into ARVN officer's hooches. These must have seemed like first-class accommodations to the Vietnamese. All of the homes were adorned with motorcycles, TVs, toys, and an assortment of demur women who looked like wives or prostitutes. Around the women ran squads of children laughing and screeching. For them this place was a real leg-up from the villages from which they came. Twangy music, discordant and otherworldly, poured out of each doorway as we passed. Ahead we saw a turning in the road and the signs directing us to the PX. The place needed a sign since it looked suspiciously just like another hooch.

It was a low wooden building with a corrugated metal roof. The stenciled sign, Dodge City West PX, in not too legible letters, hung over the open door. A short distance away was the perimeter wire and beyond that, the noisy throng of the streets of downtown Da Nang. Out there, mopeds roared and hookers, working the early lunch shift, beckoned to us across the distance.

Stepping inside was like entering a cave. Dark, gloomy, and redolent with the stench of something near death, the place had the look of a dumpy country store in Bumfuck, Arkansas, complete with dangling coils of fly tape hanging from the ceiling. There was an air force sergeant behind the counter, and he looked up in surprise, shocked, in fact, to see us.

"Good Mawin' Lootenants," he drawled in mock respect. He sported that indistinct semi-southern drawl that one associates with bigoted sheriffs who kept a chaw of Red Man in their cheeks. He looked us over and was not impressed. We needed his goods a lot more than he needed our scrip. No salutes and no concern on his part, "Where in hell didju two drop from?"

Phil told him, and the man just shook his head in disbelief.

"Sirs," he said with something between respect and incredulity in his voice, "didn't no one at the other gate stop you?"

"Stop us? Stop us, why?" asked Phil.

"Well, sir, on account of how that stretch of road you walked down is VC country most of the time. When they get inside the wire at night, they hide out during the day in that tall grass."

"Fuck me," I groaned.

We bought what we came for. Toothpaste, brushes, soap, deodorant, and a razor we could all share—it would be enough for the time we would remain on the beach. That is, supposing that we got back to the BOQ at all. Once outside we faced an intensifying wall of heat. Somehow, in the few minutes we had spent inside the store, the Asian sun had switched on to full blast. Going back we set a brisker pace, behind us the noise from the streets receded and, as we passed the ARVN hooches, it seemed that everyone had vanished. Not a great sign, I thought. Phil and I seemed to read each other's thoughts as we passed the last of the houses and stepped into the open. Two Americans walking along a raised dike and silhouetted against the skyline—a blind man with a slingshot could have popped us off.

"Well if they did see us walk out before, I bet they would never think we would be stupid enough to just walk back," I said with no conviction. But like everything else in this war of incongruities, this seemed to make some kind of sense. Back aboard the *Enterprise* days later, Phil and I laughed about the incredulous looks that we got from the Marine guards at the gate when we returned. At that moment, though Phil and I thought that we should have sent Shit-finger on the errand.

I had to have a souvenir for all of this, for who knew when, if ever, I would get back to this place. When we got back to the Q, I went down to the shower area, where the two girls were moping the shower. I spoke no Vietnamese, but, through some expert pointy-talky, I negotiated the purchase of the younger girl's coolie hat. When we were able to fly back aboard the next day, I held it on my lap, and, just as Ted called the ball, I slipped it over my helmet. The air boss and the rest of the men in Pri-Fly saw it, but no one called me on it, and it remains with me to this day.

Back aboard the ship, with our airplane struck to the hangar deck for a complete inspection and life resumed its normal pace. While we were ashore, flight ops had continued, and, with five crews to fill the schedule, several of them had to double up in order to make up for our absence. We were unrepentant. Let them deal with being in country and see what it was like to be there.

Life between air strikes was lived in a sort of limbo state. The ship's onboard TV station kept up the late night horror movies on *Eighth Deck Void*, hosted by some sailor in monster make-up. This just made things even more surreal. Before flights we could catch episodes of *The Bob Newhart Show*, man up to fly for ninety minutes, and then return for a late-night breakfast and a dose of Bella Lugosi in *Dracula*. Two hours later we would do it all again. At times it seemed like flight ops was an almost secondary effort on the ship.

———

That trip was not to be my last overnight stay in Da Nang during the cruise. About a week later, I was part of a pick-up crew, flying in support of the *Saratoga*. We were doing a lot of coverage for the fleet's RA-5C Vigilantes, the nuclear bomber cum reconnaissance plane that took pictures of bomb damage and potential targets with its SLIRR (side looking infrared and radar). We were getting better known around the fleet, and, whenever we could, we would support other units from other ships. As usual this would be a night launch, except, instead of an in-flight rendezvous with the *Sara*'s plane, we were to fly to their ship and land. Then we would brief face-to-face with the Viggie's two-man crew for the hop.

These planes had speed to spare and so went through the Vietnamese night like bats from hell. In fact, our sister squadron on the *Enterprise*, RVAH-13, used the Bacardi black bat as its squadron logo. At one point, they had one of the Filipino survival instructors snare a giant fruit bat in the jungle and they took it to a taxidermist who mounted it for them. Since it was a male bat, the taxidermist stuffed the night creature's penis as well. When they hung the bat from the bulkhead in their ready room everyone gasped. There was this huge, ugly bat stuck to a board and sporting a two-inch penis.

Our launch from the *Enterprise* was no big deal—everything was normal. On this night, Bill Woods was in the front seat, and Bob Wheelwright was the pilot. I was just going along to watch the circuit breakers. We had just reached a mid-level cruising altitude when the call came in from our ship that the *Sara's* mission had been scrubbed. No big deal, we would just go home, or so we thought.

The *Enterprise* had launched us just before going into a twenty-four hour safety stand down. The good news for us was that we did not have to sit through a day of safety lectures and films, but it also meant we could not recover aboard our own ship. There was no provision for us to go to any other deck, so off to lovely Da Nang we went.

This time, there was no welcoming small arms fire as we approached. We taxied to my favorite revetment and, without much ceremony, headed for the rickety old BOQ for the night. I had regaled the squadron with the tale of the co-ed shower, and so Bill, at least, was interested in finding out what might happen in the morning. Bob Wheelwright was a bit of a prude though and thought most of the rest of the squadron degenerate sybarites. He spent nearly all of his off duty hours compiling the complete works of Johnny Cash and Merle Haggard on reel-to-reel tapes. I'm not sure if he ever set foot in Olongapo and seldom, if ever, saw him at the Cubi O club.

The Q had the same bare mattresses and flak jackets as before, and we settled down for a night's snooze. But alas, it was not to be. At sometime after 0300, as the night, humid and drizzly, went on, and we tossed and turned on the thin mattresses, the siren announcing imminent artillery or rocket attack went off. Someone was pounding on the door to the room. "Everyone to the bunker," someone else shouted. I had been sleeping in my shorts and t-shirt so, slipping into my fetid flight suit; I opened one of the lockers and grabbed a flak vest and a steel pot.

For the next hour we stood, surrounded by some other lost souls, up to our knees in stagnant water, inside a sandbagged shelter. The flak vest weighed a ton, and the helmet rang with the raindrops that hit it from open shrapnel holes in the corrugated roof. The others, some wearing protection and others simply in their skivvies and t-shirts, stood around trying to stay comfortable. I heard a splashing sound, and a pair of rats, the size of small dogs, paddled by and ran up the steps to the open area beyond. Fifteen minutes later, the all clear sounded, and, like the rats, we went to find drier nests.

During the late autumn, the services of our EA-6Bs were in high demand from other carriers, and grudgingly from the air force as well. The guys who wore wings of lead never liked to acknowledge that the navy might have an edge on them in anything. Since they had the lock-hold on strategic combat aviation they seemed to think they knew everything. As we often said, they were legends in their own minds. Their air combat excellence was disproven one dark night up along the coast near Cap Mui Ron.

We had been tasked to provide cover for a string of attacks over a sixty mile long stretch of the coast. Apparently, some of the senior commanders believed that we contained special magic in our jamming pods and that we could conjure up some cloaking device to protect any attacking airplane in the sky. They would have to wait another thirty years for airplanes to have that trick up their sleeves. Still, we went out to do our best. Since the targets ranged the length of the coast, we flew a racetrack pattern about fifteen miles off shore and retracing our route as we reached the upper and lower turn points.

The strikes were to be made by one or two planes coming from seaward and hitting various points within a few miles of the water's edge and our job was to assess the weapons threat and apply jamming as required. That night the North Vietnamese were unusually sparing with their use of radar, apparently not wanting to give us a signal to home on. As usual, their large surface search radar, the one we called a Tall King was up and giving the SAM and AAA gunners preliminary data on what was about to hit them. Because the attacks were so spread out, the control of the anti-aircraft weaponry on the ground was less than precise and I heard the telltale signature of a Fan Song coming up and swung the jamming antennae to the proper direction. This action I repeated several times over the next ten minutes as our planes swooped down to annihilate large plots of jungle that had been designated "suspected Truck Park" on the briefer's charts. No telling how many jungle creatures died that night.

After twenty minutes of these in and out jabs by A-6s and A-7s from our ship and the *Ranger* we were getting ready to pack up and head for home. The targets had been hit and there were a few secondary explosions that left large patches of flame where a village or storage area had once stood. That was when we heard a radio call from an air force A-7 who had seen all the commotion along the coast and wanted to play. Apparently, he was carrying extra ordnance and had not seen any moving targets to bomb along the pitch-dark roads that rand out of the hills toward the beaches. If he had turned back for his base in Thailand, he would have lived to fly again. Unfortunately, he was suckered in by the most obvious of flak traps.

At a point a few miles south of Mui Ron, I could see flames leaping up into the sky. Even from our altitude, we could see the outline of a small convoy of trucks surrounded by flames. The only problem with the scene was that no one had bombed there that night. It was clearly a set up. The North Vietnamese gunners had apparently set fires around some unserviceable vehicles and no doubt had a couple anti-aircraft guns close by.

The air force pilot saw the bait and like a trout rising to Royal Wulff, took it. Just as he pitched over to make his bomb run, my indicator lit up with the 1875 PRF signature of a Fire Can radar. That meant there were at least one if not two or three 85 mm guns hidden around those wrecked trucks. As soon as I swung the jammers toward the target, the sky lit up with streams of tracers. There were so many of the glowing projectiles in the air it looked as if the sky was filled with dancing red snakes. The North Vietnamese gunners did not need radar guidance to hit their target; he had flown straight into them. They had the poor son of a bitch in their sights and bracketed him with flak and shells of all calibers. An instant later the sky lit up as he was hit and the ordnance on his wings cooked off an exploded. All that was left was a shower of sparks falling down on the jungle.

Later, we were called into CAG's presence to explain what happened. Some air force type was screaming that we had not done our job and that our lack of performance had led the death of one of his ace pilots. Once again, we explained the geometry of keeping the attacking airplane between our position and the target for the jamming to be effective. Christ, he came out of nowhere and had not been part of the mission. The fact that this yahoo came at the target from the landward side and about ninety degrees out of our protection zone meant we could do little to help. Add to that his stupidity in attacking an obvious flak trap and he never had a chance. I have often thought that stupidity should be painful, well for that poor son of a bitch it was on that night.

BACK ON THE LINE

The rich and mouth-watering aroma of roast turkey was drifting past my nose. Lovingly, I poured out the brown gravy and watched it ooze across slabs of succulent white breast meat and then run like lava in slow rivulets through mounds of mashed potatoes and sausage stuffing, then circle the pile of green peas only to come to a stop at the deep burgundy slices of cranberry jelly. The happy haze of family gathered around was set aglow by candlelight, while outside a raw November wind blew. As we ate, more delicious aromas wafted from the kitchen, promising new treats for the palate. The deep, rich autumnal scent of apple ....

"Wake up, asshole!"

In an instant the cozy scene of home dissolved into the reality of the gray steel bulkheads of the squadron ready room. Again, the voice boomed at me, "Hey, wake up!"

Blinking and stammering, I tried to wake up. With one hand to shield my eyes from the glare of the overhead lights, I tried to speak to the faceless voice. Why was the aroma of roasting turkey still there if I wasn't dreaming?

"What? What's going on?"

"Happy fucking Thanksgiving, boomer—we're going flying tonight! We brief at 1800." It was Ted Steele, my plane commander and the squadron's Ops Boss.

"I thought this was a stand down day—isn't it Thanksgiving?"

Ted shook his head, "and this is Yankee Station. If you can't take a joke, you shouldn't have signed up. We can have all the Thanksgiving you want after we get back from the hop. The skipper will make sure they save us some."

I closed my eyes, hoping that I would reawaken in that happy place of family and food, and no gray ships, but the dream eluded me. In any event, the dream was merely that, some illusion of a life that I had never had. Maybe Norman Rockwell had experienced that warmth in his life, because he painted it so well—I hadn't.

Well, there was no joy out here sloshing around in the Gulf of Tonkin, just the camaraderie of weary shipmates. That today was a major holiday made it all the worse. No place could be as weirdly obscene as aboard a warship during the holidays. The gaudy paper decorations that hung on the mess decks were designed to raise morale, but mostly they served to remind us of where we were and what we were missing back home. A big gray warship festooned with paper pumpkins and turkeys is still a big gray warship. The fact that our entire reason for being here was to make war made the festivities all the more ludicrous. It wasn't as if the North Vietnamese had attacked America. We were just inflicting massive punishment on their country in support of a corrupt regime that had not the will to defend itself.

Home was ten thousand miles away. My wife and I could only communicate through letters or cassette tapes, which we continued to number so that if one is lost or delayed in the mail, we would not lose the threads of our lives. Her letters to me seemed more and more scripted and mechanical. There was nothing in them of the desperation or loneliness I thought she might be feeling about our separation. She recited the factual, the trivial, and the mundane of her and my daughter's daily life back there. In turn, I didn't write much about what we were doing at sea, trying always to keep things light and mentioned nothing about the activities ashore. I felt numb when I wrote home and almost wanted not to write at all, but that would not have been fair. At some point, this would be over and we, she and I, would have to take the time to put things back together. I remained at a loss as to who I was at that moment and what the future was for us. Beyond my uniform and my job, I don't seem to know. Maybe, once away from the war and all this I would find myself. In the meantime, I would have to be whom I needed to be to survive out here.

Ted called me a boomer. He liked to be around people who pushed the envelope either in flight or ashore, and I guess I had become that person. Being a boomer was not my natural self, but to be accepted by this group of rampant over-achievers, I had to act like them as well. For Ted, being a boomer meant someone who will fly the worst missions, and then, when on the beach, raise hell by drinking and whoring with the best of them. I put up the façade of a hell-raiser, and Ted seemed to believe it, so I continued to pretend. In truth, though, I read too much for his taste, and while he was off getting blasted, he has no idea what I was up to. I just made it a point to show up at the right moments, when we were creating our squadron legends, so that he believed that I was one of the ringleaders.

And so it would be that night, while everyone else aboard the *Enterprise* was comfortably digesting his turkey, old Ted and I would be bouncing around in the night sky, trying to avoid becoming the impact point for a SAM-2 missile. Maybe we'd get an air medal for tonight's work—some reward, a hunk of bronze. It was just like Ted to volunteer us to take the worst possible mission. Well, my snoozing was over, and the duty officer had no idea if we would get mail today, so I left my comfortable chair and headed forward.

The after mess decks, where the enlisted men ate, were swirling with the mixed aromas that had featured in my recent dream. There were mountains of food from which enticing vapors rose. Walking forward past the mass of food was like a low-level run through Happy Valley with mountains of mashed potatoes, stuffing hilltops, and broad expanses of shrimp cocktail forests. The men were to be treated well that day. Up in the dirty shirt wardroom however, there were cheeseburgers for lunch; the officers would have their turkey dinner served later in the evening. Ted and I would get ours, after all the skipper promised to make sure some was saved for us.

It was hours until launch so I drifted up to the hangar deck. The massive hangar deck doors were opened to reveal a gleaming silver sea. Streaks of gray cloud marked the eastern horizon, but even at sea the air hung thick and humid. Above deck, at least, one got a sense of fresh air before the recirculators pulled it in and pumped it into the below deck spaces. There it would swirl through the ducts and emerge, dank and clammy. On the hangar deck I stood by the open doors with the raised elevator serving as a shade against the glare of the sun. The steel slats of the elevator decking gave me the feeling of being in an arbor, if I forgot about the rest of my surroundings. We were heading south at about twelve knots—an easy day. We must have looked like we were on a holiday cruise to the Soviet AGI that dogged around in our wake. The AGI captains did not want their crews to see us having any fun, so, on holidays or stand-down days. Perhaps they looked at their Playboy calendars or sensing that we were not going to launch, they would disappear just over the horizon until we resumed flight ops. But then they would miraculously reappear to resume their job of noting our side numbers and ordnance counts, and so radio the information to Hanoi. In that way the defenders would know what to expect. It was indeed a very stupid war.

There was no sign of our destroyer escort on this side of the ship, and I was wearying of being alone with my thoughts. I had received no mail for over a week, and I felt in sore need of company. The perpetual breakfast up in the dirty shirt wardroom on the O3 level was operating, so I decided to eat. I walked across the hangar deck, under the wings of the parked airplanes, and up the portside ladder. I saw no one in the passageway as I drifted through officers' country. I found the wardroom mostly empty, there were just a few souls scattered about munching breakfast and writing letters home. The steward told me that there were only a few moments left before the galley shifted over to lunch. If I wanted to wait, I could have the promised cheeseburgers and fries. I opted for breakfast instead.

It was a short wait, but the steward flopped my eggs on a plate and splatted some potatoes on the side. I snatched a sheaf of bacon from a warming tray and poured tomato juice from a chilled carafe into two glasses. Then I took a seat along the bulkhead and drew a well-folded wad of paper from my pocket and re-read my wife's last letter. Nothing much new there—nothing had changed since I had read it yesterday. She said she and my daughter were fine, the second pregnancy was coming along as expected, and Jake Beltran's wife was going to be her birth-coach. She said they all missed me, especially the dog. Did they? What were they doing this morning; well it was still last night for them, wasn't it? The time difference was always tricky out here. I stared at the now smudgy words on the paper as if they were a pattern or a picture. There hasn't been a letter in so long.

Bill Woods walked into the wardroom and waved. He was the kind of guy you liked right from the first hello. My daughter, young as she was, thought of him as Uncle Bill. He always showed up at our house with a toy or book for her, and he always brought flowers, wine, or something else to share with us when we had him over. I think he was homesick for some kind of normal life. We had gone through pre-flight together and had spent many hours at our tiny apartment's kitchen table during advanced training studying, while my wife made coffee for us.

"Mail?" he asked.

"No." I folded the papers away, "At least not today's, last week's," I replied.

"Oh," he said flatly, and then his eyes searched for some place over my head.

"I see you made the cut-off for cheeseburgers. Happy Thanksgiving."

"Yeah," he replied. "I'm getting tired of eggs. That's all I seem to eat on this midnight to noon flight schedule."

"Well count yourself lucky, Bub. At least you will get a turkey dinner later tonight. Ted's got us flying tonight."

"No shit, tonight?" Bill just stared at me and shook his head in commiseration. He knew the routine with Ted, and he knew we

155

were all subject to the inconveniencies and exigencies of the war, but tonight seemed a stretch to him as well. The lunch conversation continued gliding around any somber thoughts of home and family to the really important question of the day—which ready room had the best movie.

"I don't want to see *Two Lane Blacktop* again," I groaned.

Bill leaned over the table looked each way and then began to whisper conspiratorially, "I've heard that the admiral has *The Godfather*, and, for ten bucks, the stewards will let us hot-reel the movie.

He leaned back and smiled. He appeared to be all fresh-faced innocence to those who did not know him. Yet he had arranged to bribe the admiral's stewards so that our squadron could see the one movie that the rest of the ship was anxiously awaiting.

"What time will you begin the show?" I was hoping that Ted and I would be back in time to catch some of the film.

"About 1945 I figure. It depends on when the admiral starts. Each reel is a half hour long, and then we have to have runners bring the reels down from the O3 level to the second deck, then rewind and mount. When do you brief?"

"Ted says 1800 for an 1845 launch. He asked the skipper to make sure they saved some turkey dinner for us. Maybe you can hang on to the reels, and we will catch the show after we land."

"Negative sweat," he said with a smile.

The rest of the day passed at a slow cadence. I had completed all the enlisted men's performance evals for my division, so I had nothing to do but stroll around the ship as if it were my village. Each of the men I saw seemed to be, like me, off in his private world. One morning I saw Phil Celsius standing by the starboard elevator doors staring out to sea. He was speaking into the microphone of a cassette tape recorder, making a recording that he would mail to his wife, in Whidbey. In 1972 these recorders were a hot item and tapes containing blubbery words of love were sent back and forth across the Pacific bearing the flutterings of lovers' hearts. For me the day was all tedium and anticipation of action, and I remembered the ancient adage about flying: Hours of idle boredom, punctuated by moments of sheer terror. It seemed to apply to war as well.

I was the first to arrive for our brief. It had been a year since lunch, and the wardroom was getting set for the promised turkey dinner they were about to serve, so I ate a Snickers. The after-mess decks had been cleaned after the crew's huge midday meal, and they would return to the normal routines and menus of shipboard chow soon. At least I could get a cup of coffee from the continuously brewing ready room pot. Hot, thick, and slightly rancid; the flavor was uniquely navy. Hopefully no roaches had been in the grinds today. Ted arrived along with Phil. why was I not surprised? Phil, the perpetual ass-kisser, kept his nose buried in the senior officer's butt. If he thinks that action will help his career, well, I thought he was entitled to try.

The brief was all of that, brief. A routine hop and a routine intercept, we were going to escort the *Saratoga*'s RA-5C on a recce run south of Vinh. Launch at 1845, climb to twenty-eight thousand feet, and proceed directly to the northwest to Cap Mui Ron. That was it, simple. The *Sara*'s RA-5C would communicate on button twelve. Once we made contact with them, they would drop down to fifteen hundred feet and go feet dry for a high-speed run through the Kiem Long Valley and on up to Vinh. Our job would be to remain feet wet and trail them up the coast while providing a shield of electronic jamming against the Fan Song radars that controlled the SAM-2 missile sites along the Viggie's route. With luck we would catch the movie and the turkey dinner before any of us was too much older.

There was nothing more to be said, and Ted nodded to the passageway. We kept our flight gear in a tiny locker room across from the ready room. There, we strapped on the forty pounds of survival paraphernalia that made us look like oddly formed green pumpkins. Other officers from the other squadrons stared at us dumbly as we clambered along in our flight suits. They clearly thought a stand down day meant that we were all standing down. They clearly did not know Ted.

In part we were flying because, since our Prowlers had come on the line in the Gulf, no planes had been lost to SAMs on missions during which we provided direct support. This fact was troublesome, because our sister EA-6B squadron, the VAQ-132 Scorpions, was embarked on the USS America, a non-nuclear powered ship that had been suffering through a lengthy list of engineering problems, the latest of which had required that it be towed into port at Subic Bay. The Scorpions seemed to never be available for this fun stuff. With only our squadron on the line, we were being called to do a lot of business.

Our Prowler was spotted portside just aft of the number four catapult. A soft drizzle swept back along the black expanse of non-skid on the flight deck. A miserable night, the sea was beginning to churn as the wind rose. The horizon was lost in the murky darkness, and only the running lights of the plane guard destroyer just abeam told me that we had not entered the nether world. The pre-flight checks were brief; I had done them so often I could have done them in our sleep, which had happened on some occasions.

Our launch was keeping the deck crews from their evening meal, and they cast snide sidelong glances at us, as if that would hurry us into the air and they could go to chow. To my mind, their inconvenience was minor compared to ours. None of them had the remotest possibility of encountering a barrage of SAMs or anti-aircraft fire in the next two hours. Merryman, one of my best petty officers, and one of the men for whom I had recently completed a four-o evaluation, came up to me as I began to mount the ladder and climb into the cockpit.

"Evening, sir. Sorry to see you've drawn this hop. Not much fun for Thanksgiving day."

"No it's not. But I guess we all have places we'd rather be today."

"Good luck sir," he said with more enthusiasm than the remark warranted—an evil omen.

I closed the canopies as Ted started the engines while Phil, in the back seat, read off the start checklist. We noted and responded to each item, flicking switches and dialing in numbers to their proper, pre-launch settings. As Ted taxied forward on to the cat track, we armed our ejection seats. Below us, the nose wheel tow bar gave its reassuring thud as it connected with the catapult shuttle and took tension. Ted rode the brakes as he increased the throttles to one hundred percent as the ship turned into the wind and gain an extra forty knots of headwind over the deck. That wind and our end speed off the catapult would easily us get airborne. Ahead of us the catapult officer, in his yellow sweatshirt, spun his finger in the air for final run up and then saluted Ted. Ted returned the salute, and the cat officer, like the count in Swan Lake, made a slow pirouette, crouched, and with his outstretched left arm, touched the deck. He was our last sight of humanity as we shot forward down the flight deck and into the black night.

"One potato, two potato; thank you God, I've got it," Ted intoned as we recovered from the force of twenty-seven transverse Gs of the cat shot. He put slight backpressure on the stick as we climbed, and I completed the checklist. With the gear raised and flaps up, we had a clean airplane, and we were climbing.

At twenty-one thousand feet we broke out of the undercast into brilliant starlight. I had Cap Mui Ron centered nicely on the radar at seventy miles. Reaching down, I punched in button four on the UHF.

"Red Crown, Skybolt Three."

"Roger Skybolt, ident," came their reply.

Complying, I hit the IFF switch, which would send the signal identifying us on their radar. We were now under the watchful eye of Red Crown, the seaborne air and sea controller for the navy's portion of the Gulf of Tonkin and North Vietnam. Calling Red Crown was always required, although once we began jamming the North Vietnamese radars, everyone would know we were there. But Red Crown was our mother hen, and if we had to eject, they would be the ones directing the rescue choppers.

I then punched up button twelve, so we could go tactical and talk to the *Sara*'s RA-5C. As we passed 26,000 I looked over at Ted and I immediately knew something was wrong. He sat hunched over the stick and with one finger was tapping the hydraulic gauge.

"Fucking flight hydraulics are going," was all he said.

I had the emergency checklist out and punched in button four on the radio. In the back seat, Phil had the checklist out and began reading, while I called Red Crown again.

"Red Crown, Skybolt Three."

"Skybolt Three, go ahead."

"Skybolt Three is declaring an emergency. Request immediate return to Climax."

"Roger Skybolt three, cleared for immediate descent and return. Climax at one six three degrees, fifty-five miles. Switch to button two, good-day."

We were indeed in trouble. High performance jet aircraft are controlled in flight by a series of servomotors that drive another series of hydraulic cylinders. These raise and lower flaps, ailerons, and other control surfaces. The flight hydraulic system controlled these cylinders, providing them with pressurized fluid to move the needed controls. Losing the flight hydraulic system was a pretty routine emergency—ashore. At sea, at night and in a combat zone nothing was routine, there were no long runways to land upon, just a pitching deck. And to make safely to the deck you needed hydraulic pressure to lower the hook that would engage the arresting wires there. The loss of the flight hydraulic system was survivable as long as the combined hydraulic system, the main system, remained functional. It would have to serve as back up until we made it back to the ship. It was dicey, but we thought we would make it.

Except that now when I looked at the gauge, I could see that the flight hydraulic system needles had drooped completely and were pegged at zero. This meant that the combined system was all we had left. As we maneuvered to get back to the ship, I could also see that, each time Ted moved the stick, the combined needles would move slightly and then settle back, but each time at a slightly lower, as we bled away hydraulic fluid. I had practiced ejection at sea several times, and Ted had done it for real once. I did not like going into the water in training exercises under controlled circumstances, I would like it less if we had to tonight. Remembering the sea state at launch, we had at best a fifty-fifty chance—if we lost flight control and had to jump out into the night.

I punched button two and called the ship.

"Climax, Skybolt Three. We have a flight hydraulics failure. Declaring an emergency—request a ready deck."

The next several minutes seemed like a lifetime as we talked to the ship and reviewed the emergency checklist and conferred with, our squadron safety officer, about our condition and what we could expect. I could just about visualize the pandemonium on the flight deck as the men who had launched us a few moments before had to forego their dinner and reconfigure the deck for our return. Quickly, aircraft spotted aft had to be moved forward in order to give us room to land once we made our stab for the flight deck. Ahead, we had the ship on our radar, and I could see it turning into the wind to receive us.

"Skybolt Three, Climax ready deck. Standby for case three recovery." That was music to my ears.

"Roger."

The voice of the approach controller, brisk and business-like came over the air. We were now twenty miles astern and descending as instructed to ten thousand feet. If we had to eject short of the ship, ten thousand was the best altitude. Once we went lower we would have less time in the chute to deploy our rafts or let the ship spot our survival homing beacons.

Ted moved the controls again—the needles kept dropping.

"Shit, I think we are going to go for a swim," I said.

"Not quite yet," said Ted, but there was little confidence in his voice.

I reviewed our ejection procedures again, but I was still not reassured. If the hydraulics were to go completely, my last radio call would be to give our position and hope they might find us in the dark ocean. If we made it to the ship, but somehow failed to catch the arresting wire, we would have climb to ten thousand and eject alongside the ship and hope the plane guard helo will find us. That is if the hydraulics didn't crap out at that time. Either the hydraulics would hold or they wouldn't. Either we would land or we would not—like the man said: you paid your money and took your chances.

At fifteen miles we pushed over for final descent, straight in toward the ship. The storm that had been lashing the flight deck during our launch had turned benign, and we were spared a bumpier, and from a potential loss of hydraulic fluid, a costlier ride down. The needles were still dropping, and Ted was fighting the growing weight of the controls as their responses became more and more sluggish as the fluid and pressure began to dissipate.

The controller made his final call to us. It was time to use the emergency blow-down system to lower the tail hook and the landing gear. We could not afford to waste hydraulic fluid on them. One pressing question remained, would there be enough hydraulic pressure to hold the hook down in order to engage the arresting wire? Time would tell.

At five miles we broke through the undercast. It was time to make our final flutter at the deck. Rain streamed along the curve of the canopy, while ahead, we could see the ladder line of the ship. Below the sea looked dark, an oily angry black, waiting to suck us under us if we plunged into it.

Two miles left to go.

It was busy in the cockpit. Radio calls, speed adjustments. Adjustments to our attitude as the needles dropped lower, and the sea came ever closer.

At a mile astern, a low cloud passed in front of us and blocked my view. At three quarters of a mile and the ship disappeared in the mist. At a half mile the ladder line emerged from the mist, and I could see the landing mirror.

"Quarter mile, call the ball," the controller insisted over the radio.

"Skybolt Three. Prowler Ball, state two point oh," I droned.

The horizontal line of green datum lights of the landing mirror embraced the orange ball that reflected our image relative to the flight deck. We were on speed and at the right attitude—just a few feet more. "Jesus, Ted don't blow it now."

"Attitude," I whispered to Ted.

On-speed, one hundred eighteen knots, three hundred feet of landing space ahead, and now over the ramp, then a clunk as the hook catches the wire—Home.

The whiplash caused by catching the arresting wire pulled the hydraulic needles to zero. Airspeed evaporated, and the armored flight deck held Skybolt Three securely. Happy Thanksgiving.

We wrote up the debriefing sheets in the maintenance office next to the ready room. As we finished, the line chief walked in to let us know that he had inspected the tail cone of the airplane and found the burst hydraulic line. There was less than a quart of fluid left in the entire system. We should have dropped into the sea ten miles astern in that condition.

It had been a bad day and the night even worse. There was no mail in the ready room, so we walked up to the dirty shirt wardroom for our promised turkey dinner, but there was none, the skipper never asked them to save us any. Seeing the three of us standing there, the stewards looked confused. There was no turkey, they had nothing ready. Then Aquino, our squadron steward, looked up and asked, "Eggs to order, sir?"

We were back aboard, safe for now—and hungry. The stand down day was officially over, and normal operations were resumed. And, great: we were on the flight schedule for a zero three hundred launch.

———

Keeping a warship on station requires an extensive series of logistical maneuvers. In the Navy this is known as underway replenishment or UNREP. Supply ships filled with beans, bacon and bombs and tankers filled with jet fuel must rendezvous with the carrier and transfer their cargoes to the hungry warship. These evolutions must take place outside of normal flight operations, so generally they go on from noon until midnight. The supply ships come alongside on the *Enterprise*'s starboard side and match course and speed with the carrier.

Once the ships are in position, less than one hundred feet apart and steaming on course parallel to each other, lines are shot from the replenishment vessel to the carrier and then heavier lines are strung across the gap, from these, fuel hoses or slings are hung. It is a busy exercise on both ships. Skids of MK-82 bombs, bomb fins, missiles encased in fiberglass, spare parts, food, and whatever else a warship with five thousand souls aboard might need is slung across the space above a frothing sea. Since the *Enterprise* was powered by eight nuclear reactors, it never required oil to fire her boilers, but she did need fuel for her air wing. It was a constant requirement so that every other day or so more fueling vessels were brought alongside to refill the tanks. Our consumption of fuel was in the thousands of pounds of JP-5 jet fuel and AVGAS, a rate of consumption that exceeded that of some small cities.

While the supply ship and the carrier steamed side-by-side, tethered by the lines and hoses, other supply vessels showed up off *Enterprise's* port quarter. These supply ships have cargo helicopters aboard that carry out a VERTREP or vertical replenishment. With their cargoes dangling below them in slings, the choppers moved back and forth from the cargo vessel to the carrier to drop their loads on the open after area of the flight deck. The ballet can go on for several hours, then, when all the cargo has been moved aboard "The Big E" the tethers are disconnected and the vessels part company. It remains then for the carrier to resume its course back to its operating area while the deck crews move frantically to stow all the supplies before flight quarters is sounded and the ship's war resumes.

One of the byproducts of these replenishments had been the introduction of a band of pesky stowaways. No one knows when the first of them came aboard, and it might well have happened during the ship's construction but by 1972 generation upon generation of these vermin have been living quietly in the dark spaces of the ship. These creatures were now the healthiest bunch of cockroaches that had ever lived. Brown with a bronze cast to their shells, the ones we saw were always two inches long, and if you saw one, you could be sure its close relative was near at hand. It was rumored that perhaps the ship's nuclear power plant had some hand in their phenomenal growth. Personally, I thought it was simply that they fed well off the copious amounts of food being served on the mess deck just forward of our ready room.

It seemed that Ready Five, our ready room, supported the largest colony of these little beasts. They crawled out of the bulkheads and skittered over the deck to disappear somewhere else. You found them swimming furiously in the coffee and, worse, during movies, they came out of the dark to scuttle along and run up your pant leg. There wasn't a movie night during which someone didn't jump up yelling that a roach was heading for his balls.

One of our new skipper's brilliant ideas was to buy a popcorn machine and sell popcorn to moviegoers and others on the ship that wanted to snack. He saw it purely as a monopolistic ploy to make money, as he certainly did not believe in altruism. Roaches love any kind of food, and raw corn and the peanut oil in which to pop it were magnets for such vermin. The skipper would not be deterred by these six-legged corn-guzzlers. The bulky machine emblazoned with bright carnival colors came aboard on one of the VERTREPS, along with an ample supply of peanut oil, corn, and colorful paper serving bags. He shanghaied one of the seamen to be in charge of the machine and serve as the vendor in charge. Each night that it operated that poor bastard had to nurse the thing to life and hope that he would make enough in sales to satisfy the skipper's concept of return on investment. The profits went into a squadron fund, and we did make a little money. The trick though was to never eat your popcorn in the dark, just in case that extra crunch in your mouth had six legs.

———

Flying and breathing one hundred percent oxygen from engine start to shut down gave us incredible appetites. Despite eating at every opportunity, we never gained any weight, the humidity of the region and tension of combat aviation burned off calories faster than a cyclist at the Tour de France. Given our nightly cycle of flight ops, we often ate late, close to eight o'clock on most nights. That the dirty shirt wardroom was open around the clock ensured there was always something available. If not the posted three-meal menu, the infamous eggs-to-order-sir offering was always on hand.

Occasionally one of the ship's chaplains would stop by for a chat with us. I suppose that was their job, keeping a finger on the pulse of the men, and for the most part the conversations were innocuous enough. In none of them did he seem to push any religious nonsense. As far as I knew, very few of the men aboard ever went to the tiny chapel to pray or seek spiritual counsel. The chapel was hard to find, but then again, I only went there once, to learn about the birth of my daughter. The only chaplain who most of us recognized was the Catholic chaplain. He was a garrulous sort, Irish and florid faced, with big hands and a rough laugh. One night he came by and told us how we amazed him when he was up on the bridge watching flight ops.

"Standing up there I look down and see all those red lights on your instrument panels and wonder how you can make sense of it all. I am very proud of you boys, we all are." So went the benediction.

But then each night, at twenty-two hundred, he would give the ship's evening prayer over the 1-MC from the bridge. Given that we would be launching at midnight most of us would be getting ready for the first flight of the night, when he spoke. And so he would come on the air with his prayer for our safety and the hope that our "good bombs would kill the heathen Commies." Nothing subtle about him, and yet I often wondered how many Catholics, in religiously divided Vietnam, we might be annihilating that night.

————

Since as men we only thought about sex once every two or three minutes, each day, and with no females in sight, food became the great elixir of our lives. This was all the more so, because as officers we had to pay for our food aboard ship. Each month right after being paid in cash, we had to pony up our share of the mess bill. Each man's share was allotted evenly, but it came to a couple of hundred dollars a month. For that we expected a reasonable variety and quality of food. No one thought of the ship as the Ritz, but the food was not supposed to resemble the offerings of an SS *arbeitslager* either. During the early part of the deployment, no one had much to complain about, however, sometime after Christmas, a new mess officer came aboard. He was an ensign, a lowly brown bar, straight out of supply school. Had he been a conniver straight out of the Ensign Pulver School of shenanigans no one would have cared, since that would have made him a regular guy. But as it turned out, he was a weasley bastard and he seemed to think that our monthly contributions to the mess fund were deposits into his personal bank account.

When he was ashore, this young man seemed to live pretty extravagantly, much better than most of us. He was filling the cold storage lockers with custom-made furniture ordered from the cabinetmakers in the PI, buying exotic stereo equipment, and generally living large—far beyond his ensign's pay. People noticed.

Little by little, the quality of the food in the officer's mess, especially the dirty shirt, began to deteriorate. The most visible sign of this was at the Big E salad bar at the end of the chow line in the dirty shirt wardroom. We all were aware that fresh vegetables and fruit were hard to come by at sea, and some wilting of the lettuce and tomatoes was to be expected in the heat and humidity, but the offerings soon began to resemble the scrapings from the inside of a rotary lawn mower. Unripe green tomatoes, shreds of something that might be lettuce and rotten apples soon appeared. Then, it was announced that we could no longer get ham and eggs for breakfast, although you could order a ham omelet where they would toss in some sliced ham with the powdered eggs. The crowning glory was that boiled macaroni was being served regularly, sans cheese, or any other flavoring. This was followed by the ominous announcement that the weekly steak night was going to be cut back to twice a month. That tore it. Men at war can put up with a great deal, but fucking with their stomachs is dangerous business.

It all came to a head when someone noticed that filet mignons and lobster tails were being regularly flown in on the C-1 COD (Carrier Onboard Delivery) planes along with the mail. A couple of officers took it upon themselves to find out what was going on. It seemed that there was a little cabal between this supply officer and several of his and his boss' chosen friends. Not to sound homophobic, but it seemed as if the new ensign might literally have had his nose up his boss's butt.

While we all were enjoying the nouveau macaroni cuisine, the ensign, his boss, a supply corps commander, and several their other chums were having lobster and steak delivered to the supply officer's stateroom. This coterie convened several times each week and certain of the senior line officers were also invited to join them. No one was sure if the parties dissolved into circle jerks, but the rumors began flying.

One night, after another of the sauceless pasta feasts, a group of the A-7 pilots had enough. They knew where the young ensign lived, and they decided to have it out with him. Rumors of what happened that night got back to us over the space of several days. What the two or three pilots did or did not do was a matter of conjecture, however the results were not.

According to the rumor, they waited just down the passage from where the supply ensign had his tiny office. As he came strolling along, stomach filled with buttery lobster and wearing smug smile, they grabbed him. Using the best SERE School technique, they tossed a canvas helmet bag over his head to blind him and, with his arms gripped in a full-nelson, frog marched him out to one of the fuel stations on the starboard-side catwalk. Someone said they put a gun to his head, maybe so, but in the spirit of the Godfather, they did make him an offer he couldn't refuse. Either the food would immediately go back to normal, or the next time they would simply toss him overboard. What he told his boss, or what he had to do to make things right, no one ever learned, but suddenly steak nights were back on, and the macaroni vanished from the menu. Sometimes men have to do what men have to do.

———

Deck loading, the over abundance of airplanes on the ship and where to put them, was always a problem for carriers even on the *Enterprise*, and we often shuttled aircraft back and forth to Subic to allow for repairs and to permit ease of movement of the eighty-plus aircraft that comprised the air wing. One of the side benefits to sending planes to the beach was that the ship needed to establish a shore detachment to look after them, and so each squadron was asked to rotate a few enlisted men to the beach to assist with the work. This was a plum assignment for a lot of the men. The men assigned to the shore detachment went along grinning, as it meant that they could have all the beer they wanted and access to the women in Subic every night. Of course, the shore detachment needed an OIC, officer in charge to oversee the operation. For any aviation officer, this kind of non-flying duty was a career killer, and our CO, who liked to think of himself as a Michael Corleone look alike in more ways than one, deviously offered up the squadron's worst performer. Shit-finger, aka LCDR Ralph Carpenter who found himself on the next COD to the beach. He wasn't known as

Shit-finger without reason. Shit-finger had been along on every in-flight emergency the squadron had suffered since we were reactivated two years before. In the past year there had been eight such incidents, and he had been along on all of them—he was simply a Jonah—jinxed. Shit-finger had only to point his finger at an airplane and it would have problems—hence his squadron nickname.

Shit-finger was married to an English teacher. We all knew her from squadron parties, and she seemed like a nice enough person, well, at least to us she was. For poor Shit-finger married life must have been pure hell. He had grown up in Southern California where his father owned a small chain of auto parts stores. He spent his high school days tooling around in a customized '32 Chevy and lived the hot-rod life. He had gotten by with Cs in high school and college and really only liked fast cars, airplanes, and tennis. When he wrote home to his wife, she would correct his letters with a red pen and mail them back to him.

So, seeing that he could dispose of the man the skipper sent the orders went through. The skipper chortled and said that the next officer fitness report that he would write on hapless Shit-finger would look like a strip of the man's own shit-spattered toilet paper. Unfortunately for his plans to ruin the man, he had severely underestimated the breadth of Shit-finger's accomplishments.

For all of his bad luck with airplanes, Shit-finger had something good going for him—tennis. Since high school, he had been an avid and excellent tennis player. In fact, it was his skill at tennis that kept him from being flunked out of college, so one of the things he was going to take advantage of back in Cubi was the officer's club tennis court. Back in those days, officer's clubs were run much like country clubs, especially those that were located in exotic places. Bougainvillea and palms surrounded the well-maintained courts, and officers, wives, and their children used them throughout the day.

When Shit-finger arrived in Cubi, he found himself a set of nice quarters in the BOQ. Being a lieutenant commander, he was senior to many of the Q's inhabitants and he got the pick of several rooms and ended up with a small but comfortable suite. The daily duties of the shore detachment OIC were minimal, and he had a reasonably competent chief petty officer to rely upon, so he would check in first thing in the morning and again at the end of the workday, and, unless there were flights coming in or departing for the ship, he had little to occupy his time. The skipper had thought this would be a punishment leaving the man stultifyingly bored, but Shit-finger rose to the occasion and spent most days in his tennis whites.

It was also about this time that Shit-finger's wife decided to give him the heave-ho. She was one of those driven women who need to have a man was constantly over achieving and who, ultimately, would die young, leaving her a fortune. She didn't see that happening with Shit-finger, and when he sent word that he had been sent to the beach, she knew his naval career had come to an abrupt end; so, she filed for a divorce and Shitfinger granted it, smiling all the time to himself.

Shit-finger took the news without a whimper. So much so that he staged a small celebration in honor of his imminent emancipation. Several of us, who had flown in with one of the planes cycled from the ship, were there while he drank to his soon to be ex's health, keeping a shit-eating grin on his face the whole time. With the paperwork dissolving his marriage speeding through the legal system, he began to socialize with the senior officers stationed in Cubi.

Shit-finger was by no means an idiot, event though he did little in the squadron to prove it. He knew what to do with this assignment and went about setting new goals for himself—all of which involved playing tennis each day with the admiral's wife and their teenaged daughter. He acted as the long-lost uncle, and they soon accepted him into their family. He taught the pair of women how to play better tennis. The women were happy for the lessons and the attention, which was missing because the admiral was engaged in real naval business. Since his wife was happy with the arrangement, the admiral also benefited, especially in the bedroom.

Shit-finger never laid a finger on either of the women, what he really wanted, in fact needed, was the admiral's good opinion; he knew what our skipper was going do with his fitness report. Despite what we often said about the noxious documents, those dreaded green sheets, which reported on our effectiveness; *the only way you can hurt me with a fitness report is to roll it up and stick me in the eye with the pointy end,* Shit-finger did need a good report in order to make the next promotion to full commander. That is, if he was going to make his long naval career pay off. It turned out that the admiral not only liked Shit-finger for what he did for his family, but he liked him as a man, as a friend.

Months later, when we were back in Whidbey the whole story finally came out. Shit-finger had orders to London, as one of several naval attachés assigned there. It was a dream job that came with a hefty clothing allowance and other perks. It seems that the skipper, true to his word, filed a mercilessly atrocious fitness report about Shit-finger, however the skipper was only a junior commander, and his comments were trumped by the concurrent fitness report that the Vice admiral filed, recommending Shit-finger's promotion and transfer to London.

So Shit-finger found himself in England, with an extra gold stripe on his sleeve, which made him equal in rank to the skipper. He was now single, and because of the embassy connection on every hostess's guest list. For the ex-wife who dumped him, Shit-finger's revenge was even sweeter. Not long after the divorce his parents sold their chain of small auto parts stores to NAPA for an exorbitant sum, and then within a year they conveniently passed on, leaving their fortune to their only son, who immediately retired from the navy as a full commander and moved to a lake in the Rockies and built a dream chalet for him and his new British wife.

———

There were two locations in the combat zone into which no one wanted to fly because the expectation of survival or even a future return appeared to be negligible. These were Mainland China and the Chinese island of Hainan. Because of length of time the war had carried on the Chinese had reinforced their bases in both locations. Although they seldom provoked return fire either by trying to intercept American vessels in international waters or in the airspace above, they did their best to shoot down any errant Americans who might penetrate their territory. Several A-6 Intruders mistakenly wandered too far north when hitting targets in North Vietnam and then vanished.

The navy, using Red Crown had set up a warning system to alert anyone who was heading in the wrong direction. If the radar controllers on the Red Crown picket ship saw an American plane heading toward the Chinese coast they would issue a "Waterloo" call. These calls carried a color code, yellow, orange and red. The colors increasing in alarm as the plane neared the forbidden airspace. From time to time we might hear a "Waterloo Yellow" call. But until the night we all heard a "Waterloo Red" call applied to one of our squadron's planes no one had been too exercised about the problem.

Occasionally, the Chinese tried to trick Americans into flying into their airspace. They did this by imitating the TACAN homing signal that each American ship put out to assist aircrews in navigation. The *Enterprise* had its own discrete signal which we used religiously to get a bearing to and from the ship. A TACAN is basically a system of electronically separated radians centered on the TACAN station. So for navigation purposes, the aviator dials in the correct TACAN frequency and he can receive a bearing from his position in the sky to the station. At the same time, TACANs emit a second signal that activates a DME, or Distance Measuring Equipment, that tells the flier how far he is from the station. Its as if there are invisible lines of direction pulsing out through the sky and all the flier has to do is match the bearings to the course he wants to fly and the TACANs with their DMEs will lead him safely home. That is, unless some nefarious force tries to hijack the signal and lure the flier into a trap. The published Instrument Flight Rules, (IFR) describes it as follows:

"The aircraft's TACAN receiver electronically measures the aircraft's bearing from the station in the proper 40o sector and then measures the aircraft's position within that sector. If the aircraft's TACAN is malfunctioning or the signal reception is weak, the receiver may measure the wrong 40o sector. This is known as "40o Lock Off." The pilot must recognize this phenomena when it occurs."

So it occurred on one dark and stormy night over the Gulf of Tonkin that Bill Woods and his crew were coming back from a strike up in the north and as usual had dialed in the *Enterprise* TACAN and commenced to follow it home. What they did not know was that on Hainan Island elements of the Chinese air force were experimenting with sending out a very strong signal on the same TACAN frequency as our ship. Slowly, Bill and his crew began to drift toward the hostile island, sitting, as we would say, *fat, dumb and happy* as time went by. In the cockpit, the image on the radar between the pilot's knees was ignored and no one crosschecked the navigation with the most primary of flight instruments that sat in front of their faces—the wet compass. For had they done so they would not have been assaulted by a series of Waterloo calls of increasing severity and incurred the wrath of CAG when at last they awoke to their condition.

In truth, they had a very close call. They were within twenty miles of Hainan Island when they realized where they were going. They made a quick one hundred and twenty degree turn and jammed the throttles to full power as the MiGs were being scrambled from their revetments on the island. What the event meant to the rest of us was that even in the frantic pace of an air war, all of us had become somewhat complacent, as if this was a safe occupation. From that day forward many of us would cross check all of our compasses, even the tiny wrist compasses we wore for survival purposes.

STEEL BALLS

D ays and nights melded into one another, one hop, two hops, sometimes three hops a night. Ted, with his fluttering of the wings on approach, could turn a night recovery into a daylight trap when we would have to go around once or twice in order to land. Fatigue was getting us all. Operating complex aircraft under combat conditions, especially at night, taxes the body, as it demands the utmost flying skill.

Once a month, depending on the flight schedule, which in turn depended upon the perverse whims of the senior operational commanders in Saigon and back at Pearl, the air wing would have an evening meeting. All of the aviators would pack into the main wardroom on the second deck to hear the latest from CAG and his officers, as well as to receive awards for the number of traps or, in some cases, real medals and citations for heroism or number of missions.

I had already received my *Enterprise* Centurion patch, awarded by CAG for one hundred arrested landings on the ship, and so I was not expecting to be called to the front of the room to receive an award. As it turned out, Ted, Phil, and I were to be singled out. Somewhat sheepishly we stepped forward and faced the crowd of smiling faces.

CAG cleared his throat and with great solemnity began to read a citation. "And now gentlemen, we come to a most revered award to be bestowed upon these three gallant aviators."

Who the hell could he be talking about, we wondered, the three of us—gallant aviators? What had we done?

Undeterred by a smattering of snickers and smirks from the crowd, CAG went on, "For bravery untold in the annals of naval aviation, we must bestow the Order of the Steel Balls on Commander Ted Steele and his crew of steely-eyed naval aviators." Then, holding up three large steel ball bearings suspended from gaudy blue ribbons, he recounted the events that had taken place two nights before.

It was a normal escort mission, we had briefed around 2200, and, as was becoming a routine part of our war, we were to escort a RA-5C Vigilante on a reconnaissance run north up the coast to Cap Mui Ron where the Viggie would go feet dry and proceed inland to check out possible targets. The Viggie planned to hit the coast and then descend and make a high speed run through the karst valleys and out again about thirty miles south of the cape. Our job was to fly just offshore in a racetrack pattern and jam any SAM-2 sites that might pop up to shoot at the Viggie.

We shared an overlarge ready room with the RA-5C squadron, so for our briefing we simply pulled apart the accordion doors that divided the room and sat with the Viggie's pilot and the

RAN, the back-seater who operated the sensors located in the jet's belly. The weather was fair to lousy with lots of cloud decks over the target area. This wouldn't be a problem for the side looking radar and other infrared sensors that the Viggie carried, but it was doubtful that any clear pictures would result from the mission.

So, with our call signs and frequencies all worked out, we prepared to man up. Strapping on our gear and waddling to the passenger elevator, we made our way to the flight deck. There were several independent operations taking place with this launch. One of the A-7 squadrons was sending two divisions to hit some coastal targets and the A-6 squadron had a section going up to around Haiphong to hit the docks there. Both F4 squadrons had CAP duties, and there were a few Iron Hand strikes scheduled. In all, about thirty aircraft were scheduled to launch along with us.

Mist swept along the deck, but with the humidity, it was hard to determine if the dampness inside my flight suit was from the weather or simply from my constant perspiration. It wouldn't matter once we started the engines, the onboard air conditioners, so necessary to keep the electronics cool, would chill us to the bone, and add to the discomfort.

The weather was deteriorating rapidly. The ship, generally stable in average seas, was pitching slightly up and down as it was steered into the wind for launch. Like the F-4s, the RA-5C was a gas burner and would have to be refueled in flight before heading out. VA-196 put up two KA-6D tankers to serve as "Texaco in the Sky" before any of the fighters launched. They would climb to a position overhead, and the gas-guzzlers would fly in to top off before proceeding to their missions. Our EA-6B had gas to spare, so we were next to last to launch, only the turbo-prop E-2C Hawkeye, the air control aircraft, went after us.

The launch went smoothly, the Viggie was topped up, and off we went in loose formation to the point just north of Cap Mui Ron. Somewhere south of the cape we broke out of the clouds and found ourselves flying between layers of gray clouds. A last quarter moon gave a slight shimmer to the upper sides of the decks, and from time to time we could see the darker coastline below, with the tiny filaments of light from fishing sampans moving out into the gulf. It would have been the epitome of tranquility, were it not for the war.

The Viggie called to let us know he was beginning his run. All the way from the ship, I had been monitoring the radars along the coast. A Tall King surface search and acquisition radar, used to feed acquisition data to the SAM's Fansong radar, had been visible on my panoramic display, and I had assigned a Band 4 jammer to it, so that an electronic firing solution could not be made until the Fan Song showed its hand. As the RA-5C dropped down below the cloud decks, I monitored several of the Fan Songs in the area. They were reaching out in search mode like insects using their antennae to find their prey. I had all the Band 7 jammers on and assigned to the locations of the target radars. These sites had come up on the computer, identified by number from their latitudes and longitudes. These I had entered into the ALQ-99 system, as we warmed up on the flight deck before launch. It was a classic electronic warfare confrontation. They would try to find us with their radars, which when I detected them I would jam in such a way that they would either be totally masked or see so many targets that their computers could not differentiate and find the real target, the RA-5C, until it was long gone.

Electronic warfare had been around since the Second World War as a kind of passive process of trying to elude an enemy's radar by dumping chaff into the air and hoping that the feathery tinfoil would drift through the air and distract the operators on the ground.

Unlike that, active electronic warfare is like a three-dimensional chess game. You have to think three moves ahead of the enemy and know how he will employ his resources. To the old-line brass hat "iron bombers" in command in Vietnam, our approach to warfare seemed beyond comprehension. For them, you saw a target and you hit it. Perhaps this new, thinking man's style of warfare seemed a little unmanly to them.

I suppose we were full of hubris, a sense of our importance based upon our knowledge of the Soviet order of battle. We knew what to do and when to do it. The enemy on the ground, using its array of radars, was trying to fix the position of attacking aircraft so it can shoot them down. They needed to determine altitude, direction, speed, and numbers, so they could launch the appropriate weapons. Our job in the jamming their air defense was to deny them the ability to get that data so that they failed to compute a firing solution. In truth, we were talking about buying seconds. For in the matter of ten seconds a warplane moving at five hundred knots has traveled nearly two miles from its original location. Add to that the bobbing and weaving, something we call jinking, and you are in and out of the kill zone in a few heartbeats.

We flew on up the coast to a point at which we could put the Viggie between the known SAM sites and ourselves. As soon as they called "feet dry," we turned and, with four Band 7 jammers going, I assigned each to a known SAM site. My panoramic display was alight with indications of imminent launches. The well-known warble of the Fan Song targeting frequency was ringing in my ear, and Ted could see the SAM light going off on his side of the cockpit. The target was hot and the Viggie called that he was going into afterburner. That was when the whole sky lit up.

The missiles that were launched that night never made it near to their target. We were jamming them and the Viggie, in afterburner was outrunning them. None of the sites could use their radar to compute a firing solution so they just launched the SAMs ballisticaly, firing more at the sound of the passing jet than at a hard target. The SAMs were designed to be armed in flight, but by the time that the arming sequence could complete the Viggie, which was flying low, was long gone. Up in our plane, the radar battle was still raging. SAM radars, one after another, were coming up, and the radio calls of "SAM, SAM, vicinity of ..." were loud on the shared operational frequencies.

Just then, below us and coming out of the cloud, I spotted the telltale signs a missile. A streak of orange flame was swooping up at us from the undercast. I yelled into my mike, "SAM, starboard side."

As soon as I made the call, Ted turned right and into the oncoming flame. Like turning into a skid on an icy road, the technique seemed counterintuitive, but the most effective method to avoid a SAM that was coming for you was to turn into it and then turn sharply again, always watching for the second missile that would come from below. As soon as he did, the flames vanished and the voice of the Viggie came over the radio, "feet wet" then "Skybolt, is that you up there?" We, moreover I had been had.

There was an old story about the Viggies. Based in rural Georgia, they often took advantage of their evangelical neighbors in the backwoods and swamps by giving them a taste of fire and brimstone. The RA-5C had been built with its fuel-dumping nozzle in the tail of the aircraft, right between the exhaust pipes of the two jet engines. One of their tricks, especially on cloudy nights, was to dump fuel and light it off with a touch of afterburner. The vaporized jet fuel, tiny particles hanging in the humid air, would flare and burn, sending a stream of flame for miles across the southern Georgia sky. Within moments the phones would be ringing at local police stations and preachers, frantically called by parishioners who were sure that the end had come. Meanwhile, the Viggies would return to base and, if asked, plead ignorance to any airborne shenanigans.

And so we lost in this little game of aviation gottcha. Now we got to stand up before our peers, stalwart aviators who had endured the heat of battle and the flaming fuel dump trick of our shipmates.

The event for which we should have received the award, however, happened several nights later, and it happened on the flight deck, not in combat. It was a wet, nasty night with the seas running high—again we trapped aboard in the dark. Everything on the flight had gone according to the script, and all we had to do was to taxi forward to the bow to park and the respotting of aircraft. Ted retracted the flaps, and when I saw they were up, I unlocked the wings and pulled on the wing fold handle. We had forty seconds to clear the landing area. Normally, we would be spotted toward the middle of the pack on the bow, but for some reason that night we were going to be the first airplane on the starboard side, just behind the Van Zelm arrestors, with our nose pointed toward the centerline and our tail swung off over the starboard catwalks.

We had been back at sea for several weeks, and the non-skid paint on the deck was worn and greasy. In places the paint had flaked off completely leaving bare steel exposed. Ted was coaxing us forward with small applications of the throttle. The pitching of the deck was not helping, and we were making slow forward progress. As Ted was about to steer the nose toward the middle of the deck, so that we would face the row of parked airplanes on the port side, the ship rolled slightly, and our right main mount tire skipped over the cat track's rim and smack onto the track itself. By necessity this stretch of smooth metal, which allows the catapult shuttle to glide and to hurl airplanes into the air, is kept well lubricated. On this night, the track was extra slick with grease floating on the rainwater. The surface was like a skating rink, and, because of the rise and fall of the bow, we were sliding forward. Ted applied some power, but that made it worse. We were caught in the track and moving sideways, with no control. A second later the port main mount hopped into the track. Only the nose wheel was on the non-skid and it did not create enough friction to slow us. The deck crew saw what was happening even before we did.

Here we were, fifty thousand pounds of airplane sliding ever so slowly toward the bow of the *Enterprise* with nothing to stop us from simply dribbling off the bow and into the dark churning sea. The pitching of the deck only magnified the problem. That thought, and my subsequent realization that we would either be entombed in the airplane as it sank or ground into shark-bait by the ship's massive screws, got me to call on the radio for chains to stop us. Airplanes on aircraft carriers are secured to the deck with a combination of chains that are hooked onto hard points under the plane's wings and to steel pat-eyes, small indentations with welded steel rods forming a star on the deck. Our plane crew ran toward us, chains dangling around their necks and hooked onto us; they furiously tried to hook the other ends of the chains to the pat-eyes.

In the cockpit, with the canopy open despite the rain that was now soaking us, we could see the men swarming under us, trying, as they fought to keep clear of the engine intakes and exhaust, to secure us to the deck. There was the sound of clattering chains being dragged toward us. Then, it seemed the plane had stopped. Suddenly the ship lurched and, with a tremendous crack, one of the chains snapped, and we started forward again. *Jesus, we're going over the side,* I thought.

From where I sat in the right front seat, the deck edge at the bow was slowly coming closer and closer. I could hear the shouts of the deck crew calling for more chains as they tried to slow down and stop our progress toward a watery oblivion. Should I blow the canopies? That would make for an easier escape if we hit the water. Ted looked at me. He hand retarded the throttles and he was nearly standing on the brake pedals, but we were still moving.

More clunking sounds as more chains were connected, then our side of the ship rose and that seemed to stop the slide. Within a few seconds, and before the ship could roll back, more chains were attached, and we were finally stopped. Ted shut down the engines and began to unstrap. The deck crew had let down the ladder on his side of the plane, but on my side, the ladder remained up. No one dared to come to that side in the dark. There was no room to climb down without the risk of tumbling into the ocean sixty feet below. I nodded at Ted and waited for him to get out. Then I followed him and climbed over his seat and down the portside of the Prowler. The deck crew had already left us, another A-6 was coming forward to park, so there was no one to thank. On the flight deck, the remnants of two heavy tie-down chains lay with their links spread apart as if they had been made of pasta. It was a near thing.

Hong Kong Phooey

The peaks of Hong Kong Island were wreathed in gray. An early morning fog rose above us as the *Enterprise* rose at anchor. We were out in the Lamma Island channel, far from the view of most of the inhabitants of the Crown Colony. Being kept at such a distance was a prudent and necessary step, given the vitriolic anti-war, anti-American, and anti-nuke sentiments of the locals. It was just as well that we anchored so close to the sea-lanes, as we were within a stone's throw from the People's Republic, and Chairman Mao's rhetoric about capitalist running dogs was *au courant*.

But all of these issues paled when compared with the magnificence of the view of the harbor from our flight deck. This was the Orient that I had imagined, the one that William Holden and Clark Gable had used as their backdrops in films like *Soldier of Fortune*. Somehow the stinking cesspool that we had visited in the Philippines and the smoke rising from destroyed targets in North Vietnam didn't make as deep an impression on me as seeing this city first-hand.

Soon I would be ashore, just another tourist amid a sea of strange people and sights.

The problem that morning was getting ashore. Liberty launches had been contracted by the navy to ferry the crew ashore, but there seemed to be no organization on the ship as to how we were to get aboard these small boats. A mess officer, that weasely ensign, had been put in charge of the embarkation. The bastard would steal your eyeteeth but was too afraid of the enlisted men to admit to the officers assembled on the hangar deck that officers had priority on the launches. I stepped up to him, along with several others, to set him straight; moreover, I had drawn Shore Patrol that night and was toting my uniform along with some civilian clothes. I had to get ashore ahead of the rest. Our squadron had made room reservations at the Bayside Hotel in Kowloon, and he wasn't going to slow me down.

One of the Red Baroon's special duties while we were out on the line had been to fly into Hong Kong on the COD. He was always finding a way to nab on to some special, generally cushy assignments. Tagging along with the ship's advance party he had arranged to book our squadron several suites of rooms. Like Major Blank de Coverly in *Catch-22,* the Baroon had a knack for finding and arranging accommodations ashore long before we made port. He had gotten wind of the problem of boarding the launches and joined me as we pushed past the cringing ensign. With a strong hand at my back, he pushed us down the gangway and onto the camel that floated alongside the ship, where the launches were docking. What would amount to several hours of waiting for many of the others was thus avoided. Soon we were basking in sunshine on the top deck of the launch as it plunged through the choppy waters of Hong Kong's inner harbor to the fleet landing at the China Fleet Club in Wanchai.

PROWLER BALL

Visiting with their husbands in Hong Kong was a real treat for the spouses of sailors sent to Vietnam. Unlike the army, the navy did not offer R&R during a cruise, so liberty ports served the bill. Many of the officer's and NCO's wives had made the long flight, and there was a line of them waiting at the pier when the Baroon and I stepped from the launch. He and I were not expecting our wives, and those of our squadron mates who were holding up signs with their husband's names on them seemed less than pleased that we had somehow beaten their spouses ashore. We warned them of the long delays on the ship and then went off to find telephones from which to call our spouses back in the States.

What struck me as we walked along through Wanchai to the post office to find the phones was how cosmopolitan the place was. It was the women mostly, every shape, every nationality, every style of dress passed us on the street. I felt as if I had just landed from years on Mars. We had only been away from home for three months, and yet it seemed like ages since I'd clapped eyes on an attractive woman. Today, little is left of this part of old Hong Kong, and even then, most of the old was fast disappearing, replaced by glass and steel edifices dedicated to making money. But there were clear contrasts. Even rickshaws were common, and not just for tourists snapping photos in front of the White Star Ferry terminal.

The Baroon always traveled first class, or so he liked to boast, and the best first class ride in town was on the top deck of the White Star Ferry over to Kowloon. There, for one Hong Kong dollar, the equivalent of twenty cents, you could ride across the harbor seated on wooden slat benches and take in all of your surroundings. First, though we hit the post office where we both made our calls home, keeping the talk brief and everyone's emotions buoyed. When we finally said goodbye to our wives we both had misty eyes.

What really struck me as we made our way to the ferry landing was that even with the gaudiness of the signs and banners in English and Cantonese, there were Christmas decorations everywhere. After all, it was mid December and the colony was still a British possession. Christianity had a strong hold in the place. I suppose that it was just that I had not expected to see Santa and Rudolph prancing around streets filled with Chinese people. Since that time I have made the harbor crossing dozens of times, and still the sights have always impressed me. In those narrow roadsteads the world's commerce sails by. Trading vessels of all types plied the waters, their cargoes from all over the world, brought in and shipped out as had been done for centuries. I felt as much an alien interloper there as anywhere I have ever been.

Later that night I was to find out how much of an interloper I was in this cultural crossroads. The first night in port I had been assigned to the local shore patrol as the night duty officer. Not that I had any training in dragging drunks from bars or breaking up fights in whorehouses, but the navy thought it would be appropriate that an officer be present to lend a little official weight to any police proceedings.

The job was simple enough, I had to dress in my blues and ride around with the real SPs as they made their way through the brothels and bars of Wanchai. First, though, I had to get to the Shore Patrol office at the fleet landing, which meant that I had to walk from our Kowloon side hotel to the White Star Ferry, and go back over to the Victoria side, and then walk several blocks into Wanchai. At that moment in history, walking through an Asian city dressed as a US naval officer provoked a lot of stares, curiosity and outright resentment. The air war in Vietnam was not popular anywhere, least of all here, and I could see in the eyes and faces of the Chinese who I passed on the street that, though my money might be welcome, as a representative of US foreign policy, I was not.

The evening with the Shore Patrol went pretty much as expected. I rode around with them in a Land Cruiser, picking up our sailors and depositing them back at the landing so they could be loaded on boats and taken back to the ship. Most of them were docile, drunk as skunks. After they spent a few hours aboard, sobered up, and if they had their liberty cards were renewed, they would be back for more of the same, in the meantime, off the island they went. The real goal of the Shore Patrol was to keep our sailors out of the hands of the Hong Kong Police. The Hong Kong Police were really tough bastards. They were not very big men, but they could kick the shit out of anyone who put up any resistance. If those guys got them, our sailors were likely to be beaten with truncheons before being released back to the navy.

About an hour before I was to go off-duty, we drove around a corner to find a bunch of sailors fighting with a couple of whores in the middle of the street. Three burly SPs bailed out of the truck and began to break up the fight. Most of the sailors gave up at the sight of the Shore Patrol and meekly got in the back for the obligatory ride to the landing, but one tough guy decided the whores were not about to get the best of him and kept wrestling with one of the girls. One of our SPs got him in a headlock and was dragging him back to the truck.

"Calm down, sailor, and get in the fucking truck!" I said to him.

"No, fucking way, Yank! You can't boss me around, I'm an Aussie."

Well, that made it a different story, so we let him go, and he lunged back after the girl who screamed. At that moment the Hong

Kong Police showed up. Three of them, each half the size of the Aussie sailor, jumped him and began to perform a drum symphony on him with their thick rubber clubs. He fell in a heap on the street and we drove away. Once we got our clutch of sailors to the landing, I took a cab back to the ferry. In less than an hour I was back at the hotel, I found one of the unoccupied beds in our suite of rooms and collapsed into it. Sleep was not going to come, though.

I had not been in bed long before the door to the room opened and, amid giggles and sighs, two of the guys came in with a couple of girls from the Bayside Club downstairs. They were as surprised to see me, as I was to see them. We had taken several rooms on the seventeenth floor of the hotel, so there was plenty of bed space for everyone. While one of the guys went off to find a private room, I got to sit and "talk" to the girls. Mostly they giggled and seemed to want to know if I wanted to join their little *ménage a quatre*. But I was just too tired. Soon they went off to another room and banged away the night. Then at last, I dropped off to sleep.

The next morning, after breakfast, the Red Baroon and I went off to tour the city. I had a long list of things to buy and places to go in the city. Under his guidance we strolled about and went to the various shopping areas to buy things for my wife—opals, tiger-eye topaz, a silk dress—all the things that a dutiful husband-sailor should bring home. After being at sea so long, it was strange to be in a real city, with concrete buildings and paved roads among throngs of people, traffic, and the bustle of normal life. The smells of the place were as exotic as they were strange. Walking down the street you could suddenly find yourself among hanging carcasses of pigs and chickens in an open-air butcher shop or wandering among piles of silk and batik at a street vendor. The Baroon wanted a new pair of shoes, and the only place to go was Lee Ke's, for, as they were known in the fleet, a pair of squeaky leakys. After that we went for lunch.

The Baroon was a fastidious tourist and had the day well mapped out, so we found ourselves in Jimmy's Kitchen, The Original Go Down for lunch. The name came from the old days in the colony when workshops and restaurants in Kowloon were in the lower level or basements of buildings, so that upon entering, one literally had to go down to get in. Jimmy's was world famous. It turned out that several of the other old hands among the squadron's officers had the same idea, so we were eventually seated at a large round table while drinks arrived and we decided what we wanted on the menu. Naturally, the Baroon with his stentorious voice presided and ordered a variety of starters including satay chicken and shrimp, something very new to me. I never thought of peanuts and cinnamon as a good combination until that day.

The day advanced toward evening, as we shopped and walked and finally bought more liquor to take back to the hotel. One of the sitting rooms in the hotel was decked out with liquor bottles and glasses, and several of the guys were and already plastered. Most of us were keeping our alcohol levels high. For the five days we were scheduled to be in port, free from any duty, everyone was making the most of it. Booze, in Hong Kong even single malt whiskey, was cheap enough and the bar was kept well stocked.

After my previous night's forced sobriety, I decided to drop in at the Bayside Club downstairs from the hotel. Paul Hazlet decided to join me and we were, as Ted Steele would say, "big." We were showing our pesonality, but this time with Hong Kong dollars. We paid for the drinks, the girls, and eventually, after giving the mama-san her cut, we took the girls back to the room. A couple of hours of grappling and giggling ensued, Paul and I, each with our damsel of the evening, finally wore out and, after making sure the two girls left without taking our wallets with them, we locked the door and went to sleep. The story that went around about that night was that I had spent so much money there I must have bought the place and for the rest of the liberty call the place was known as "Pierre's Bayside".

The next morning I woke feeling very hung over. The girl's perfume, cheap flowery stuff, filled the room and her sweat was still on my body. I badly needed a shower. Paul was snoring, and I looked over at him and blinked. Something shiny was sitting atop a hassock next to where he slept. It looked like a tooth. I looked again, it was a tooth, a single tooth with a piece of flesh colored plastic attached.

"What the hell is that?" I said a little too loudly, even for my ears.

Paul woke and looked around. "What?" he was groggier than I was.

"What's that? A tooth?"

Paul reached out a hand and took the thing and popped it back in his mouth. "Yeah, its mine," he mumbled and rolled over. In a moment he was snoring. Later he told me he had lost a tooth during a college rodeo event and no one knew that he had it.

Before we left to go sightseeing that day, I took myself to the barbershop. In Hong Kong while the barber cuts your hair, a young lady gives you a manicure while another uses her strong tiny fingers to massage you everywhere it might hurt. I spent an hour in the chair and when at last I was done and heavily tipped the ladies and the barber I felt rejuvenated and ready to press on.

Someone had arranged for a tour that we could go on. So we embarked on a bus trip out to the New Territories and up to the border with Red China. A relaxing drive might be a good cure for our hangovers, so off we went. At that time, anything about the People's Republic was still very much a mystery to most Americans, even to those of us who read the secret messages and annexes. China was the evilest of evil empires. Nixon may have recently gone there, but for us, it was very much enemy territory. For us to stand on a hill within sight of the red flags and the watchtowers filled with armed PRC soldiers that stood along the border was a bit off-putting, if not outright frightening. What would it have taken for a squad of Chinese soldiers to come across the wire and snatch a bunch of Americans? So we were wary.

Gordy Verdunne, our corpulent Crimson Tide ex-lineman and resident southern bigot, was along for the trip. His verbal pronouncements came out like a cross between George Wallace and Strom Thurmond. He might as well have had the Stars and Bars tattooed on his chest and a plug of Red Man in his mouth. Every other word out of his mouth was what we today would describe as politically insensitive. At the time, all of us thought that he must keep his white hood in the closet, taking it out only for special occasions. Blacks were coons and Asians were slopes in his lexicon, and none of us were too comfortable around him. He was married to a real bitch of a southern belle who oozed mint juleps and pecan pie, until she let loose with a series of four-lettered invectives when she was crossed by anyone. She could turn the word 'fuck' into three syllables. It was his wife who was the one who finally ratted out the married officers who were out with their Asian girlfriends during the Singapore port call. Strangely, that earned her no credit with the wives back home who more or less ostracized her for what she said. They would care of their errant husbands in their own way.

On the bus and at each stop Gordy was being effervescent in his own disgusting way, and most of us gave him a wide berth. At the overlook into the PRC there were several older Chinese dressed in traditional garb and offering to pose with tourists for photos. Gordy decided he needed a picture with "the chink" and approached the man in the costume. He was wearing a flat-topped hat and long white robes with embroidered designs on the sleeves. Gordy handed his camera to Paul, who snapped the photo. There were smiles all around. Then the old gentleman put out his hand for money. Gordy looked at him in surprise. I suppose he thought the man ought to have paid him to have his picture taken with a white man. Nevertheless, in a moment Gordy figured it out and reached in his pocket for some money.

He placed the bill, a Hong Kong dollar in the man's hand and started to turn away.

The old gentleman looked down at the money in his hand, spat on the bill, and threw it on the ground.

"No one dollah Hong Kong, one dollah US!" he shouted at Gordy.

No one of color had ever spoken to Gordy like that, and he was instantly aware that he was in the minority up here. Several of the other Chinese began to close in around him and Gordy began to sweat despite the coolness of the day. None of us felt like intervening in this clash of cultures. Gordy looked hesitant, then with a sick smile on his face, pulled out a ten-dollar bill decorated with Alexander Hamilton's face on the front, and pressed it into the old man's hand. The crowd, seeing the money edged closer and put out their hands for a share. Gordy then executed a perfect head and shoulder fake and ran to our bus. There he remained for the rest of the day.

Later in the afternoon, we stopped at an ancient village and walked around the absolutely appalling conditions. Animal and human excrement were spread on small garden patches and the place reeked of shit. Nearby we visited the flat-bottom steamboat that was used in the John Wayne and Lauren Bacall film, *Blood Alley*, but Gordy chose to stay on the bus, away from any of the locals. There was a snack bar on the boat that served tepid tea and weak coffee. At the gift counter I bought a copy of Mao's Little Red Book. I figured, I had read Mein Kampf and The Book of Mormon, why not another piece of propaganda.

Back at the hotel Gordy had settled himself with a bottle of George Dickle, sippin' whiskey and proceeded to drown his troubles. He was pretty far along when the call came for him to return to the ship. Apparently, he had forgotten that he had the duty the next day. For him to even be able to stand up was going to take a major effort on his part. His bulk was turning to fat even at the age of twenty-six. Somehow, he got to the fleet landing and onto the liberty boat running back to the ship. Tossing about on the launch on the long ride out to the ship did not improve his lot. He began to puke over the side of the launch. He puked and puked to the point that drowning might have been a blessed relief. And there he might have really drowned in his drink, or at least in the Hong Kong harbor, if it hadn't been for the long arms of one of the RA-5C pilots.

Gordy might have been able to step from the liberty boat and onto the camel that bobbed up and down next to the ship. But the camel, caught in the rise and fall of the harbor currents, was moving violently, and, as Gordy tried, in his inebriated state, to step across the narrow gap and onto the gangway going up the side of the ship. He missed and suddenly he began to drop into the water. He could have been crushed between the camel and the ship, or simply have vanished into the dark water, but a large hand reached out and grabbed his shirt collar. A second later he was thrown onto the ladder, dripping wet from the waist down, but alive. Panting and grabbing at the ladder hand over hand he made his way up the side of the ship and to his bunk.

As for me, I came back to the ship a couple of days early, sick as a dog. Perhaps whatever germs were lurking in that quaint Chinese village had infected me, or, more likely my last trip to Da Nang had brought me in contact with a female Anopheles. Two days later I went to sickbay to get something to stop the fever and pain. I was standing by the pharmacy dispensary window when I heard a loud bang, like a heavy object striking metal. It was me, collapsing with malaria—down for the count and nearly unconscious. Hong Kong? Phooey!

THOUSAND PLANE RAID

We had a stand-down day for Christmas, twenty-four hours of peace, but that night the gloves came off. They called it Linebacker II. It was Nixon's plan to intimidate the North Vietnamese and get them back to the Paris peace table. He was fed up with the North Vietnamese and if the later accounts were correct with Henry Kissinger as well. For those of us who were going to carry out Tricky Dick's strategy, it was hard to see where what we had been doing all these years left off and where the new effort began.

It wasn't as if the military had defined aerial combat campaigns in Vietnam. Everything about this war was run on a political basis, and mission and operational labels were designed as much for home-front consumption as for mission needs. Oh, maybe the generals and admirals and those in the press who wrote about such things called what we did in the day-to-day drudgery of the air war by exalted names, but we just did our jobs. For the most part by late 1972, we had run out of hard targets, or even symbolic targets in

the north. There was no Berlin or Tokyo to bomb. There were no
stirring speeches from the brass to convince us of the strategic
importance of what we were doing, we simply flew the midnight-to-
noon cycle missions that we were assigned and hoped that soon the
whole thing would be over.

Coming out of our liberty call in Hong Kong, there did seem
to be a new urgency aboard *Enterprise*. It was not so much what
anyone said or did, you just felt it. Since Nixon had put the entire
map of North Vietnam back on the target list, we knew that
something serious was about to happen, and we were in it. The steel
beneath our feet vibrated excitedly as we rushed south around
Hainan Island to get back to Yankee Station.

There were no more olive branches to be extended. We were
going to reopen the war with a punch from a mailed fist. That first
night's target was to be a bridge complex south of Haiphong.
Bridges, especially those in the coastal estuaries, had been a regular
and early target for carrier air strikes. As I walked into our ready
room for the first briefing, I saw Jake Beltran starring at the TV
screen where the Air Wing's AI was showing strike photos of the
target. Jake had tears streaming down his face as he looked at the
images of a twisted river pocked with giant watery craters and a
spider-web of rickety walkways on either side of a bombed out
concrete bridge.

Jake was muttering to himself and wiping at his eyes, "How
many fucking times do we have to keep going fucking back to the
same fucking places?" His question was directed at the screen, but
then he looked at me. "Do you know how many times I've flown
against that bend in the river? Three times in seven years—three
times—and each time I lost a wingman. A friend lost. Lost for

fucking what—a stretch of swamp with bicycle bridges?" He looked at me and then stalked out of the room.

Later, Jake came up to me and apologized. He was one of the many veterans aboard who had been to this lousy war too many times, and no amount of flag waiving and chest thumping was going to convince him of the need for us to continue. But he was a professional and as such, none of us made policy, we just executed it.

And so, it began in earnest. Our job was simply to fly and to attack, until someone gave in at the Paris peace table. It wasn't a great tactical problem, just an application of blunt force—we were simply going to put more ordnance on the targets than the North Vietnamese could absorb. Round the clock bombing, thousands of sorties flown by navy, Marine and air force units from Guam to Thailand—this time Nixon meant business.

Our Prowlers were in constant demand, now every attack needed electronic warfare support. We had been too successful for our own good. For twelve hours a day, from midnight until noon, every other launch the *Enterprise* put out was an alpha strike with Haiphong and Hanoi and every building inside them targeted. Our squadron's skipper was flown down to Saigon to meet with the senior planners there, so that optimally we could coordinate our electronic warfare with the onslaught of the strategic bombers. SAC's B-52s were slated to fly into the target area and replicate their famous ARCLIGHT missions, and somehow we were going to have to protect them.

When the skipper returned from his meetings in Saigon, he just shook his head. The brass had no time for tactical considerations, the President said, "do it" and they were ordering it done. We would just have to do the best we could, because the 52s were going to be flying higher than we were, and we could not keep them in the jamming envelope when they did so. Worse, it seemed, the North Vietnamese would have plenty of time to get ready for them, because the planes leaving Guam for Thailand via targets in North Vietnam were forced to file ICAOA flight plans with turn points, time of flight, and altitudes. Even if the North Vietnamese gunners didn't get this information, the radar sites operated by the Chinese on Hainan Island and the Soviet AGIs would have clear radar pictures of the flocks of bombers. They would stand out on their radar screens like whores in church.

Launch followed launch, cycle followed cycle. For each of our crews two a night, then three—after the first few strikes the sky to the north glowed orange from the burning docks and warehouses of Haiphong. When we climbed away from the ship, I set the new radar coordinates for the mission, but we only had to fly toward the raging flames to get to where the action was.

Each night we headed north, launching in clear tropical winter weather and climbing up to thirty-five thousand feet. We had to get close enough to the Buffs (big ugly fat fuckers the sobriquet with which the B-52s had been dubbed) to jam for them. To get that high took a lot of gas, even with our large fuel capacity. The EA-6B had a hard time getting above forty thousand feet, even on a good day and with no external stores, but with drop tanks and jamming pods, thirty-five thousand was just barely doable. And still it was not high enough to do our job properly.

Red Crown was so busy checking flights in and out and it sounded like LAX at Thanksgiving. It was really hopping; aircraft were all over the sky. The guys down in the communications and control area of the ship on Red Crown duty had no time for idle chitchat, and we were checked in and out in seconds. Nearing the coastline, the fires from the repeated bombings became distinct as individual targets. You could see the areas in flame as curving arcs of tracers from eighty-five millimeter cannons snaked into the air trying to protect what was left of the battered targets. Near Haiphong, there was a huge pulsating mass of brownish flame burning. It had been on fire for at least twelve hours and seemed to be growing in size as if it were a canker eating the earth under it. The fire was the result of a hit by some lucky F-4s. They bombed the area and had hit the storage area for the SA-2 missile boosters, and it was the solid fuel for the boosters that were burning with no hope of the inferno being extinguished.

The strike was devastating to the North's air defense network that was supposed to protect Hanoi. With the loss of the boosters they were rapidly running out of launch capable SAMs when the fuel storage fire finally went out having consumed itself, they had no replacements. For the defenders of the cities, whatever munitions might still be on the Soviet replenishment vessels now anchored in the harbor those munitions might as well have still been in Vladivostok as anywhere. Nothing was going to be allowed to get ashore. With the docks on fire and the harbor strewn with aerial mines, there would be no movement of ships for months.

As we leveled off the airplane bucked and rolled as the pressure waves from the detonation of flak at all altitudes collided with us. Every radar that the North Vietnamese had was up and functioning, at least until the Iron Handers with the Shrikes and Standard ARMs hit them. At the same time, time-trusted Soviet-style anti-aircraft defense discipline had simply gone out the window. Soon, with their radars destroyed or damaged, the defenders on the ground took to launching all their missiles at once as if they were shooting at ducks with shotguns These barrages were, we supposed, meant to inflict damage by proximity to their explosions. In truth, there was more damage on the ground from falling debris than against the tactical air forces that were laying waste to the region.

Ted and I bounced through these missile attacks as the blast concussions first tossed us about in the air, and then pelted us with clouds of descending fragments and debris from the detonations. The torrents of cascading metal banged into us and bounced along the wings tearing at the paint and denting radomes. I was just hoping that we would not ingest the metal fragments into the jet intakes, which would result in the destruction of the Prowler's engines. Jumping out of the plane at this point would have put us in the water in close proximity to a lot of very angry enemy soldiers and civilians. Below us, sections of VA-196's A-6s were hitting the port complex on the south side of Haiphong harbor. These attacks we could cover with our jammers. The AAA was intense at times, but the Intruders pressed in and delivered their ordnance

The B-52s were the main anti-aircraft targets on these nights. It quickly became a major coup for the North's gunners to hit and down one of these massive beasts. Unfortunately, the air force made it too easy for them to hit the big bombers. The Stratofortresses came over in waves of three cells each containing three planes. We heard later that the first wave was flown by the colonels and senior lieutenant colonels, the second wave by majors and captains, and the third by junior lieutenant colonels and senior majors. It turned out that the first wave took the lightest hits, while the gunners on the ground got the altitude and courses fixed, so the second wave had the shit shot out of them, and, by the time the third wave arrived to drop their bombs, the gunners on the ground were reloading.

The first night over the target I saw several of the big bombers hit. High above us I saw the flash of the blast and then the shape of huge wings, engulfed by flame and floating toward the ground. As the fragments of the 52 headed toward the ground, the emergency radio frequency crackled with the calls of each of the crewmen as they descended in their chutes. It was an odd sight to see, huge bombers, three times the size of their Second World War predecessors falling to earth. Then, hitting the earth these planes broke up when hit and burned furiously. Having been raised on the premise of the supremacy of the Strategic Air Command and the massive bomber fleets that had kept the Soviets at bay for decades, it was difficult to assimilate the destruction that I was witnessing.

By the third day we were running out of targets. The North Vietnamese had fired off their entire supply of SAMs and most, if not all, of their heavy anti-aircraft ammunition. Of course, they still had plenty of small arms and light anti-aircraft ammo, but cruising the skies over Hanoi had become less and less of a challenge. So much so that F-4s were escorting the Jolly Green SAR choppers into neighborhoods around the Communist capital to pick up downed American airmen. The North Vietnamese citizenry seemed at last to be reeling in shock from the attacks, and, with no way to shoot down American planes, it appeared to us that maybe, just maybe, this war could be over.

With the intensity of the attacks waning, there was the inevitable let down. A combat aviator's worst enemy is complacency, and that's when little mistakes begin to creep in and cause big problems. Worse, fatigue from just too many launches and difficult landings begin to erode efficiency and effectiveness. Some people handle the shifts in stress well, and some men, despite outward physical prowess, succumb.

Jake Beltran collapsed on his way to the ready room on the fourth night of the bombing. He was a healthy male, just thirty-three and had just been selected for commander. Maybe it was just fatigue, maybe it was something worse. The flight surgeons in sickbay ran him through an EKG, but they couldn't be sure if he had a serious heart problem. Jake looked tired like the rest of us, his face drained and drawn, and he was as weak as a kitten. Ordered to bed in the hospital ward of sickbay, there was nothing for him to do until he could be air lifted back to Subic. He would have to take the next COD in two days time. Meanwhile, the flight surgeons suggested that we have a pacemaker kit on standby.

The closest pacemaker was at Clark Air Force Base on Luzon. The military, in anticipation of the probable release of our POWs by the North Vietnamese, had stockpiled a massive amount of medical equipment and personnel at the hospital at the airbase. We needed to get our hands on one of the pacemaker kits. However, this was not a job for a couple of aviators. We couldn't just barge into the lobby of the base hospital and snatch a pacemaker. We had no idea what one looked like, and it was highly likely that we would come back with the wrong thing. We needed to take a flight surgeon with us.

We had made several runs to the PI over the months at sea, using our fourth seat for a special passenger or cargo. Someone finagled the flight schedule and Ted and I, along with a startled flight surgeon were scheduled to go on the next launch. It was about nine hundred miles from Yankee Station, south past the Paracel and Spratley Islands; we left the ship around midnight and touched down at Clark just before three a.m.

"You stay with the plane, and get us refueled. We may be leaving in a hurry," Ted told me. Until that moment, it had not occurred to me that we might have to steal the device. He and the flight surgeon disappeared into the transient line shack and commandeered a truck to take them to the base hospital. The ship had sent a message to the Air Force hospital asking for a pacemaker kit to be available upon our arrival. So they went off to collect it.

I stood by and watched a drowsy air force line crew refuel the Prowler. I then had them bring up a huffer, so that when Ted and the doctor got back, we could fire up the engines and head back to the ship. I also went inside the operations office and re-filed a flight plan for the return trip to the ship. The *Enterprise* was expecting us back by early morning.

I had been waiting about a half-hour when the truck with Ted and the flight surgeon came screeching to a halt next to the line shack.

Ted came running toward the plane, the flight surgeon in his wake carrying a small attaché case in arms.

"Let's get going!" Ted shouted.

Both of them looked back over their shoulders apprehensively.

"What's up?" I asked them, as I waived to the line crew to come and get the huffer started.

"We need to go, now!" Ted shouted as he pulled on the last of his flight gear.

I helped the flight surgeon get settled into the rear ECMO ejection seat and made sure he knew about re-arming it once we started engines. Then I crawled into the front cockpit and watched the line crew to make sure they latched the ladder on my side, while Ted did the same on his side of the plane. We both took care of latching the small platform below our canopies. If that came off in flight we would have a hard time getting out of the aircraft once we landed.

Ted gave the signal to the linemen to rev up the huffer, and I went through the engine start checklist. Once we were under our own power, we called for taxi and takeoff. Within five minutes we were climbing and I was calling departure control for vectors.

Once we leveled off I asked Ted, "What was all the hurry?"

Ted looked over at me, I suppose with a grin, but his oxygen mask covered most of his face.

"A bit of a midnight requisition. We had to steal the pacemaker, isn't that right, doc?" he said over the intercom.

Another voice came over the intercom and the flight surgeon replied. "Well, it seems that no one passed along the message from the ship about our urgent need for this thing, and we were going through a lot of needless talk about approvals with the night duty staff in the hospital. So, I asked Ted to talk to them while I went to the bathroom. I ducked into the supply room off the ER and found what I needed. They had dozens of these stacked up just waiting for customers."

Ted interjected, "Then it got a little hairy. When the nurse went to call the on-call cardiologist, we just took the kit and ran. No sense asking for more trouble."

I just shook my head and waited for the inevitable radio call instructing us to return to Clark, but it never came. We arrived overhead the ship as the glow of dawn was beginning to fade and made a routine trap. The flight surgeon took the pacemaker down to sickbay and checked on Jake, who, it turned out, did not need it after all.

As far as we knew there were no repercussions from our felonious act, and we went on with our war. Jake got a trip to the PI and eventually back to Whidbey. Several months later he was processed for early retirement based on an undisclosed medical condition.

LOSSES

No warship that steams into harm's way can escape taking casualties. We were no different than all the naval vessels throughout history that had put to sea with orders to seek and destroy their enemies. At sea, casualties could be caused by accidents or from hostile action; it was part of the job. No one liked to think about it, but even when I had made my inspection tour of the ship's spaces and was shown the cavernous freezer lockers with the stack of empty coffins in the corner, it was clear that someone calculated there would be losses.

During our combat cruise, most of the losses came in late December and early January. The intensity of air operations and the ferocity of the level of air combat during those weeks made it inevitable that we would suffer casualties. During those hectic weeks around the Christmas bombing campaign, planes from Air Wing Fourteen were in the air all through the night and sustained hits from ground fire and one seemingly impossible shot from a MiG-21.

One of my principal means of relaxation aboard ship was to climb up to the O-11 level on the ships island. I had always been drawn to lofty perches and high above the flight deck I found one from which I could watch air operations and simply chill out after flying. On a good day, standing on the backside of the phased-array radar installation, which crowned the island, I could find a place that was isolated from my regular duties and catch a few moments of peace. I was up there late one afternoon just before New Year's Day, dodging the demands of my job and trying to settle my nerves a bit. I had been sick for days, then flying two to three hops a day, and finding myself a tad hypoglycemic by early afternoon. My cure for that was downing a long series of heavily sugared glasses of iced tea and then pissing up a storm.

This particular afternoon the air wing had been tasked to fly more daylight support operations to help the air force's jolly greens to rescue the many downed B-52 crews hiding out in the outskirts of Hanoi. The two F-4 squadrons were putting up iron-handers during daylight hours to suppress any anti-aircraft fire that might be directed toward the lumbering green air force helicopters. From where I stood, the pattern of returning airplanes seemed to be normal, until a blast from the flight deck loudspeakers told of an airplane in trouble. I scanned the skies, looking for incoming planes. F-4s were easy to spot, since they trailed sooty black plumes of jet exhaust, especially at slow flight power settings. I looked aft to see if there were any approaching the ship, and, sure enough, there were a pair of F-4s, with their tailhooks down, coming up the starboard side toward the break. The lead Phantom was putting out a lot of black smoke, much more it appeared than just exhaust. It had been hit by small arms fire somewhere over Hanoi. The massive yellow MB-5 fire truck had been moved into position on the flight deck just ahead of the landing area. It was set to douse the burning F-4 with light water as soon as it landed. The MB-5 crew were clad their silver flame-retardant suits and ready for any eventuality. The Air Boss had cleared everyone else from the flight deck as we waited for the arrival of the stricken fighter.

From where I stood, nearly a hundred and fifty feet above the water, I had an unobstructed view of the situation. The F-4s flew up past the bow and dropped their gear. Everything looked normal, except for the growing plume of smoke from the lead F-4. It was essential that the damaged fighter should make the first approach, while his wingman would stay with him through the approach matching airspeed and attitude as the damaged plane came down the chute to the flight deck. If the pilot of the damaged Phantom was wounded, he might need the voice of his wingman giving him control corrections to land.

Off to port, the pair of jets leveled off abeam of the ship and headed downwind to the final turn toward the flight deck. The *Enterprise* sped up to get more wind over the deck and make the approach for the wounded F-4 easier. Everyone was standing by. The plane guard helo was on station and our escorting destroyer had come up to offer instant assistance if needed.

The two Phantoms turned toward final approach, gear down, hooks down, and full flaps. Normally, the F-4s were able to engage an auto throttle system whereby a computer on the ship could control their speed on final and allowed for near-perfect three-wire landings, but with battle damage that was impossible. Unless the pilot was wounded, when auto throttles could be a lifesaver, their use in this situation was not recommended.

The pair made the turn and were lining up wing to wing for the final stab at the deck. At about a half mile astern, the pilot of the wounded F-4 must have moved the throttles, or perhaps the heat from the smoking area toward the tail finally melted enough of the airplane to reach the fuel tanks. There was a sudden puff of oily black smoke and then a long lash of flame—it was time for the pilot and his RIO to get out. Instantly, the air boss, in his tower in Pri Fly just below where I stood called out "Eject, eject!"

A second later there were two small explosions and the ejection seats soared up away from the burning plane. Then the white plumes of a pair of parachutes appeared. In the air, the surviving F-4 waved off, climbing to avoid the hulk of the rapidly disintegrating Phantom. Another second passed, and then engulfed in flames the fighter plunged into the sea a quarter mile behind the ship. By then *Enterprise*'s plane guard helo was overhead the pair of downed aviators, who had disengaged themselves from their parachutes and were bobbing in the sea held up by their yellow Mae Wests.

On the flight deck and in Pri-Fly all motion was momentarily suspended, as all eyes looked toward the plume of smoke that rose from the Phantom's impact point and then toward where the rescue helo was now raising one of the F-4 crewmen to its open hatchway. In another instant the frozen tableau on deck dissolved as the process of recovering the other F-4 commenced. As we kept steaming into the wind to complete that evolution I focused my eyes on the scene astern. The plane guard destroyer had heaved to windward of the man in the water in order cut off the swells in the area of the two aviators so that the helo crew might have an easier time of rescuing the remaining flier. As the rescue continued the destroyer remained hove to and stood by in case the rescue helo needed assistance. The remaining F-4, now low on fuel, came around and made an uneventful recovery. As the crew of the surviving Phantom stepped from their parked plane to the flight deck, the plane guard helo arrived, landing aft of the arresting wires a moment later the surviving pair, soaked to the skin, stepped onto the non-skid of the flight deck. White shirted stretcher-bearers were waiting for them if necessary, but the two gave the medics thumbs up and walked themselves to sickbay for medical evaluation. We lost a plane, but no lives—that kind of luck was not going to continue.

––––––

I lost two friends during our cruise. One was a friend with whom I had gone through Pensacola, and one was a man I first met the day he was killed. I met Clark Alwin just as we stepped into the hell that was the first morning at Pensacola. As we were hit with the din of the screaming drill instructors inside the stately building that housed Indoc Battalion, we barely said hello before we were ripped apart and were faced with our own private humiliations, but I will never forget his devilish grin when he looked at the chaos around us. He was going to make it no matter what happened.

As part of class 27-70, we had suffered together with all the other new volunteers. We made it all the way through commissioning and on to primary training at VT-10. At Sherman Field in Pensacola, we got to choose the airplane we wanted to fly when we graduated from primary training at VT-10. Choice of airplane was made by your place in the class standings. I was number two in the class, and so I chose the newest plane in the fleet, the EA-6B Prowler. Clark was lower down, probably in the top ten though, and he chose the A-6 Intruder, this meant we were both bound for Whidbey Island, Washington, to join different units. We ended up going through SERE (survival, evasion, resistance, and escape) school together, at Warner Springs, California, and both of us had the crap beaten out of us.

Once at Whidbey, our flying careers diverged. But as life would have it, he and his wife moved in just down the street from us, on Glacier Court in junior officer's housing. Our wives became close friends in that pressed-together-by-necessity atmosphere that military bases created for spouses. We did things together as couples do, going to movies and such, until he deployed with VA-52 aboard the *USS Midway* about ten months before I too deployed.

Just before I left for Westpac, his wife gave birth to twin boys. The sons that as it developed Clark would never meet. I saw Clark about a week before he was killed. We had flown over to the *Midway* for another of those escort missions that were making the EA-6B so popular. VA-52 hosted us, and, as we waited to brief for our flight, Clark and I talked. He was not the same man I had known back in Whidbey. He had become very gaunt, his skin almost convict gray. He, like all of us had aged, but was also fatalistic. He said to me, his voice very matter of fact, "I've flown almost two hundred missions, and I am going to die here."

I knew enough to keep my mouth shut about that being crap. Somehow men knew these things, knew that their time was up. Nothing would shake him out of that sense of doom, and no one in the navy was going to do anything about it.

As it turned out, we did not fly support that night. So, at dawn we flew back to the *Enterprise*. A week later we got the news that Clark and his pilot had flown straight into a karst ridge outside of Vinh and exploded. They had been dropping bombs on suspected truck parks and pulled off the target a few seconds too late. No sign of survivors and no wreckage were ever found, so the timeless jungle consumed them, like so many others who fell from the sky there.

————

I had seen Brad Watkins around since the beginning of the cruise, but until that day we had never conversed. Our squadron was small compared to others on the ship and we shared an enlarged ready room with the recce squadron, RVAH-13. Brad was a RAN, radar officer who flew in the encapsulated rear seat of a RA-5C and operated the sensors and cameras, taking pictures of bomb damage and possible new targets. The RA-5Cs went in low and fast and, it was hoped, avoided the worst of the ground fire. On that day, the day he died, we happened to have breakfast together in the dirty shirt wardroom. With the big push on to finish the war, our flight schedule included more and more dayhops. Truth be told, air Ops were now going around the clock. He was scheduled to make a run up through the Haiphong area looking for anything else that we could bomb. The recce bird would go in with two F-4s flying CAP just in case the North Vietnamese thought to put up a MiG or two. But the likelihood of that was slim. Since Randy Cunningham had bagged his five MiGs the North Vietnamese air force had remained grounded.

Brad was good company. We laughed over our eggs and talked about our families. We shared our thoughts about a naval career, and the kind of things that men at war share with ease, without ever really knowing the other guy. It was good talking to someone other than the guys from Whidbey. He provided a new set of eyes on the world, and we said we would see each other later.

There would be no later. The RA-5C went north with its fighter escort and made its run through the target area. Somewhere along the route one of the F-4s saw a MiG-21. It was a rare chance for the Phantom, a chance he might never again get. The MiG was alone and had come up to see if it could nail an American. The pair of F-4s was hungry for a kill and set off in pursuit, abandoning the Vigilante as it pulled off the target. But there was a second MiG-21—as the F-4s should have known, ought to have known. The second MiG spotted the Viggie climbing out and fired on the RA-5C and, as was later reported, the pilot and RAN ejected at close to five hundred knots, far too fast for survival.

The pilot's chute opened, and although he had two broken legs from the impact of the airstream upon ejection, he was picked up by North Vietnamese troops on the ground. No one knew what had happened to my friend, Brad. Worse, the F-4s never looked for the missing RA-5C. They chased the MiG, but never caught him. From there everything broke down. Red Crown never reported the Viggie missing, and the F-4s came back to the ship without having engaged the other MiG.

When later it became known that the RA-5C was lost, all hell broke loose in CAG's office. Not only had a plane and its crew been lost, but also so had any attempt to rescue them had been missed, all because, when the F-4s returned to the ship, they had implied on the radio that the RA-5C was with them. The two Phantom crews were chewed out and had letters put in their jackets about the incident, none of which helped the downed RA-5C crew. The pilot was lucky though; he made it back several weeks later, injured, but as part of the first wave of returning POWs.

There were more losses, some totally avoidable. Like the young sailor who drowned in his own lung fluid because, coming back from a night in Olongapo where he had bought some street drugs, he began to convulse. His shipmates, unwilling to admit to what they had been up to ashore, put him to bed and left him there, to die alone. As he lay there unconscious, he continued to convulse. He brought up fluid into his lungs, and drowned in his own lung fluid. The ship's XO was so enraged by the incident that the kid's body was put on display and all the enlisted men in his unit were forced to look at it. I saw it too as they wheeled the gurney down the passageway from sickbay through the mess decks. A sheet covered the body, but it was stained with his bloody mucus, and the fabric was stretched over his open mouth in a live-action version of *The Scream.*

———

We lost an A-6 and its crew off Haiphong during one of the massive raids at Christmas. They had been hit by ground fire pulling off the target and ejected near the harbor entrance. Our SAR helos could not reach them before the troops on the ground had captured them. It turned out to be the gentlest kind of loss though. No one died, and, because the pilot was an Asian–African American, the North Vietnamese could not see how they could use the capture of him and his B/N as propaganda. Ironically, the pair made it back from captivity and to Whidbey long before we did.

———

One of the most avoidable of our losses, one that was so stupid and caused by the sheer bravado of its victim, took place on the very last day of combat. As the North Vietnamese poured their troops south into the DMZ, the fighting increased around Quang Tri. The south wanted to hold the city at all cost. All of the carriers along the coast were mounting support missions to help throw back the surge of invaders. It did not help very much that the ARVN forces were collapsing and falling back to safer positions so that each of the *Enterprise*'s strikes were becoming increasingly futile.

Several F-4s armed with MK-82 five hundred pound bombs were sent to hit the NVA troops. They had made one run and dropped several of their bombs on enemy formations. The situation on the ground was going bad and remained chaotic at best. The front line was dissolving minute by minute, and the FACs, forward air controllers, were having a hard time pinpointing where the F-4s should attack. The troops moving south were overrunning the smoke the FACs had dropped to mark the targets.

It is one of the dictums of aerial ground attack, learned the hard way over the years of air combat, that an attacking airplane should make only one run at a target from the same direction. Watch William Holden in *The Bridges at Toko-Ri* buy the farm after making several runs on the same target from the same direction. It is idiocy at the highest order. Sooner or later, the gunners on the ground get more accurate in their fire, or they simply get lucky.

Well, leading the F-4s that day was one of the legendary fighter jocks, a commander named Halston. He was well known for his bravado and swagger, and he was soon to be promoted out of flight operations and into a desk job at the Pentagon, as he was groomed for further promotion. He typified the fighter jock, sporting a golden ascot under his custom designed blue and gold flight suit. Some of the officers on the ship liked him and others, tired of his pomposity simply called him the lounge lizard when he dressed like that.

Of course, he knew better, but after his first run at the enemy troops, he decided to come around again and repeat his first run. If his RIO in the rear seat of the Phantom objected, no one ever said. So, Halston pulled his Phantom back up to altitude and then started down to attack. The ground troops saw him and began an intense barrage of small arms fire. The F-4 plunged down, dropped several of his bombs, and pulled off, hitting afterburner to claw back up to altitude.

It's at this point that the story became apocryphal. The section of F-4s had long before broken up. Halston's wingman had expended all his bombs, and kept circling above waiting for Halston. But Halston had one more MK-82 on his wing, and he was determined to use it. So he sent his wingman back to the ship, and Halston decided to make one last attack. He was running out of war—as today was to mark the end of hostilities. Another air medal would look good on his uniform, maybe even a new DFC.

What happened next could have been foretold and played back in slow motion. The F-4 did a split-S and swooped down from the west, as it had done twice before. The jet came on and, at the same altitude as in the previous two runs; the bomb separated from the plane and went on its way. Halston hit the afterburner; at the same instant several shoulder mounted SA-7 Grail missiles shot up from the ground. The missiles guided by infrared heat seeking warheads followed the hot afterburner trail hit the F-4 and it exploded. The FACs over the target area reported seeing two chutes leave the F-4.

Months later, Halston's RIO was back in the States undergoing rehabilitation at the San Diego Naval Hospital and was debriefed. He never said a word against his pilot's decision to make the third attack. All he knew was that from the moment of his ejection, he was a target for small arms fire. He had been shot and wounded in the right leg on the way down. The NVA troopers who captured him gestured with their weapons that he should walk to a waiting truck or be executed where he was. They were not prepared to fool with prisoners. He hobbled to the truck, but felt that in the confusion on the ground that either Halston had been killed by ground fire on the way down. Perhaps, thought the RIO, Halston with his usual bravado, had tried to fight back and was executed. No one ever knew and his body has never been recovered.

————

I heard about the suicide from one of the boatswain's mates. Like most suicides, it made no sense, but even less so in this case. We were moored at the carrier pier at Cubi. Everyone knew we would be going home soon, so there was a relaxed atmosphere on board the *Enterprise*, still, who can tell what goes through a man's mind.

It had been another hot and humid day, but the air seemed a little lighter than usual, so people were out on the flight deck in larger numbers, if only to facilitate a speedier crossing from port to starboard or bow to stern. The seaman, a young kid, really, had been standing by the deck edge aft of the number three elevator, just behind the LSO station on the ship's port side. For quite a while, he just stood there staring at the water below. At first, there had been some supposition that he had simply fainted in the heat and then had fallen from the deck.

From where he stood, it was nearly eighty feet to the water, a more than Olympic dive for anyone. But to dive or jump from the ship, you have to clear the catwalks and, in his case, the safety nets and framing around the deck edge elevator that was, at that point, in the lowered position.

He dove, or jumped, or simply fell. When they read the suicide note that they found in his locker it confirmed that he wanted to end his life for reasons that were as murky as the water in the Olongapo River. Whatever he planned to do, the impact of his head on the steel edge of the lowered elevator popped his skull like a watermelon, and his fall was reversed. Several of the mechanics who were on the lowered elevator and saw the impact lost their lunches immediately, while a few others made the man-overboard call. The kid's body was fished out of the bay and sent to the Cubi hospital. Nothing more was said about it.

PROWLER BALL

They said that the war would soon be over. The POWs were
going to be released any day, but there was a little more
fighting to do. The North's goal was to take as much territory in the
south as possible before any cease-fire line could be established. For
us, it meant business sort of as usual. While we were flying
unopposed in the North, there seemed to be a lot of activity moving
south along the Ho Chi Minh Trail.

Only the previous night we had almost bought it, and it was
the fault of the air controllers on the ship. They had become
complacent. The *Enterprise* had launched a couple of strikes toward
the Than Hoa Bridge area just to keep some pressure up on the
supply routes to the south, and we provided cover jamming. It had
been a normal night hop. We flew up the coast, established ourselves
in a ten-mile long racetrack pattern at twenty-four thousand feet.
Then the ALQ-99 receivers began picking up the night music from
the defending weapons systems on the ground. The high-pitched
tweeting of the Fire Can radars that controlled quad-mounted

antiaircraft guns and whose PRF (pulse repetition frequency) was so steady that you could set your watch by it filled the audio in my headset. There was a lone Tall King somewhere to the north, tracking and reporting to ground controllers on the various sections of attacking airplanes.

As we cruised up and down the coast we set jammers on the missile sites and kept one band seven on the Fire Can, just in case he was feeling frisky. Each of our attacks went off as planned. Feet wet, feet dry, drop your bombs, and goodbye. A little later, we heard Red Crown check out all of the *Enterprise* planes, and we were good to go home.

The weather had deteriorated as seemed to do each night lately and it was becoming a messy night. Because of the weather, the ship had declared that we would have a case-three recovery, and that meant an instrument approach all the way down to the ball. Like civilian airports in bad weather, the ship had a routine set of established holding patterns some distance from the landing area. We carried the most gas, and so we would be next to last to land. Only the E-2C Hawkeye, the turboprop early-warning plane that stayed aloft for two cycles or nearly four hours, normally landed after we did.

The holding locations were called "marshal," and if you drew the pattern out, it looked like an inverted wedding cake, with us on the widest and highest point. That night, what no one seemed to consider was that, because the ship was within twenty miles of the coast of North Vietnam, our marshal position was seven miles inside hostile territory. If we had flown there, we would have been circling for ten minutes in full range of a half dozen very active SAM sites.

When the controller on the ship gave us the bearing from the ship for our holding position, I looked down at my kneeboard chart and swore.

"Fuck me!" I declared, and then called the ship. "Climax, Skybolt Six one four, negative on the marshal vector. That puts us overhead Dong Hoi."

"Skybolt, Climax—ah roger," came the hesitant reply.

I could sense the confusion in the controller's voice; he probably had never looked at a chart of North Vietnam. Several seconds passed, then a minute. Ted was keeping us well off the coast and away from any lucky gunner on the ground.

"Ninety-nine Climax, stand by for new marshal vectors."

At least they were fixing the mistake. They had to redirect most of the airplanes still aloft. The new bearing that they gave us put us well off the coast, and we could settle back and wait our turn to land.

Next morning Ted was waiting for us in the ready room, wearing a sly grin. "We have something special this morning me buckos," he said. The first thing that was special was that we were flying in daylight, whoopee. The second was that we were going southwest into Laos and Cambodia—certainly not our usual territory—and looking for a SAM site. It had been rumored that a SAM site was about to be set up to shoot down aircraft approaching Saigon. The CIA had thought that this might be a real possibility and pushed the question up the line to the military in Saigon. They in turn sent word to Pearl Harbor, Pearl got back to the commander of Task Force 77, which then meant us. Simple flow of shit up and down the chain of command. Therefore, we would be glad to go looking for the source of the rumor. The improved SAM2 had a range of up to twenty-seven miles, and if the North Vietnamese were successful in erecting a missile site close enough to Tan San Nhut airbase, they could interdict flights at will, commercial or military.

There were to be three of planes flying in this gaggle. An RA-5C to take pictures of anything interesting, an F-4 to provide some air cover and firepower, and ourselves to run the electronic spectrum and look for any telltale radar signals. Our route was generally toward the southwest, across the length of Indochina, so the ship moved down the Gulf south of Da Nang for our launch. Once we were airborne both the Phantom and the Viggie topped off from the duty KA-6D tanker. They would need to stretch their fuel for the nearly nine hundred mile round trip.

We joined up in a loose formation, the Phantom from VF-142 flew off our port wing, and the Vigilante took up a position on our starboard side. It was a clear day over the mountains and jungles of Vietnam. Below, we could see isolated hamlets and narrow roads—bandit country for all we knew—but no sign of the war that had ravaged the country for decades. The natural growth quickly reclaimed bomb craters and burnt houses. I had the sense that I was flying over Appalachia, not the Annamite Mountains of Vietnam.

What I was looking for with my sensors was a signal from a Tall King radar. This Soviet-built radar was being used more as an early detection source to feed information to the SAM sites to improve their speed of acquisition and launch of their missiles. If I found one of these in our travel south, I was halfway to discovering that the North Vietnamese were indeed planning to move missiles into the area.

At cruise speed of 420 knots we had about an hour to kill in the air before we reached the area of interest. The briefers told us we should look in an area of narrow valleys running southwest to northeast, west of Saigon. This was a rugged area, long occupied by the Viet Cong and NVA infiltration teams. It was remote, but close enough to Saigon. With that in mind, the job was to simply make a run through the area to see if anyone might turn on their radar and "paint" us.

For most of the ride down my scopes indicated nothing. The various telltale signals, which were so prevalent in the North, did not appear. In fact, nothing popped up on the display. We were used to flights that lasted merely an hour and forty-five minutes, this hop would be close to three hours, so we occasionally reached for a Snickers or other candy bar and washed it down with the tepid water from plastic bottles in our survival vests. The chocolate bars had, of course, melted in the heat on the flight deck, but if you placed them near the cockpit air conditioning vents, they would harden up, even if they were a bit misshapen they tasted like Snickers. The water, well, it just tasted like plastic.

The eight of us in the three airplanes were bored. This was like taking a plane back to the PI to adjust the ship's deck loading— just sky and clouds to watch. The serenity of flight was like a drug. I was feeling a bit logy, not a good thing at altitude in a combat zone. But nothing happened, no stray MiGs, no AAA or SAMs, just sky and jungle.

We were flying a direct route to the IP (initial point) from which we would turn about 150 degrees to the north and start our descent into the valley. The plan was simple; the RA-5C would descend to about a thousand feet AGL (above ground level) then light off its afterburner and torch through the valley, while we chugged along behind it trying to detect any radar signals. The lone F-4 would slow flight above us, and, from its eagle perch, look for any targets it might deign to attack. Once we made the run, we could head for home.

There was none of the normal plane-to-plane radio chatter; everything we needed to say to each other was communicated NoRDo, no radio, and using hand signals. On the radar, the turn point looked to be about two miles ahead, and we pitched down. Because the RA-5C was much faster than we would ever be, even without going into afterburner, once he pitched over he was soon almost out of sight. As we streaked down, the increasingly humid air closer to the ground became compressed by our speed. We were leaving telltale wingtip contrails, perfect for ground gunners to sight on. At the IP the Viggie banked hard and entered the lower end of the valley. We saw him level out as we followed the turn, and then he lit off his afterburners and shot up the valley at below hilltop level. So far none of my sensors had detected any radar signals from the surrounding area.

It was our turn now, and Ted had the throttles all the way ahead, any more and the engines would have to be replaced when we got back aboard. The heavy Prowler was bucking in the thick air as we dipped into the valley. Out of the corner of my eye on the right, I could see some twinkling of light. Then a plume of smoke shot across the open space between the rapidly departing Viggie and our nose. Small arms fire opened up all along the military crests of the hills, thirty-seven millimeters, seven point six twos, RPGs, the VC that had lodged in those hills were throwing everything they had at us. We were at five hundred knots and somehow between the meteoric speed of the Viggie and our comparative plodding, the gunners got their lead wrong. The firing seemed to go on forever, and, if we had been hit, we would have instantly been dead meat. At that altitude, perhaps five hundred feet, and at that speed we would have simply come apart. But the entire evolution must have lasted about three minutes, and then we climbed back up to where the F-4 was flying in lazy circles just watching the show.

As far as I was concerned, there was nothing in that place except a lot of angry Commies. No radars, no missiles, and truly no reason for us to have been there. Now all we had to do was get back to the ship.

The weather out over the Gulf was again deteriorating as the day wore on, and we were encountered decks of dense clouds the further north we flew. In the meantime, the ship had moved back up the Gulf to be closer to Haiphong Harbor for the continuation of the aerial mining operations that had helped to bring the North's emissaries in Paris to the peace table. Nixon was not giving up until all the POWs were home.

The escapade down into South Vietnam had consumed a lot of fuel. We weren't in trouble yet, but the Viggie and the Phantom needed fuel in order to make in back. We radioed Climax for a tanker, and as we neared the coast south of Da Nang, a KA-6D showed up with gas for our wingmen, but it had none for us. Ted had been watching the gauges and was getting a little concerned at how much fuel remained, especially when the ship advised that we would have to wait another thirty minutes for a ready deck. Now, we really needed fuel.

The only other plane available that had any fuel was an A-7 with a buddy store on his port wing. Inflight refueling from a KA-6D was tricky enough, especially after being in the air for a few hours, but taking gas from a buddy store was even trickier. The problem was that, although the refueling tank and drogue were on the outboard wing station of the A-7, in order to fuel and keep in the proper position you had to try to avoid putting your wingtip into the A-7s tailpipe exhaust.

Ted was very tired by the time we hit the tanker, and we kept stabbing at the round target on the end of the refueling hose. Each missed attempt ate up more fuel. Every time we got close, he would drift right just a little, and the right wingtip would hit the A-7s exhaust and pitch up throwing us off to the left. We were now getting down to bingo fuel if we didn't get some soon. This went on for about ten minutes, until finally Ted approached the basket with enough roll to keep the right wing up. We sucked the buddy store dry, but it was enough. Then we heard the ship call.

"Ninety-nine, Climax. Ready deck!" Ah, sweet music.

The F-4 was first down the chute. We dropped down under a deck of clouds at about five thousand feet when we saw the long white wake of the *Enterprise*. Everything below the cloud deck was gray, painted into different shades by a diffused sunlight that added a little shimmer to the simplicity of the color.

We could see the F-4 head for the ship, followed about a mile astern by the RA-5C. Ted slowed a little to give us time at the ramp.

"Hook down," I called as the airspeed bled off.

Ted lowered the hook, and we went through the landing checklist.

At a quarter mile astern I called, "Six-one-two, Prowler Ball, state two point three." We had indeed used a lot of gas.

A little wagging of the wings, five extra knots for the wife and kid, a whoosh, the thud of the hook point on the deck, and we were hanging in straps as the arresting wire brought us to a stop.

CARRYING THE MELON

A ir operations at sea often lent credibility to the absurd, we were a floating island after all, and not every flight that was launched was destined to rain down death on the enemy. In fact, many flights were simply scheduled for the benefit of some of the air wing's and admiral's staff officers so that they could get their minimum four hours of flight time each month—a requirement if they were going to draw flight pay. Some of the staff officers were pretty rusty, and often they ended up as passengers in multi-seat airplanes where they could log flight time and their aviation skills would not be called upon nor affect flight safety.

Then there was the case of the admiral's change of command ceremony. The ship was scheduled to have a full-dress change of command at while sea, and those of us who were dopey enough to have packed our swords and dress whites in our cruise boxes were drafted to be present. Well, no one told us not to bring the hardware along, after all we were naval officers going to sea, why not bring one's complete uniform suite? That of course, included the obligatory fifty-caliber sword and dress whites with the choker blouse.

Mercifully, the ceremony was to take place during the relatively cool morning hours. The ship would be steaming at a leisurely pace and the sea breeze would keep things tolerable. The ceremony would be on the hangar deck, so the sun would not be a problem, still we would be wearing our dress whites, which made me sweat just looking at the thing. Starched and tight around the throat, they were the least comfortable of any of the uniforms in the service. Still, we would have to act a bit military for a short while, and the rest of the ship would go about its business, with men gawking at us from behind parked aircraft or gazing down on us from the catwalks overhead. The only benefit of our participation was that, since we were in our whites, we were automatically invited to the reception following the ceremony, which is where the story of the melon flight comes in

The departing admiral's wife, the short female with a leathery tan and who lived in one of the big colonial-era houses on the Cubi Point side of Subic Bay, the woman who Shit-finger had taught tennis, wanted the change of command reception to be a grand affair, even if she was not going to be there to oversee the function. To that end, she had obtained a huge watermelon from the brother in law of her gardener. But that bit of agricultural produce was in the Philippines, nine hundred miles away.

So, a mission was created to go and fetch the melon. Since the COD had already departed for Cubi, and there was no way to ensure the safe transition of the said melon by any other means that to have someone hold it on their lap for the trip, the use of a fleet jet was required and VAQ-131 was given the honor of carrying out the mission. There was some debate about whether the melon could travel on its own, strapped in and resting on the fourth seat of the Prowler, or whether it absolutely needed to be held by someone. Since several of the line crew had been begging us since we left the States to go aloft, we held a drawing for the privilege. One of the young third-class POs had the winning ticket. He was beaming at the chance to fly. His job was to sit tight for the ride to the PI, where he would get to spend the night ashore. The next day we would fly back, with him holding the melon in his lap. The last thing we needed was for a watermelon to break loose when we caught the arresting wire and explode in the cockpit so we made sure he knew the serious nature of this assignment.

The flight over to the PI was a normal hop—bright blue tropical skies over the expanse of the South China Sea. One of VA-196's planes was flying along with us in a loose formation. At one point we thought about doing a little bit of ACM, air combat maneuvering, with them, but we were just too mellowed out for any hassling in the sky. As a section, we climbed to twenty-seven thousand and settled back for the trip. Once we were at altitude, I dialed in the HF radio and fiddled with it until I came up with the BBC. They were playing the latest hits from the UK, so we had music in our ears throughout the long, boring trip. This would have been a great time for a stewardess to appear and offer "Coffee, tea or me?"

Finding Subic Bay when coming from the west was sometimes a hit or miss affair. Given that you had to fly over a vast expanse of water before finding any recognizable landmark, and that the TACAN at Cubi was notoriously weak, it took a quick eye on the radar return to make out the right bit of Philippine coastline to line up with. The coastline was full of inlets and curves that often fooled even veteran fliers who were familiar with the area. Too far south and you could even miss Manila, too far north and you might see

Clark AFB or end up over the mountains of Luzon. Often the coast was covered in thick clouds that forced you to drop down and look for the right landmarks, especially if it was in the rainy season.

We made our landfall, and, after giving our passenger a few last minute aerobatic thrills landed and gave the plane over to Shit-finger and his line crew. He knew all about the melon from the admiral's wife and laughed along with us. We officers made for the BOQ and the pool there, while the line crew took our passenger in tow for a night out. We were going to lounge at the Q's pool, where the infamous Cubi Hot Dog Machine was located. Their dogs were four for a dollar, and it was another twenty-five cents for beer as a chaser. It was a great place to pig out, swim, and get plastered without going broke. There were also girls at the pool. Most of them were female officers and nurses who lived there in the Q, so that if you made the right connection, an evening in Cubi could be very entertaining. I ate a prodigious number of hot dogs and then I fell into a long sleep only to wake up incredibly hungry.

The next morning I found myself at the BOQ mess for breakfast. My eyes bugged out at the display in front of me. There was an incredible array of food there, as if a cornucopia of fresh fruit had burst forth. I stacked my tray high with fresh orange juice, melon, bananas, and grapes along with some fresh rolls and butter. I sat alone gulping and munching happily when another officer came by sat down across from me. Eying my heaps of fresh fruits he grinned and asked, "Been at sea long?"

It took me a minute to catch on, but it was true. The "Big E" had no way to keep fruit fresh, and, though I liked fruit well enough, until that moment never knew how much I missed it.

After lunch, which gave me enough time to call home and check on my wife and daughter and the imminent arrival of our second child, we flew back to the ship. The weather on the trip back was very different. Gone were the soft tropical breezes and gentle seas. A strong cold front led by a line of thunderstorms had moved out of Asia and over the South China Sea. We would have to skirt a long way around the line of storms. I had never seen the Himalayas, but the mountains of pure white clouds to the north of our track topped out at nearly sixty thousand feet, twice the height of the mountains in Nepal. It was a spectacular sight. The piles of white cloud rose higher and higher, and the base stretched for at least a hundred miles. The sea below the mass of cloud was black and streaked with whitecaps and froth. At one point, I spotted lone freighter that was having a tough time in the swells, and I could see its bow pitching and plunging through the wave troughs. At that moment, I thanked my stars that I had chosen aviation over being a surface officer.

I knew the clouds were like massive machines, sucking up moisture and energy from the warm seas below, but inside them, the electrical energy served to block out all radio signals for about twenty minutes. It was only when our wingman from VA-196, who was flying about five miles to our north, passed in front of the wall of cloud that I became aware of how immense this storm was, and still it was just a large thunderstorm cell, not even a tropical storm or a cyclone. As it passed in front of the brilliant pillars of white, the A-6 seemed to shrink to the size of a model airplane in relation to the pile of cumulus behind it. It dawned on me then that our existence as humans is very fragile. I suddenly began to think about my own mortality, not in terms of the war, but in terms of how man survives under the weight of such forces of nature. I hoped that we would not ever have to go down under such a storm. The sheer force of the wind and rain could tear a man to bits, and it was likely enough that if you were to fall under this mountain of elemental forces your body would never be found.

We found the ship in the peaceful twilight of a late afternoon. They were waiting for us. The kid in the back seat maintained a death grip on the green oblate form of the melon. It would have been priceless to see what would have happened if he had to eject with that thing on his lap, but we made it aboard, and he never lost his grip. As soon as we pulled forward into our spot on the deck, several hands appeared to take charge of the melon ensuring its safe passage up to the admiral's mess so it could be refrigerated. Perhaps there should have been a melon medal struck for our mission. At least the kid in the back seat should have gotten one.

One of the make work jobs we had during this twilight period of semi-peace was called rigging ships. This is a job that is normally given to the patrol and anti-submarine forces that are charged with maintaining maritime surveillance. They know their trawlers from tankers and scows from submarines. However, since we were still looking for spurious uses of radar-guided weaponry at sea, we were assigned to do it. The idea was simple: fly as low and as close to the unidentified ships at sea and record the names, nationalities, and homeports if we could. One of the intelligence guys found us a camera to use for this purpose. Unfortunately, he did not have enough film for more than one or two missions. The tried and true method of rigging involved making a quick sketch of the ship, noting the locations of booms, hatches, stacks, and anything that would seem to help the intelligence officers decide if the ship and its possible cargo was a threat.

At one point we were directed to a freighter slowly steaming south in the Gulf. The ship was an old, break-bulk freighter flying the Polish flag. Once painted white, and perhaps used as a Gdansk to

Havana cruise ship, it was streaked with rust and was limping along, barely making headway. We asked ourselves, why was it out here? There was no cargo visible above deck, no telltale cylindrical shapes under wraps that might prove to be missiles or aircraft fuselages.

On deck, there were a number of passengers strolling about. We observed men and women taking the air and idly chatting with one another. The sight of them made us think it must be some kind of excursion. Take a honeymoon cruise from one peoples republic to another? Yuck. Why would a bunch of Poles want to wallow along aimlessly in the South China Sea seemed an apt enough question. Maybe they were on some socialist-inspired cultural exchange, or else they were technicians, brought in to repair the damage of twenty-five years of war. Perhaps they had an engineering casualty below decks and could not make headway. Whatever it was, we never found out. The next day when we looked for it, the ship had vanished.

A PEACE OF WHAT?

We were told that, with the major players back at the peace table and the first contingent of POWs was on their way home, the ship could go to Singapore for a diplomatic port call and liberty. The State Department's diplomats wanted us to put on an airshow down there They were keen to impress the locals that, that despite the wind down in Vietnam, America was still as strong as ever and remained committed to the region. Certain dignitaries were invited and would be flown out to the ship so we could display our might.

Before we left for the Lion City, we had a short stay in Cubi. It was to be the usual drunken carouse through the streets. Luckily for me, for our one in-port night I had drawn the flight deck watch from midnight to 0800. This duty was designed simply for the ship to have someone to hang in case a disaster occurred while we were safely moored at the carrier pier. I say luckily for me, since by that time in the cruise, I had not had a woman in quite some time, and it was likely that I might have finally succumbed to one of the bar girls and shown a lot of "pesonality."

As it was, I was able to sit in one of the large yellow flight deck tugs all through the tropical night and watch the incredible display of the winter Milky Way in the heavens above me. Each hour I was required to call the various fire watch stations below on the hangar deck to make sure they were not asleep. These watchers were enlisted men, who, like me, had drawn the short straw for the night. They were perched in armored and fireproof boxes located at intervals high above the hangar deck. Their job was to sound an alarm if smoke, flame, or anything dangerous appeared in their sight. The night went along without incident, and each hour I made a call to the OD on the bridge that all was well.

At 0700, the main gate opened, and a flood of people poured through. Civilians and military personnel came aboard the station to start their workday. Our sailors who had used their pesos to sleep with their chosen bar girls returned to the base and boarded the white Blaylock taxis for the trip back to the ship. From my perch on the flight deck, I could see the cabs arrive and their cargoes of sailors and officers spill out, all trying to get back aboard and into clean uniforms before they were put on report. As I watched this sad parade of soiled and disheveled uniforms, one of the cabs drew up to the officer's brow, and out came several of my squadron mates, all the worse for wear. As I watched, the face of Paul Hazlet peered up at me in a San Miguel–soaked confusion and smiled wryly. Apparently, he had found his girl of the night.

Going ashore in Singapore was like re-entering civilization after a long stint in the wilds. Again, the Baroon did us proud. He conned his way on to the COD with the pre-arrival delegation that was setting up our port call. As a result of his negotiations, we had a suite of rooms at the Shangri-La. The lodgings appeared to be equipped with a rotating bevy of Qantas stewardesses in the hotel pool. This was my first experience with Aussie culture and I found it educational, strange how many of these women seemed to lose the tops of their bikinis while in the water. The bottoms disappeared as well later on inn the rooms upstairs. The Baroon had also arranged that we would receive invitations to all the diplomatic receptions for the ship that were being held in conjunction with the air show. That meant booze, food and a bevy of attractive females of every size, shape and national origin. Truly, the Baroon was a genius.

Real food, real women, and places to spend money on stuff that was worth taking home, those were my first impressions of the place. The airshow had been a big success, and we were enthusiastically welcomed to the city. The *Enterprise* anchored offshore amid a small fleet of freighters and coasters. In this port, we used our own launches to run the liberty parties ashore. Going back years later I realized that the city-state had reclaimed that part of the harbor and massive hotels now rise from where we once dropped anchor.

My wife was due to deliver our second child at any time, so I called home almost daily, but there was no news. I felt even more at loose ends not knowing about the birth and being so very far away. Food and drink seemed to be the best antidote for the ennui I was feeling and I ended up having plenty of both. As promised, the various high commissions and diplomatic services coughed out a plethora of invitations and put out a list of parties to which we, as American officers, were welcome.

Singapore was going through its first socio-economic tightening phase, and, to a large extent, officially tried to proscribe many public human interactions. Public displays of affection, chewing gum, and any kind of risqué behavior were verboten according to the authorities that had clearly studied the methods Heinrich Himmler. Still, we were American sailors on liberty and we could turn anything into a good time. In fact, by the time it came to sail away I think most of us were more home sick, because the place seemed so normal to us, not like the wild-west atmosphere in Subic.

A day out of port, the ship suddenly seemed to take off out of the water. The *Enterprise* moved northward form the equator at full speed. We soon learned why. Apparently, the Communist negotiators in Paris had become reluctant to release any more POWs without some additional quid pro quo. Upon hearing this, Nixon hit the roof. For the first time since I had come aboard the ship, *Enterprise* conducted a nuclear-weapons drill. And it was done in full view of the crew.

For any Russian spies in the air or on our ever-present shadowing AGI, the meaning was very clear. Nixon was done with fucking around with the North Vietnamese. Let them eat protons seemed to be what he was saying. With each hour that passed, the ship seemed to be leaping across the waves as it sped northward. Our bent propeller shaft was not spared, and the resultant vibrations from its wear on the bearings added to the sense of urgency. Throughout the day the nuke drills continued, making sure that the watching Soviets and their Vietnamese allies knew score. The *Enterprise* had nukes, and we were preparing to flex our muscles. Within twenty-four hours, the situation in Paris was resolved. The nukes disappeared into their cradles in the magazines and we went back to our desultory patrolling of the South China Sea looking for stray communist ships.

With no urgent mission to occupy our minds, we went back to flying patrols off the coast between Haiphong and Dong Hoi. A daily ritual of manning up and then drilling holes through the sky, looking for strange ships, ate at our effectiveness. Complacency set in, and the danger of an accident grew proportionately. Time grew heavy for all of us. If there was to be no war, why were we still here?

One day, the chaplain sent word to the ready room, looking for me. He was the same cleric who prayed nightly for "good bombs." I was to report to his office near the chapel immediately the message said. It took me a while to find the space as it was tucked away down a passage I had never before noticed. When I came in, he was reading at his desk. It took a moment before he put down what he was reading and looked up to see me standing there. When I told him who I was, he put on a very somber face. He was not smiling and I knew that something terrible must have happened at home.

My mind and heart were racing. Had my wife died? Had the baby died? From the look on his face, I thought it had to be likely that I was now facing a tragedy. He looked at me a long moment, appraising and I thought judging how to give me the bad news. My heart skipped again and yet he said nothing, but fished around in the debris on his desk for a piece of paper. Finally, he extracted a flimsy sheet from among others there. It was a naval message from the Red Cross in Whidbey. Without a word he handed it to me.

I had to read it twice before I saw that my wife had given birth to another girl, and both she and the baby were fine.

"Thank you, sir," I stammered.

"Everything okay, son?" he asked. He could not have cracked a smile for me even if he had seen the second coming of Christ.

"Yes sir. Everything is fine." I just wanted to get out of there, fast. Since we were at sea, there was no chance to call home until we made port in a few days. When at last we reached Cubi, I made the call. It took a few tries before I was finally able to complete the call and speak to my wife and find out that everyone was indeed fine. The unreality of that conversation reality hit me like a ton of bricks. What was I doing half a world away?

———

It seemed as if the navy liked to play with our minds. The skipper of the ship, the same man who had for months said "I don't know when we are going home," finally came on the 1-MC and announced we would be offloading our ordnance the next day to the

USS Coral Sea. The "Coral Maru", as she was known, would be our relief ship on Yankee Station. Once we transferred the ordnance we would make a short port call in Subic. Then, free from the obligations of combat the *Enterprise* would proceed to Alameda with a stop in Pearl Harbor. As soon as he was done speaking, the ship rocked with cheers for ten minutes.

The next day everyone watched anxiously as the *Coral Sea* came alongside and the slings of mark 82s and Aim-9 Ds swung out over the water to our relief. The offloading went on for several hours. With each moment that passed the reality of going home began to sink in.

The next night we were in Subic and for some, I expect this would come to be an emotional moment. Fortunately, most sailors had treated the place as the hellhole it was, but a few thought they had found true love and were going to miss "their hooker." For a few of the ship's crew, and for one of our squadron's chief petty officers in particular, this would be their last stop for a while. They were not going home soon. That is, not until the virulent strains of NSU that they had developed could be cured and cleared from their bodies. The navy was not going to risk their going home and infecting wives and sweethearts with the latest strain of the virulent Philippine Clap.

A few others, men with really no home to go to or no desire to see their spouses, took up the offer of a cash bonus to "cross-deck" and went to squadrons on the *Coral Sea* or one of the other ships coming out for the postscript of the war. It was hard for me at that time in my life to fathom their desire to do so, but for some people the war and the being aboard the ships that fight was more comfortable than being back home.

The *Enterprise* had taken aboard a number of "hangar queens," airplanes damaged beyond the ability of the facility at Cubi Point's to repair. Some were simply those for which the rework facility at Alameda was the last stop before the scrap yard. The ship's decks were now crowded, as it was on the trip out. The airplanes were packed in every available space except for the waist catapult area where a pair of F-4s stood by. They remained in that position for the entire transit, armed and ready to be launched in fifteen minutes notice.

It was a brilliant, sunny day, when we left Subic Bay for the last time. Those crewmen with no other duties milled around on the flight deck, enjoying the fresh sea breeze. All the while up-tempo rock music played from the flight deck loudspeakers. The ship made a wide circle outside the harbor entrance, waiting for one of the SH-3 helos to return and land after having deposited the port pilot back ashore.

The loudspeakers blared and the flight deck was momentarily cleared, to allow the chopper to land and shut down. Then the mood began to change. Had they changed their minds, were we going back? Silence fell over the flight deck as we watched the ship make way out from the shore and begin to head in a northwesterly direction. This was the way we always turned when we headed toward Yankee Station, and for a few minutes, the crew's collective heart sank. Then suddenly, the bow began to swing to port, to the south, a new direction, decidedly a new direction for us.

The silence ended when the loudspeakers on the island broke out with "Are you going to San Francisco?" and a cheer went up from the crew. For hours following this, as long as there was light to see by, people stood at the edge of the deck and watched as one by one the Philippine Islands slid by. We were steaming south to the San Bernardino Straight and beyond into the Pacific. In five or six days, we would be in Hawaii.

COMING HOME TO A FOREIGN COUNTRY

I had been away at sea for almost nine months, but it seemed longer, and perhaps it was since I had thought of little else but flying since I had won my wings. Aboard the ship, the routines of a military life filled the long hours so that each day had seemed a week. Nine months was just enough time to have a baby, so a very human span of days. A lot had happened during that time and I had yet to make sense of it. Still, it was a shock to me to be re-entering a once-familiar world.

We had drunk up the last of our booze on our last night out and we were pretty hung over, but someone had turned on the TV in the bunkroom. Instead of the ship's TV broadcast, I saw the grainy, but welcome, image of Frank Blair reading the news on the *Today Show*. We were back in civilization! What a way to come home. Dressing quickly, I raced to the portside catwalk, and there across a few miles of the warm Pacific was Oahu. Looking east, I could see the postcard-familiar shape of Diamond Head in the distance.

The sight transfixed me. I stood and watched as the massive ship neared the coastline. Soon, tugs appeared to ease our bulk through the entrance to Pearl Harbor. My first thought, in looking at the approaching harbor, was that the place was so tiny. It was a shock. That so much history stemmed from the attack here seemed almost impossible. The *Enterprise* inched into the narrow space between Ford Island and the long carrier pier near where the *USS Pennsylvania* had been docked during the attack of December 7, 1941. The tugs had a big job to do as they pushed and pulled to maneuver the giant ship into its berth. *Enterprise* seemed even larger in the narrow waters between the piers and wharves of the base. Getting into our berth became a deft dance of a giant, but soon the ship was moored, and truly back from danger.

My cruise was to be over once we docked. A number of the sons of the ship's company officers and NCOs and of the embarked squadrons were going to come aboard for what the navy called a Tiger Cruise. The navy had flown them out from the mainland and they were waiting on the pier. The Tiger Cruise was a chance for the sons of naval officers and senior enlisted men to see how their fathers had lived at sea. With all the extra people coming aboard there was a need for extra berthing spaces, and I had been asked if I wanted to go ashore at Pearl and catch a flight home. Of course, this was to be at my own expense. It was either that or I could remain aboard for the transit to California with all the visitors and then wait for the general disembarkation at Alameda. We were a squadron of only four airplanes, so that just sixteen officers could make the fly-off to Whidbey as soon as the ship neared the mainland. Apparently, I had neither the seniority or done the right amount of ass-kissing to make that evolution, so I was invited to leave early. Though I would have to pay my own way, the idea of getting home a week early seemed worth it. I packed and locked my big blue cruise box and gave one of the aviation bosun's mates twenty bucks to make sure it made the offload of our squadron's gear at the pier in Alameda.

I dressed in tropical whites for the flight. I filled my suit bag with the gifts for my wife and daughters that I had accumulated over the months and caught a cab to the airport. Pan Am had a flight to Seattle in two hours, and, when I forked over my fare—it was normal to pay cash for an air ticket back then—I was immediately given a first-class seat at a coach price just because of my uniform. Five hours later, I was looking down at a cool, rainy Tacoma as we made our approach to Sea-Tac. During the flight, the pilot and co-pilot had stopped by my seat to chat one of the flight attendants must have told them I was aboard. Both were air force types who had flown in Vietnam and wanted to know what I had been doing there. I expect my impressions were pretty raw, and they had been away for several years, still, it was nice to be noticed, and we chatted amiably for ten minutes or so.

I had called my wife from Honolulu to tell her I was coming home, and I let her know I would find my way from the airport to the house. So, I was in a fairly jubilant mood as I walked through the terminal looking for the car rental desks. As I walked past a small group of, well, there is no other term for them but hippies. In the military, we referred to these kids as derelict hippie-freaks, but I gave them little thought as I passed. Then one of the long-haired, fringed-deerskin-and-bead bedecked young men yelled out at me, "fuck you, baby-killer." Then he spat at my shoes. I had never been spat at or upon, not even in the streets of Hong Kong, where clearly the sight of my uniform produced visceral reactions on the part of some of the inhabitants. I stopped in mid-stride and gave the group of them; well they had to be kids, maybe at most twenty years old, my coldest withering, war-weary stare. I was glad I was not armed, as they would have been too easy to pop. Then I walked on to the Avis desk to find a way home.

The girl at the rental car desk was pert and pretty and reminded me of everything one hopes to find in the wholesome girl-next-door type. I had a credit card for the rental. I knew I could return it to the Avis office in Oak Harbor in the morning. As she finished up the agreement, she chattered in her happy voice and asked, "Where are you coming from?"

"Vietnam," I replied, thinking of my recent encounter with the hippies.

"Vietnam?" she was perplexed and said, "I didn't know we had anyone over there anymore." She was being honest, and her naiveté showed, but I was filled with a growing sense of futility and disgust, and I replied curtly. "Well there are a couple hundred thousand men still there." With that, I got in the car and drove up to the island.

It was getting on dusk when I arrived. She had been dosing, waiting for me. The girls were asleep, lost in their happy world of childhood. We spoke little and made love like the strangers we had become.

Death and Remembrance

It has been forty years since these events took place. Forty years for me to screw up three marriages—forty years and five kids later, time to drift through a dozen different jobs with a dozen different employers. In forty years, I have moved nineteen times and lived in nine states. I have gained and lost weight and gained it again, become a diabetic and, along with my hair, lost any sense of direction. But, I have kept these memories.

We are a nation that likes its celebrations; and we mark our historic anniversaries with parades and speeches. The media grasps events and re-tell their significance in fifth-grade English. Since the attacks of 9/11, the news cycle has accelerated to an instantaneous flow, obliterating understanding with its constant and repetitive prattle. In 1972, there was a similar event. The media at that time had decreed that 1972 was the Watergate Year. It was an event that eclipsed all others that year. The media did this as much because it was their own victory as it was an indictment of power gone amok. For them it was a clear-cut victory over the dark forces surrounding an unpopular president: it seemed to all that was the result of the heroic efforts of a pair of journalists digging deep into the political septic tank that is Washington.

So, the magazines were printed, television and radio talk shows were broadcast, while the accused made the perp-walk and gave the news magazines their photo-ops. But there were other events in that year—events of life and death proportions that the average American often ignored. Out in the South China Sea we knew nothing of the Watergate break-in, and, if you had asked us about it, we would have simply shrugged our shoulders. For us, the focus of life was living to the next day. Home had become a place, warm and hazy in the imagination, of lovers and wives and for some, happiness. But we were still a part of half a million men at arms on duty in that fetid place called Vietnam.

We did not make the evening news much anymore. Being at sea, we were not bloody enough or controversial enough to fill the few seconds that the news networks needed to draw the public's attention away from sitcoms and game shows. In Vietnam, officers primarily fought the naval air war and perhaps that made us just too elite for the networks. Only bullets and flak do not distinguish between ranks or by how much your paycheck is. I wondered what my parents might have thought if they had seen their son on TV interviewed by some field reporter on the evening news. But this naval part of the air war never saw any reporters, except for the spooky types from *Aviation Week* who were looking for technical information that they could publish so the North Vietnamese could read it in the next issue of the magazine. But all of this that happened—all of it was very real. Every day we flew, staggering out, exhausted on to the steaming flight deck to the waiting aircraft, generally carrying the burdens of fatigue and hangovers with our fight gear. No outsiders saw us. Occasionally a reference to Yankee

Station might have crept into a TV reporter's voice-over, but that was it.

For Christmas 1972, they even kept Bob Hope away from us. The Saigon Command had said that it was too risky to send him up to Yankee Station. After all, who would be able to explain the icon of American entertainment's being caught on the wrong end of a Styx missile shot from a Komar patrol boat. Worse yet, all those young tits and asses that he hauled around the world with him, just to remind us fighting men of what white women looked like, would have to be fished out of the Gulf. So, we continued to drink and fly and slept until the days ran into nights and the days of the week were lost in our memories.

Our lives ran in a series of cycles dictated by fleet operations, and through the labyrinth of military commands through Saigon and Pearl Harbor up to Tricky Dick in the White House. Our lives at sea ran on forty-five to sixty day periods, steaming north and south on an endless course through the South China Sea. We operated midnight to noon, day in day out, in rain, in heat, and in simmering sunshine. Fifteen launches a day, thirty to forty aircraft per launch, landings at forty-five second intervals—the *Enterprise* became the busiest airport in all of Asia as fuel and bombs were loaded on airplanes to be deftly expended on the misty jungle targets and suspected truck parks of North Vietnam.

Ashore, we drank, ate, and fucked everything in skirts. Next to the palm of his hand, the whores of Olongapo were the sailor's best friends. The Filipino girls were sweet, funny and hopelessly corrupt, and the all fucked like bunnies for twenty pesos a night. Some of them were incredibly ugly, sold by their poverty-stricken parents into the life while others had a natural angelic innocence but were so tarted up, they would have given the Catholic Chaplain an erection. Some of us fought beery brawls against the "black shoe sailors" in the Number One—USA Shitkicking Bar and then sobbed on the long distance lines back to our loved ones at home.

Looking back over the forty years, it doesn't seem that America has learned very much, and it was probably a blessing that we were so isolated from the rest of the country on bases far from the civilian populations. For naval aviators, we came to this war as volunteers. Most of us had grown up with the desire to fly; we had asked to be there, in the middle of the fight. And there was the sense of élan, of joining the lost era when aviators were indeed, knights of the air. While the street demonstrators back home called us Yankee Air Pirates, as the North Vietnamese had dubbed us, we had the phrase stitched onto patches that we proudly wore on our flight jackets. Flying was our chosen profession, and, drunk or sober, fatigued or in the best of shape, as long as you could maintain your professional demeanor, you could do no wrong.

EPILOGUE — HO CHI MINH CITY 1994

B usiness had brought me here, but also in some way I came to find out if it had all been worthwhile. In Hong Kong, where the offices of the People's Republic of Vietnam had issued my visa, there was no curiosity, no animosity about my planned visit. The once-ruined country was trying, trying its best to lure tourists and, more importantly, business to its shores. So, as an American and a representative of a major international bank, I was told that I would be more than welcome.

I flew in on Cathay Pacific, not willing to trust any Vietnamese operated airplane on the long over-water run from the Crown Colony. My first-class flight landed at Tan Son Nhut, and I looked on with wry amusement at the line of ancient Soviet-built airliners that were parked along the ramp facing the terminal. The stood there mute, like sentinels of disaster. Each of them was unserviceable and certainly not airworthy. Each of them remained rusting in the humid air, while their lifeblood of hydraulic fluid leaked out into purple pools under their wings. Behind them stretched a line of concrete blast shelters that once housed American and South Vietnamese warplanes. Ruined, they were now only pockmarked shells, filled with rubble and debris and showing the craggy holes from artillery shells in their curved roofs.

I began to wonder how I, an American and ex-Yankee Air Pirate would be received once I was on the ground, but I was soon put at ease. The arrivals area was chaotic and reminded me of Mexico City airport. Inside the terminal, it was a cacophony of voices punctuated by indecipherable PA announcements. The immigration officer, young and clearly born after the war, merely glanced at my American passport, as if the arrival of Americans in this once-forbidden city was of no consequence. Or, more likely, I was expected and was simply to be observed. If they were doing so, I never noticed. At the customs inspection area, where my bags were x-rayed—perhaps I was importing drugs or worse, who knew—I was met by smiling young women in brown uniforms who wore gold jewelry studded with rubies. Each of them seemed to be auditioning to be my personal guide and escort to the city, and they giggled like whores in a cathouse. They wore their uniforms with great laxity. Each of them was showing as much cleavage as their small bodies and tight blouses would allow. They seemed disappointed when I left and had not invited them along for the ride into town.

The local branch manager of the bank had sent his driver to meet me, so I was spared a jolting ride in a tuk-tuk from the airport to the hotel. The bank's Mercedes was cool and dust free, and riding in the back seat gave me a chance to see the former capital of South Vietnam for the first time. Being a Yankee Station sailor, I had only set foot in the country when we operated in and out of Da Nang and had no real experience of being "in-country".

PROWLER BALL

The strangest thing about being in Vietnam again was that although the severe American trade embargo had yet to be lifted, American products were advertised everywhere. On the streets sidewalk vendors could make change of a hundred dollar bill and give you tens and twenties back, none of them wanted to use the Dong, the local currency.

My job in Saigon, I could not get used to calling it Ho Chi Minh City, nor as it happened could many of the locals, was to ferret out any chance of the existence of a securities market that would permit foreign investments to flow in. Everyone was looking for the newest and hottest emerging securities markets. Vietnam's neighbors, Thailand, Malaysia, and Singapore were part of the new Asian Tigers and had vital securities markets and exchanges. My clients in Boston and New York wanted to know what opportunities there might now be in Vietnam. Our bank had an office in Saigon, and the folks on the ground had set up meetings for me with various local officials.

However, on my first night I had been invited to join some of the ex-pats in town, along with some senior cadres for a dinner. To the twangy tunes of American country western music, rendered by a Vietnamese singer and her backup band, I found myself standing along the Saigon River. I was invited by the bank and some senior Vietnamese officials to attend a full-fledged American-style barbeque. Ribs, chicken, steak, and all the standard American side dishes were being served along with 33 beer and soft drinks. Why should I have been surprised, we had taught the Vietnamese about basic American cooking just as the French had taught them to make delicate pastries. Still, it was a surreal moment; standing here and listening to everyone pretend to be just down-home folks.

My stay in Saigon continued to leap from one surreal moment to another. As I was taken by my host to one meeting with senior Vietnamese financial authorities and on to another, I found that the sessions were in reality one long meeting. For although the Vietnamese participants changed with each meeting, the agenda seemed to go on in one long single thread, it was like a tag-team match. This interest by them was perhaps facilitated by the fact that I was first an American and, more importantly, I was a combat veteran of the war here. That revelation came about quite naturally as it turned out, and it was to my advantage.

When one meets with Vietnamese officials, the atmosphere is excruciatingly polite; the first thing they do is to offer tea, along with little rice cakes, and of course cigarettes. I am not a smoker, and so I stayed with the tea and cakes. Early on in the discussion, I was asked if this was my first visit to Vietnam. Of course, I knew that they had done their homework when I applied for my visa, so I told them. "No," I said, "I was here in 1972 and '73. I was a naval flight officer and flew airstrikes in the north." There, it was out, and I had expected some resentment. Instead, their reaction was anything but. Quite to the contrary: being a war veteran and being willing to help direct foreign investment into their country had earned me a higher level of esteem, because at that instant, one of the officials spoke rapidly to one of the assistants, and, suddenly, the tea disappeared and Vietnamese iced coffee was brought in. From that point on I was treated like a long lost relation: welcomed at each subsequent meeting and feted like an old friend.

This happened again when I stopped in a small restaurant next to the Continental Hotel in the center of the city. The tables were occupied by several groups of tourists, some French, who were acting rudely, as if they still owned the place, and some of the bearded Birkenstocker brigade, who were passing out Dong to pay for their orders. The waiter was an older man, perhaps fifty, who spoke English. When I made my order for a brioche and iced coffee his eyes lit up. "You GI?" he asked. I said I was, and, from that moment on it seemed that I was the only customer in the restaurant, for he ignored the annoying French and left the hikers to work out their financial issues on their own.

Between meetings, I got to see a lot of the city and even wandered into the old part of Cholon. There, the street markets were as vibrant as ever. Daily marketing was a must for the city's households. With no refrigeration available to most of the vendors, the piles of ripe vegetables and fruit had to be sold the same day as they were put on display. By day's end only a few scraps were left. The goods were brought in to the city on old US trucks left behind when we pulled out. As I heard from one of my hosts, the Russian vehicles had all crapped out years before, so as in Cuba, the locals made the most of the residue of Uncle Sam's adventure.

On one of my guided tours, I was taken to the Banque du Indochine, a huge French colonial monstrosity. Inside I found the beginnings of a vibrant securities market, which had, in fact, existed for years under a Soviet-style barter process. What was most impressive was the inside of the huge domed lobby. Looking up, I could see that the smoke of hundreds of cooking fires blackened it. When the VC and the NVA poured into the city, they had used the bank as a campsite and had burned whatever they could. My guide, a young Vietnamese woman, assured me that in short order the place would be put right, but I wondered.

All over the floors, once no doubt highly-polished, were bales of paper money. These were Dong notes bearing the image of Ho Chi Minh. The scene looked like a large recycling plant, as the notes were wrapped in wire and baled together. The notes were printed on an inferior paper, and they both looked and smelled like used toilet paper. According to my guide, some of the bales would be burned and new notes issued. I could see why so many people in this cash economy preferred western banknotes, for between the humidity and general filth that pervaded in the outlying areas, holding one's wealth in this funny money could be risky.

One of the highlights of my stay was an interview by Newsweek reporter Ron Moreau atop the Caravelle hotel. We had drinks and dinner in the open air, while looking out over the city and the river winding northward. I explained how impressed I was with the place and voiced my opinion that America would be foolish not to get our feet back into the country, economically. Since I had not been in the city during the war, he told me of nights sitting on this same rooftop and watching firefights in the suburbs.

Like most tropical cities in the world, the older parts are the most charming. I took time to walk to the old American Embassy compound and along the shady streets that led away into the quiet neighborhoods. One of my lasting impressions was of a pair of young women walking leisurely along and chatting to one another. They were both wearing the traditional *ao dai*, the combination of pajamas and long skirt. As they walked along, their long hair swung in one direction, while their skirts swung the other. It was one of the most alluring sights I have ever seen.

Recently a friend asked me if I wanted to go back again as a tourist. I have seen the pictures of the five-star resorts along the coast, and they are very seductive. But, like a lot of things that have run their course in my life, I have no desire to go back. There are plenty of tropical beaches and resorts closer to home, and my ghosts from Vietnam are now buried.

AUTHOR'S NOTE

I have called this book, *A Yankee Station Sea Story*. As anyone
familiar with navy sea stories knows they all begin with the warning
phrase, "no shit" before the teller then goes on to recite something
extraordinary. So, for those sailors and naval aviators, who may read
these words, let me repeat that warning. One of my difficulties in
putting together the stories of a real squadron comprised of real men
at war was whether to use real or fictional names. Out of deference
to the real players, their families and descendants I have chosen to
maintain fiction as the best way to go. Although the real members of
the squadron will no doubt recognize themselves in part or perhaps
others, I have chosen to avoid any references to real people so any
inference one may make is purely coincidental. As for the events
themselves, they are as real as I can make them. Still, I have blurred
some lines and made some situations that were separated in time
contiguous so as not to be repetitive. Everything that I have written is
what I personally knew about either by being witness to or was
involved in. In the end, fiction won out as the only way to tell this
story. The reader can assume what he or she will; but this is a work

of the imagination-fueled by gallons of coffee spiced with a touch of JP5 jet fuel. The only thing that I can say in my defense is that if anyone is offended, then I must be telling the truth.

From the beginning, I had planned on a career in the navy. I would have probably never left had I not been pushed as much as pulled away. The military had taken a beating from the press and the public in the post-Vietnam era. Unlike today, when the public is falling over itself, as it should, to help the veterans of recent combat, we were called 'baby-killers" and upon returning to the states treated like sons-of-bitches where ever we went. When I looked for a job in the civilian world it I was advised to play down my war service. I ran into one sanctimonious human relations type that castigated me for not going to Canada to avoid fighting. I told him to "fuck off" and walked out of the office. The time following the end of hostilities was confused for most of us. It was a bad time. It took years of reflection before I could begin the narration of what happened out there. I know I have probably still missed a lot that might be important to others, but this, for me, was the reality of the times.

Now I am a graying sixty-five year old. I have gone through three marriages and several relationships with nice women like a drunk in a brewery. At one point along the way, I picked up an MBA. From that I went on to become a corporate executive but remained unsettled and on the move, ever restless. I have relocated twenty-five times in my life and lived in eighteen cities, from coast to coast while pursuing a career in a succession of mid-level positions. Time has taken its toll; through the years I have gained weight, developed diabetes, in the process made, and lost tens of thousands of dollars. In short, I am like a thousand other vets who carry their scars on the inside and manage to cope.

As my editor was pointed out, many of the phrases, acronyms and slang used by naval aviators are unfamiliar to the civilian reader. Where possible I have tried to explain in the text, but as this is a work of fiction, adding long lines of explanatory comments seemed to spoil the flow. So, I found myself forced to add a glossary of sorts at the end of the book. I hope that it helps.

JB

Flanders, New Jersey

A SHORT GLOSSARY OF NAVAL TERMS

Admirals/Flag Country or Quarters

These are the quarters on the ship housing the operations, berthing and mess facilities for the embarked Admiral. An admiral is a flag officer (he has a flag with stars on it signifying his rank: hence a flag officer. On the *Enterprise* this area was on the O3 level.

CAG

CAG is the Commander of the Air Group. In this story that would be Carrier Air Wing 14. The rank of CAG is that of a senior commander and is thought of as the first step toward command of an aircraft carrier. He is known as CAG, not the CAG.

Call the Ball

Pilots fly their aircraft aboard a carrier using a system that involves a Fresnel lens that lets them see a colored ball of light reflected to the cockpit. This tells them if they are low or high in the approach as they shoot for the number three or target wire. The ball changes color from green if the plane is on the correct approach to red if the plane is too low or orange if it is high. The ball moves in relation to the motion of the plane and the pilot can see the motion relative to a fixed horizontal set of lights known as the datum line or lights. On each approach to the ship, whether it is done "NORDO" or no radio the pilot must call that he has the ball in sight a quarter mile astern of the ship. The typical call would be "613, Prowler Ball, state two point four. This tells the Landing Signal Officer (LSO) that the pilot has the landing environment in sight, but it also reminds the arresting gear team to set the system for a heavy airplane. Each squadron has its own LSO and by saying that the state (fuel remaining) is in this case, twenty-four hundred pounds that the aircraft can probably only make one missed approach.

CAP

Combat air patrol. There is always a CAP overhead the ship during combat operations to provide cover in the event an enemy might attack the carrier.

Deck

For a sailor, the deck is any horizontal surface whether on a ship or on land. Vertical surfaces are known as bulkheads and ceilings are overheads.

Feet Dry/Wet

When coming from the sea an airplane is feet wet until crossing the coastline, then it goes feet dry.

Flight Quarters

Like battle stations, flight quarters are called over the ship's intercom when flight operations are to commence. All aircrew must report to their assigned ready room or aircraft.

Hack

Being in hack is simply enjoying the wrath of one's superior officer.

Iron Hand

Iron hand missions are flak and surface to air (SAM) suppression missions. The idea is to coax the enemy to turn on his weapons systems and radars so that the Iron Hander can shoot an anti-radiation weapon down his throat.

Karst

A geologic formation of nearly vertical limestone that is particularly evident in Southeast Asia. Often it is seen in oriental art, especially on the tacky wall murals in Chinese restaurants. Karst ridges in Vietnam the karst is generally covered with foliage and deadly to low-flying airplanes.

Nugget

A brand new naval aviator or naval flight officer

Overhead

In the navy, a noun or verb that describes anything above one's head. To arrive "overhead" means to fly to a point over something, like the ship.

PriFly

This is the name for Primary flight control on the carrier, the ship's control tower for aircraft operations. The Air Boss sits in PriFly and controls all air ops on the ship, not a good idea to piss-off the Air Boss with poor airmanship.

Prowler Ball

The radio call given at the position a quarter mile astern of the ship to ensure that the LSO knows that the approaching aircraft is an EA-6B and that the arresting gear has been set for the correct weight.

Skybolt

This is the radio call designation for the VAQ-131 Lancers.

Struck

This is a verb meaning to take offline or remove from service. When an aircraft is struck below decks it means it needs serious maintenance attention.

Thatch Weave

This maneuver is named for US naval aviator John S. Thatch who devised the "beam defense" maneuver to defend US F4F Wildcat fighters against the more agile Japanese Zero. Thatch and "Butch" O'Hare at the Battle of Midway first employed it. Essentially two fighters fly a weaving course covering each other's tail to ensure that an enemy fighter does not "get on their six o'clock" position.

TOPGUN

US Naval Aviation Fighter Weapons School, originally based at NAS Miramar, San Diego, CA

Transpac

This is the process of transiting the Pacific either by air or sea.

Prowler Ball

Made in the USA
San Bernardino, CA
07 February 2019